something like
Starlight

# something like *Starlight*

a novel by **elsie bea**

Elsie Bea, LLC



Aylett, VA 23009, USA

ISBN (paperback): 979-8-9906366-4-4

ISBN (e-book): 979-8-9906366-5-1

Library of Congress Control Number: 2025922911

Cover Designer: Molly Donahue

Developmental Editor: Kimberly Hunt

Copy Editor: Lori Whitwam

Proofreader: Ramona Mihai



**CONTENT WARNING**

While lighthearted with a happy ending, **this work is intended for a mature, adult audience.** This work contains on page intimacy with explicit descriptions and situations that may be unsuitable for readers sensitive to certain topics or themes. Please note that reading content tips may lead to plot or character spoilers. Read at your own discretion.

<u>**Content Warnings**</u>: Parental loss, grief, spousal loss, therapy, mention of apraxia, mutism and/or non-verbal misdiagnosis, childhood disabilities, mention of teen pregnancy, open door intimacy, vulgar and explicit language and/or sexual situations, spanking, bullying, near-death experience of a child, death, and mention of/characters portrayed having cancer, and cancer-related death.

*To all the girls who can't sit still.*
*Maybe you're meant to be the movement.*

# Chapter One

## LEMON

Listen up, bitches, this is my story, and I'll break the fourth wall whenever I want, thank you very much.

I'm Lemon. Yes, I'll allow time for that to sink in. *Lemon.*

Laugh it up. It's fine. I've heard it all: Lemonade, Lemon Cakes, Lemon Pie, Lemony Snicket.

But the worst I ever heard was...

"Sour Patch!"

When said by my arch nemesis and brown-nosing *Daddy Wannabe*, O.L. Nashville.

It doesn't even sound like a real name. It's more like a stage cover...a stripper name. And with that little nugget of brilliance sure to fire him up in all the ways I love, I saunter over to Mr. Mad-Eyes and cock my hip to the side, swinging my VIP pass around to fuck with him.

He likes things orderly, and I am the opposite of order.

"I'll pretend you didn't call me that pet name again, since you're in control of the tour and obsessed with me, but don't think for one second I'm letting up on my quest to learn your full name and exploit it seven ways to Sunday, *Nash.*"

I call him by his nickname. The name only the *men* call him, my father and the other suits he lines his boardroom with.

Most of the women at Perkins Global Records offer a more sanctimonious title to Agent Tight-Ass, and that one's even worse, a breathy, lustful, submissive *Mr. Nashville.*

Like he's important or something.

I roll my eyes as I hear it now. *Yes, Mr. Nashville; right away, Mr. Nashville;* and the most gag-inducing of them all, *anything you say, Mr. Nashville,* through lash-fluttering eyes.

*Well, fuck that.*

I raise a brow in challenge when he doesn't respond, driving in his inadequacy with one smirk, something men like him despise.

And damn, do I love being despised by men.

Like, okay, so you have balls and a ding-a-ling, whoop de do. Nobody cares. We could use your parts for reproduction and survive fine without you. We only need your sperm, *men.*

I don't want Mr. Nashville's sperm, as it happens.

And I have a theory he's a bit salty by that fact, seeing as how I just swallowed throatfuls from the band he's managing on the bus, and he hasn't stopped scraping my body with his icy blue irises all week, licking thick lips, permanently turned down in a scowl of disapproval.

I may or may not be sleeping with them. The band that is, not his lips.

And don't judge, either. Ever heard of a why-choose romance? Women can have entire harems these days.

Anyway, I'm dumping them. It's day six, and that means what it always does for me.

It's in the past.

The record label will have brand-new talent to strut soon, and who knows? With my last job being kaput and no prospects lined up to replace it, maybe I'll go on tour with them, too.

I don't do it just for the sex. My endless VIP passes to these tours are my escape. Always have been. Musicians, new cities, another chance to fall in love and feel the electricity that brings? I'm in every time.

Don't get me wrong, I *love* love.

My friends would say I'm a matchmaker. Find me a couple pining over lost time and missed connections, and I'm there for it. I will alter the elements themselves for a happily ever after. That's why I became an officiant, one of my three hundred and two jobs since I was seventeen, none of which I've stuck with, but that's beside the point.

I love *falling* in love, not necessarily staying in love. Much like my jobs, it's about the unknown...the chase, the catch, and reward. The high you get when you willingly enter the storm.

But once it's all said and done, it's like everything else...over. And the high fades right along with it.

I don't need money.

We have lifetimes of it. So much that my father doesn't notice I've given every cent I've earned since high school to those in need. It's sickening enough the thousands of dollars missing each month hardly dips the line graph his accountant keeps on my vault, but for me to simply hoard it among piles of wealth when my neighbor's kid can't afford his EpiPen?

I hate the rich, even if I am one.

I used to think my last job would be the one, a live-in care tech for a hospice patient, someone I knew on a personal level.

I was serving my community.

And unlike my other jobs, where I felt bumpered and boxed in by the oblivion of sameness, giving my attention to someone I grew to love like a second father gave me purpose.

He died, as patients in that line of work do, and I grieved him like a daughter.

*Randall Holiday.*

I can hardly say his name aloud without breaking. Regardless of whether I knew he was dying, preparing for it with the rest of his team and understanding the inherent biology behind his terminal illness, none of that mattered.

I was torn by his absence. I became part of his world, and then he was no longer in it.

Even if my own father is disappointed that I didn't *stick with a job this time*, I can't love just to lose.

I need change like I need my next breath, something Papa will never understand, being a self-made billionaire. Structure and work ethic are his pillars. But when you grow up with unlimited money and zero boundaries like me, you learn what takes most people a lifetime to realize.

Life is moment to moment.

There is no up or down or right or wrong. It's just a bunch of beings, strung together by societal standards and reason, governed by self-inflicted constraints.

But *why?*

There's so much to experience. And being tied down by jobs or projects...or people...isn't worth it when you only get one chance to live.

Jobs will replace you. People will leave you.

But adventures? You can keep them forever.

Besides, who wants one dick for the rest of their life if they can have a variety?

Does it make me a ho?

Some would say.

But *some* are patriarchal asshats, so I mean, *meh.*

I enjoy life, I love sex, and I live for my next thrill. And with more money in my trust than I can spend in three lifetimes, who the fuck cares if that's how I live?

Nash does, apparently.

He growls, a deep rumble that'd probably feel good on your clit if he didn't look so mad, and his nostrils flare when he stares, as if he can read the dirty thoughts that strip him bare inside my mind.

He sets his jaw like he's gearing up for a fight, and I take back all prior thoughts of said clit-rumbling.

I like him mad.

He's attractive and incredibly fit. Okay, he's flat-out eye candy, but he's stiff. And not in the pelvic way.

It's No-Nonsense-Nash.

Always *be careful*, and *don't climb scaffolding in heels*.

He's closer to my father's age than mine.

He *is* a father.

I won't linger on why I'm suddenly hyperaware of that fact.

"Did you hear a word I said?" Nash snaps, irritated as always, and usually at me. "The band needs to get some writing in this stretch of the tour. From now until Centerville, they are on strict orders—*no groupies*."

His eyes flick down my body, assessing my slashed-up band tee and fishnets shoved tightly into knee high, leather, zip-up stilettos because they're sexy as fuck and I do not apologize for that.

"Oh, Nash," I offer, earning an irritated groan, "You seem to have forgotten I'm not a groupie." I wave my VIP pass in the air, emblazoned with a bright blue stamp reading Quality Assurance. "I was appointed to be here."

"Self-appointed," he grumbles. "I need them focused, Miss Perkins. Your father will—"

I smile widely as I encroach on his big important man space. "*My father* will be pleased to learn how smoothly you run his events when I tell him what an amazing time everyone had with absolutely zero hiccups, all thanks to his number one tour manager."

His eyes narrow as I reach my tiptoes and whisper in his ear. "Don't worry, Daddy. When I'm done playing with my toys, I always put them back where they belong."

"Jesus, Sour Patch. If he knew the way you speak—"

"You gonna tell on me? I might be cursed to look young, but I'm twenty-eight, you know."

"I'm well aware."

Blatant desire laces his words, and I bristle as my nipples harden to needy fucking beacons and the incredulous tease of a man simply smirks.

"Well, then, you're aware I can speak to, and fuck, whomever I want. An entire band. Or two. Or three, even. And despite what you might think, Nashy-Poo, it doesn't make a woman a slut for loving her body and enjoying life."

"I didn't say it did, I said—"

"You implied I shouldn't talk sexy."

"No, I didn't."

"Yeah, you did, Papa Bear. I said stuff about boy toys, you said don't talk like that, threw in some daddy kink, and—"

"Daddy *what*?"

"Daddy kink." I blink at him. He can't be serious, right? "You know the routine. Bad girl needs punished, sugar daddy gives her the spankin' she never got, and everyone gets a happily ever after."

His mouth hangs open like I've grown three heads.

"Have you seriously never watched porn?"

"What? Of course I haven't watched porn!"

"Bullshit."

"Excuse me?" Nash's brow knits, his voice low and menacing. "What did you say?"

*Yeah, I definitely like him mad.*

Probably why I press it further.

"I said bullshit. There is not a single man in this country who hasn't scrolled some tits or ass at least once. I mean, at the very least you've watched a few casting couches, right?"

"Casting...couches?" He seems truly stumped.

*Maybe this man isn't lying.*

Maybe he really is just a silver fox, single dude who enjoys work and doesn't want to fuck anything with legs.

Perhaps that's why I plant my seed, crossing my arms over my chest so my boobs peek out the top of the cut-up band tee. His eyes immediately fall there, as predicted, and a smile steals my face as I clear my throat, and they snap back to mine.

I like it when Nash stares.

He's done it this entire tour. And the last. And the one before that. Different bands, of course, but each time, I wonder when he'll finally crack. At which point will he stop watching and join in?

Or would he take me all for himself, his salt-and-pepper beard brushing along my slick center, tasting me like I know he wants?

"I'll compromise with you," I say. "Let me ride the bus to Centerville. Papa owns a hotel there, and I have some friends I can visit."

"Do these friends have couches you'll be cast on?"

I don't miss the air of annoyance behind his inquiry. As if he has any right to judge what I do in my spare time.

"Maybe," I challenge. "Does that bother you?"

"That? No, that doesn't bother me, Sour Patch." His gaze scrapes down my body. "It's everything else about you that does."

# Chapter Two

## LEMON

The saltwater air kisses my cheeks as I glide down the boardwalk near the Centerville Stadium. My bright yellow roller blades with tiny black lemons inked across the sides shine in the morning light as the sun peeks over the ocean horizon.

A rush of brisk air launches into my body, filling the empty spaces with satisfaction. My feet turn out of their own accord into a spread eagle, and I throw my head back, soaking up the energy of the coastal town.

Another adventure in the books.

I slipped off the bus with the sunrise to work in a skate session before I scoop my luggage and check into Papa's hotel.

A sense of relief settles within me at the thought of starting fresh. Maybe I'll take up counseling. At least then my sociology degree wouldn't go to waste.

I shift into a move my old figure-skating coaches would have chastised me over forgetting the name of, as I was never much good on ice. Too much precision required.

But on the rough tread of pavement, I move with the world, not through it. My foot goes back, and my body snaps into position. I glide, skating dangerously backward over the floating docks and twisting in a double lutz that has the shipyard boys whistling and howling, as I shimmy my hips and throw them a kiss.

Eventually, I reach an opening, a wide marketplace just past the boardwalk. I veer toward it in search of new charms for the bracelets I never remove. My mother, whomever and wherever she may be, got the first for me when I was seven.

Just before she left us and never returned. Sometimes I hate the bracelets, for all they represent.

Lies.

"Every charm you add is a new adventure, Lemmy," she'd said, adding an apple for the day we'd spent at the orchard. "One day, you will have a whole set of adventures to remember. Never settle for a life you don't love with every breath."

Then she left.

No note. No kiss. Just a goodbye to my father in the night, as he ran after a car she smashed through locked gates.

I don't remember much about her.

Or that night.

Just the sound of my father sobbing while she yanked her roots from his heart and never looked back.

Guess she only loved us with half her breath.

That was in the past, but I still wear the bracelet.

And her words still haunt me, too.

I'm aware it's psychologically questionable, but I wear this dumb metal loop around my wrists like a shackle. And every day, I put it back on, adding adventure after adventure as I go, in the form of little charms like this stupid fucking rhinestone apple.

I finger the faded gem that represents the last happy memory I have of my mother, and I swallow my grief back down where it belongs. Papa and I fared perfectly well without her, anyway.

I have four full bangles now. I wear two on each wrist, and I dare a motherfucker to tell me it's stupid. These are *my* adventures.

My proof you can do whatever the hell you want and still stick around maybe? I don't know.

I'm proving something at this point. I'm just not sure what.

I skid to a halt by a tarot card stand with rows of hand-made jewelry, some of which are tiny silver charms. One of them is a guitar, which could work, but it's not the first band I've toured with, and it probably won't be the last, so I pass it by, scanning the booth for something more specific.

One of the guys is nicknamed Onyx, for the dark onyx gauges he wears in his ears, and that could be a unique way of honoring this adventure, but my heart tugs a little when I think about him.

I told the guys I was 'breaking up' with them, so to speak, last night. Honestly, it's not a breakup when you're just messing around on a tour, and most of them were privy this would come to a swift end when we got to the next city, as most tour-bus relationships do, but Onyx was different.

He got glassy-eyed when I broke it off, informing him I'll be staying in Centerville when they leave tomorrow.

Darkpath is a great band, its members all gorgeous, seasoned rock gods, but Onyx is a baby compared to the others, a replacement for their retired drummer. He's only twenty-three.

And his puppy dog eyes cast little daggers at my soul when he looked at me like I'd stolen the heart right out of his chest.

He seemed fine after we talked on the boardwalk, with the others still passed out on the bus and immune to long-term relationships, like me, but I can tell he's not over it.

He's one of the good ones.

Not for me, that's for sure.

He's a settle-downer, even if he is a rockstar.

And I'm not the girl who will be waiting for you in the bus for the rest of your life while you enjoy all the fun, I assure you that.

Still, I find myself picking up the onyx charm shaped like a puppy and smiling at the sentiment. I glide on my skates toward the vendor, an eccentric woman with silver curls bouncing around her face and bright, rosy cheeks. Rows of rings line her fingers, half of her head woven with haphazard braids and colorful feathers.

"How much for the dog charm?" I ask.

"The dog?" She closes her eyes, humming before she answers me, and I find myself looking around to see if anyone notices her odd behavior, but the streets are too busy.

Her eyes snap back open, locked on me. "Not for sale."

"What?" I scrunch my nose. "It was sitting on a platform that says *Charms for Sale.*"

She lowers her glasses on her nose, squinting curiously over the rims. "And yet, it is not."

I know I shouldn't care. I could find another charm at one of the hundreds of tables lining the boardwalk, but you haven't met me if that's where you think we're going with this story.

"I'll give you whatever you want for it. One hundred bucks."

"No." She shuts her cash box.

"Three hundred." I raise a brow.

She considers this a moment, but still, she refuses.

I chew the inside of my lip, angry and revved up to win a competition I'm not even sure I entered for a charm that definitely isn't worth more than a steak dinner, yet here I am treating it like a whole fucking cow at an auction. "Six hundred dollars." I grind out, and the old woman finally breaks.

"Deal."

"Wait, really?"

I'm not sure what happened.

Did I just agree to spend six hundred dollars on a dog charm representing a man-boy I dumped last night?

She laughs as though she can hear my thoughts.

"Are you sane?"

"Not one bit, dear." She cackles, using a shaky hand to reach out and place the onyx dog before me on a velvet display. "But you aren't either, I see." She points her knobby finger at my bracelets and brushes it through the charms, the hundreds of adventures I hold against my mother clanking together.

I snatch my hand back as she laughs again, noting that the charm is no longer on the velvet display, but somehow…it's already dangling from my left wrist.

And next to it is another charm.

One I find my eyes drawn to like a hunter to her prey, curious and hungry. My eyes dart to hers. "What's this?"

The crazy woman smiles at me, her cackling turning into a singsong of sorts as I finger the new charms that brush my skin.

"That is my one stipulation." She grabs the bills I produce from my foot pack and tucks them, one by one, into her cash box with a wink. "Think of it as a buy one, get one free."

"Free?" I balk, staring down at the new charm I didn't ask for, that doesn't represent any adventures and therefore, doesn't belong on these shackles… I mean…bracelets. "I didn't even want this charm. How can you charge someone six hundred dollars for one they want and then give them something entirely unsolicited of the same quality and size, free? It makes zero sense."

"The apple," she taps the charm my mother gave me, "doesn't fall far from the tree then, now, does it?"

I yank my arm back, turning away from her as goosebumps prickle my skin.

A loud crack sounds through the darkening sky and the clouds split above us.

"Perhaps a lemon won't fall at all. Maybe it needs to be plucked."

I whip around to face her, my body zinging with electricity and, quite frankly, the heebie-jeebies at the fact she knows my name. *Who even is this woman?* A friend of my father's? I recall the tarot cards at the edge of her display. A psychic?

But I'm stumped when I find nothing more than an empty booth where the odd woman was once standing, the only evidence of her existence, a box of charms under a sign that reads *Free to a good home.*

Every last one of them.

*What the hell?*

I stand in the square, turning on my wheels as I search for the wild woman who just ripped me the fuck off and knew far too much about me for comfort, but she's gone. Aside from the charms, it's if she was never there in the first place, and I'm left to my own, stunned, drenched, and fiddling with two new charms.

A black dog.

*And a silver fox.*

# Chapter Three

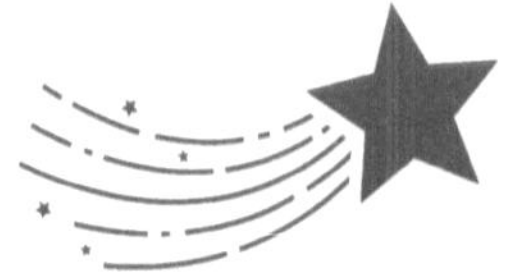

## OLIVER

"T hought you left." I zone in on the CEO's sopping wet daughter, slinging open the doorway to the bus. A white T-shirt exposes her midriff, Perkins Records across the front in bright pink gems, and my cock hardens as I struggle to peel my eyes away.

The cotton sweatpants I'd chosen—when I assumed she'd gone—now stretch painfully over my erection. I may as well be nude beneath the thin gray fabric.

My teeth gnash together at my vulnerability. Exhibiting less than professional composure is not something I'm in the habit of doing.

Not on a tour.

Certainly not around Lemon Perkins, the boss's daughter, *and constant splinter beneath my skin.*

I lean against the kitchenette, unable to drag my eyes away from her, this rhinestone wrinkle I can never seem to smooth out. It's almost compulsory how I wish I could.

Of course she didn't leave like we agreed.

She never does what she's told, but it's time someone taught her to do so. The crew need their focus. The band needs to practice.

And I need this tour to break records.

I could call her father.

I should.

But what good is accusing his flesh and blood of being a distraction right before he announces the promotion?

It's down to me and his west coast tour manager now. But I'm the one with eight years of service to the company, and more than one hint has been dropped my way these last few weeks. It would be foolish to be anything but amenable to Miss Lemon Perkins in my current position, no matter how distracting she may be.

My jaw ticks as my eyes fix on the fabric stretching across her breasts, made transparent by the rain. She's braless, and that's the least surprising thing about her. Her pert nipples stand unabashed under my watch, and I find it impossible to look elsewhere.

"Up here, Mr. Nashville," she purrs, like the interns who whisper *Milf*—manager I'd like to fuck— behind my back, a practice I would never engage in despite the rumors.

When you're a single male and keep to yourself, people assume things, but I've been with no one since my wife passed eight years ago.

And even if the thought of filling Lemon Perkins' incorrigible mouth until she can't talk back has crossed my mind more than I'm comfortable admitting, I have held back every desire to spill my load across those pouted lips.

Lips she bites right now, *dripping wet*.

Watching me.

"Why are you here?" I snap, unable to contain my rage and my cock at the same time, and I'll be damned if I let this wanton tease of a trust fund see me come unraveled.

*No.* Not when I'm this close to securing a partnership that would get me off the road, and in tenured board seat with the most influential man of the east coast music industry, her father, Emil Perkins.

This will be our ticket to normalcy. Stability for my family, allowing me to work locally, quit touring, and save money for my girls and their futures.

I've done well with the generous salaries the company sets, but this is what I've been working for since Lauren died, and it was up to me alone to see them thrive.

What if all four of them get into college? That's a price tag I can't comprehend at the pay I earn now. Cheer team, ballet, and recreational art lessons break the bank enough.

My brow creases as I stand at a stalemate with a billionaire's bratty heiress, in a bus I spend more time in than my own home.

*I'm too old for this life.*

I want to settle down, and Mr. Perkins likes me. I've spent close to a decade proving my worth at his feet, all to make my goals reality. And if everything goes smoothly through the end of the quarter, a spot at the big table will be waiting for me.

I feel it.

Confidence grips me at the thought of becoming present with my girls.

No more nannies and detentions I haven't got time to understand or resolve. No more slammed doors or missed recitals.

No more disappointed glares from eyes that match Lauren's. Eyes that beg me to do better.

It's time I paved the sharp edges created by her death. I sigh, running my hand through my hair as I think about my oldest, and the spitfire she's become.

I worry about Bryar, sneaking out and seeking her next thrill. If I'm not careful, she'll turn out like…

"I have eyes, you know." Lemon smirks, shoving past me in the doorway. She tugs her clothes off in the middle of the bus and drops them to the floor, drowning out every thought I had before this moment as she stands completely nude and twists her hair into a bun. "Check-in isn't 'til eleven, Sherlock."

"The hell are you doing, Sour Patch?" I groan at my worsening erection and avert my gaze. "Put them back on this instant."

I train my eyes away, growling like a wounded animal, likely because I am one. My cock throbs painfully at the mere sight of her, but the insufferable brat just giggles, twisting bright yellow hair around a finger I want to suck between my teeth, and...*shit*.

"This is not comical!" I will my eyes in the opposite direction. "Miss Perkins, you will put some clothes on immediately, or I'll—"

"You'll what, Daddy?" she whispers, stopping me dead in my tracks.

"Don't call me that."

"Why not, *Daddy*? Does it make you feel naughty? Because you want to put your big, hard cock in my pussy and fill me with your cum?" Her eyes sparkle as my mind reels at her words. "You could, you know. I'd let you right now."

I whip around, not bothering to cover my erection from this excruciating harlot who tempts me every waking hour, but it's mistake number one.

I lose all composure with her bare body before me, and I feel my control as it slips.

"Do you know what I see when I look at you, Miss Perkins?" I step closer, a risky move when I want so badly to feel the weight of her breasts in my palms, suck her nipples, brand them with lessons she's yet to learn from the playboys she toys with. I want her to know how I see her.

"A slut."

She says it like she believes it.

"*What?* No." I frown.

Her eyes soften, and it warms places of me it shouldn't. I've been gruff with her, distancing myself on tours, pushing her away with harsh stares and short words, but it's necessity.

This conversation alone is already more than it should be. Still, I can't have her thinking so little of herself. She's got the whole world at her fingertips if only she believed it.

"Why would you think that? That you're a...that I think you're..." She's never been shy about her promiscuity before. Lemon Perkins could give two fucks what I think, couldn't she?

"Because you like good girls, or you would have tried something by now." The hurt in her eyes spikes me in the chest even before she twists the knife. "Probably ones who don't let older men watch them have orgies while they palm their big fat cocks." Her violet eyes narrow on the tented fabric below my waist.

I don't love her.

I hardly know her.

*I know the face she makes when she comes.*

A chemical reaction.

*A physical goddamned need.*

But it's not fair to Lauren to love again.

Even if I did, ten of me couldn't sate one evening of Lemon's lascivious needs.

Not to mention she's a mess.

Tests me on a daily basis. Drives wrenches in all of my systems. She's reckless.

But the way her dripping cunt glistens beneath my stare, how I want to show her she's more than this reputation she feigns, it grows as hard as my god forsaken cock.

"I like order," I clip. "And you make everything the opposite." A growl that surprises even me rumbles from my throat and drags her eyes to mine. "But you are not a slut, nor do I see you as one."

Her eyes widen. It hurts me that she assumed I thought so little. She's free, but she loves with her whole self. I've seen it. She will be that band's biggest cheerleader for the rest of their career. She'll befriend their significant others. She'll send them birthday cards.

She may be unorthodox, but Lemon Perkins is not a slut.

"You don't think I'm—"

"No." My fists clench at my sides, hair stands on end, and my cock leaks at the tip for her. Somehow, the millions of reasons not to be with her don't exist in this moment.

*Fuck it.* I grab the back of her neck and yank her lips to mine, planting a kiss I feel all the way to the head of my cock. "You're not a slut, Sour Patch." I rub my thumb over her lips.

"But it's time someone taught you some lessons."

The twinkle in her eyes is a cosmic swirl. "You gonna teach me yourself," she teases, "or watch someone do it for you?"

With that, I flip her over my lap faster than my brain can process, feet tumbling over gravity on our hasty topple to the sofa. My fingers part her dripping cunt, and I want to hate it, to loathe her for pushing me to this moment, but her whimpers own me as she bucks her hips to meet my touch.

I don't enter her, just spread her arousal around her swollen center, in awe that it's there for me, Lemon Anne Perkins. "All for me," I growl without thought as I rub her pussy, squeezing it in my palm like it truly is mine.

Her moans become as needy as her tilting hips, and I worry someone will hear.

"Shh." I slide my thumb into her mouth. I'm rough, but I know this woman's kinks like I know my own dreams, and her grinding hips tell me she's more than spurred on by the play. She sucks and swirls her tongue over my thumb like I wish she'd do on my cock, and I try not to think about the reasons she's become this skilled. That she's practiced and learned on God knows how many men before me is a thought that makes me want to shove my length in and take up all the space inside of her, until there's no room left for anyone else.

I fume at the thought of her with any other man. The band, Onyx, the ones I've seen licking all the places I want to taste as she comes, meeting my gaze and whispering my name across the room.

It's always been for me.

Two dozen tours.

And hundreds of orgasms straight from her perfect, moaning lips.

They might get her screams, but what they don't know is, I see her eyes.

*She comes for me.*

My undoing, Lemon Perkins. She reads the room and rewrites the script, and hell if my fingers haven't been dying to flip every last page since I met her.

I slam my palm down hard across her ass, and the brat likes it. Of course she does.

The fact she can't be broken fuels my fire even more. It rages in the presence of her strength. She rides the line and tests the limits until I'm left straddling the edge of right and wrong, asking myself whether feasting on this storm of a woman will end the hunger for good or just make me a tempestuous glutton.

Boss's daughter or not, I gave my heart up long ago, and I don't think I'll ever get it back.

That's fair to no one, which is why this is a horrible idea.

She moans around my thumb, and the vibrations go straight to my cock that's pressed deep into her stomach as she lies across me, breaking up my thoughts.

"Nash! Please!" she begs for more, for the release only my eyes can bring, my name on her tongue and her flesh between my grip...but I can't do it, can I?

This is wrong.

Emil's daughter.

Yet she feels like she should be mine in all the ways I shouldn't want.

I roar, bringing my hand down as hard as I can across the right side of her tight muscular ass, one I imagine slamming against as I grind her naked body over my cock. I growl, unsure which thing I'm feeling more intensely.

That she makes me lose control?

Or how damn good it feels to hold her across my lap and use her for pleasure, to hear the moans and cries and know they're just for me.

*"Miiiiine,"* I growl the word like a curse, rocking her naked form back and forth across my lap, punishing my cock that's still trapped beneath a thin cotton barrier and

aching for the warmth of her wet cunt I can feel at the tips of my fingers.

But this moment here is as close as I'll allow myself to get. I grip harder, grinding until I explode, my body shaking violently as my fingernails sink into her curves.

I groan with instant regret as I watch the white marks across her backside turn red in the shape of my fingers, bruising before she's even left my lap, my mark on her body something she'll still bear when she's strewn across those godforsaken couches I can't get out of my head.

"I looked up casting couches last night," I growl, as she slides off my lap and throws a sassy grin my way. I don't miss the clench of her thighs, reminding me she hasn't orgasmed yet.

*Yet? What am I thinking?*

I scrub my hand over my face, blowing out a breath.

She's thrown on a band tee, seemingly unbothered by what just occurred, and I eye the shirt greedily, hating the way someone else's musk now kisses her nipples.

Nipples I haven't yet tasted.

And there it is again. *Yet.*

I grind my teeth at the jealousy and desire taking hold, over a woman who would lay with me just as soon as the next man who walks through her daddy's office door.

She picks lint from the front of the abominable shirt I ought to rip right off.

Who knows which member of this tour bus it belongs to. I don't think she cares, even if it bothers me like nothing else.

Her legs dangle from the loft bed above the kitchen nook, her usual bunk when she weasels her way onto these coastal tours. I can still see the pink glowing stars above it that she stuck there on her first one.

Guilt stabs me as I watch her there now, feet hanging with French manicured toes, like they were back then...when she had just turned twenty.

What I just did was not only professionally wrong, but morally and ethically as well. I'm fifteen years her senior.

Doesn't matter that she's a willing participant in all things hedonist, or that she's a grown adult. If some old asshole preyed on my daughter like I am Mr. Perkins', I'd end him, sexy violet eyes of an invitation or not.

If she tells her father, I could lose out on the promotion and the opportunity to settle down with my family. To glue the cracks of our foundation before it comes crumbling down.

I can't allow that.

Not for anyone.

"Your father can't know of this. We can't…" I struggle to get it out, half of my brain warring against the words that will push her away from me instead of in my arms and my bed where the deluded half of me craves her to be.

But I'll do anything for my girls.

I swallow, knowing what must be done for my family and our future.

Even if it's a lie.

"It was a lapse in judgment. It won't happen again; you have my word." I nod. "Miss Perkins."

That's who she is.

Not Sour Patch.

She's the daughter of my boss. The woman who will inherit every bit of the global enterprise controlling my family's futures without so much stepping a single toe in the boardroom.

She's a billionaire's heiress, Lemon Perkins.

And I'm the help.

Her smile slips with each word I speak. I see hurt in her eyes, just briefly, but it's gone as soon as it starts. She turns her attention to her jingling bracelets, pinching a tiny silver charm between her finger and thumb, feigning nonchalance, despite the storm in her eyes.

"What's there to tell?" she asks. "It's not like I got off or anything."

I deserve the jab. I've hurt her.

She hops from the loft and takes up all the space left within my lungs as she presses her lips to my ear. "Men come undone for me all the time. But you know that better than most."

It wounds me just like she hopes it will, but I don't react. Years of parenting taught me that's exactly what she wants. She wants to see me want her.

And I need to convince both of us that I don't.

"I didn't mean to hurt you."

She's all any man would want, and she knows it, but I'm not that man for her.

Her lip trembles, and it breaks a heart I didn't know I still had. But this is what's best for us both.

"Sour Patch, I—"

"Don't call me that anymore." Her eyes score my heart with finality, and I know it shouldn't wound me, but it does. "I'm sure there are several someone else's around here more than willing to make the left cheek match the right." She leans closer, daring me to shut her up with my tongue and finish what I began. I lean, too, before...

"They might even let you watch."

*Fuck.*

I shove away, and she gasps, stealing my breath as she retreats, hurt and surprise etched across her brow.

She's beautiful, tempestuous, and reckless, full breasts heaving, and those otherworldly purple eyes swirling and charged. I ache to fall to my knees for this woman and worship the goddess she doesn't know she could be...this tease of a yellow bow that's needled her way into my tour bus and worse, my heart.

But I don't.

And she knows very well that means we're done here. We must be. And if she thinks that's what I want in order for this to end, then I'll do what I must to keep us apart. For my family.

She doesn't bother replacing her panties, just swipes my work jacket from the wall hanger, wipes the arousal from her unsated cunt and tugs the hem of the band tee back over her thighs. She gives me one last look of pure disgust before she snatches up her in-line skates and slams the door behind her.

My chest heaves, cock hard again at the passion behind her anger. At the suggestion I'd need another man's permission to watch.

Even if it was just another one of her missiles to my defenses, it worked.

I yank my sweatpants off, wrapping my bottom half in a towel and moving to my private bunk for replacement clothes, but before I can solve one problem, my next begins.

My jaw tightens at the name on the phone.

Scrubbing my palm down my face, I throw on my slacks and polo combo as I swipe accept.

"Mrs. Kempling, yes, how are you? The girls all right?" I hold my breath when she doesn't immediately reply, familiar with the silence and what it means.

What now? Are they hurt? Is someone in trouble?

I hate that I'm not already there to know. To control and fix whatever the problem may be.

But I know—deep down, I know. And I heave a sigh as I flick my fingers to the blinds of the bus and look out at the loading dock.

"What's Bryar done, Mrs. Kempling?"

She hesitates longer, but her voice cracks and she finally speaks. "I'm sorry, but she's horrible, Mr. Nashville! I...I tried. I thought I was making headway, but she's...she's..."

"She's what?" My pulse quickens, worry still lacing my fears even as they are replaced by anger that she's done it again. I know right now, by the tone in our nanny's voice, that this will be Mrs. Kempling's last day, and my teenage daughter is the culprit. "Tell me." I'm short with her, dominance maintaining control.

It's what I'm good at. Why I'm in charge of these million-dollar tours. And somehow, despite all that experience, it's a thirteen-year-old girl who brings me to my knees for guidance.

"What has she done, Mrs. Kempling? Drugs? Alcohol? Shoplifting again?" I massage the bridge of my nose as I pace the small stretch of the bus. "Jesus, please say it isn't boys."

"It's boys," Mrs. Kempling starts, but that's as far as she gets before I curse, throwing my phone to the floor and ending the call.

I'm lucky it isn't cracked.

I dial Mrs. Kempling back and apologize, getting the full story of Bryar and the tenth grade, car-driving boyfriend she snuck out with.

My fists clench, my stomach already in knots. She could get in a wreck or mistreated.

*A boyfriend?*

I don't even know this young man.

Roadies cart tubs of lighting gels and cables into the venue as I stare out a window that doesn't open to my girls doing cartwheels on a green, sunny lawn, and I know with all certainty, this is my doing.

I haven't been home to meet this boy, even if she'd wanted me to. I sink to the floor spinning the imaginary ring on my left finger, the one I feel even if I no longer wear it.

"You would have known how to fix her," I cry to Lauren, to the fucking air as tears spring to my eyes. "I'm the one who should have died, and our children are the ones who suffer for it."

Not anymore.

I rise from the ground and straighten my clothes.

Tracing the word *Perkins* across my badge, I shove all thoughts of bratty teenagers—and adults, as it were—from my head, replacing them with one thought only. Promotion.

The Nashville family will not crumble.

"I promise, Lo."

# *Chapter Four*

## Lemon

"**F**uck that fucker." Mud sloshes up against my slick thighs and bare center, but I don't give a damn right now. I refuse to care about what anyone else considers wrong or dirty or different.

My entire life, I've been told to sit still. To obey standards impossibly opposite what I feel inside.

All I've ever wanted was to be seen for who I am and accepted for the things they shame.

*"You are not a slut."*

He does that. Mr. O. L. Fucking Nashville, whatever the hell that stupid ass acronym stands for.

He sees me.

He makes my insides melt and my outsides burn at the same goddamned time, his stare branding me as his, even if he says it's not so.

He knows where his eyes will always wander.

And now? I'll be wherever I please.

On his tour bus.

In his office.

Right the fuck in his face.

Until he stops playing games and mans up. Nothing is forever, but I know if he'll give in and let us ride whatever this thing between us is, it'll put an end to the constant ache I feel around him.

Two weeks of Daddy Nash as my personal pogo stick, and we'll both be better for it. He'll be just like the rest, in the past, and maybe he won't be so grumpy all the damn time.

He can deny all he pleases, but he wants it as bad as I do; my ass still feels the proof.

I wish my ass didn't like it.

Getting it out of our systems is the only option, whether he believes it or not.

I slide to a halt by the market from earlier, the witchy woman fresh on my mind. She couldn't have vanished into thin air. It was a trick, a sleight of hand or…mirrors. That's got to be how she got the charms on my wrist.

And if she's here somewhere, maybe she could read my tarot. Look into a crystal ball or some shit.

At this point, I just need to bitch to someone, and if that someone happens to be clairvoyant, at least one of us will know what the fuck Nash was thinking.

I duck beneath the railing and wind between rows of vendors, but after minutes of circling, I'm at a loss.

Maybe it's time for a new adventure. One that isn't O.L. Nashville.

I pull in lungfuls of air as I skid to a defeated stop. I've never been turned down.

A school sits to my left behind a tall chain-link fence. A few kids stop playing to wave, but as soon as I wave back, their fearless ringleader gives me the middle finger and mocks my wonky stop.

Glad to see mean girls haven't changed.

"Santa saw that!" I skate past, but my wheel jams beneath me, and before I know it, I'm toppling over while the little brats gather at the fence to point and giggle.

"Girls," an elderly woman shrieks, "get away from that woman! Back to the blacktop!"

I roll my eyes before I hear the last bit. "You never know what diseases women like that have. This is why you stay in school."

Wow. Good to know authority hasn't changed since I was in school either.

People think what they want.

I've learned to let them.

Soon, their snickering fades to the back of my mind as a stickier situation settles in. A glob of bubblegum stretches from my wheels to a crumpled paper, the RealiTea TV logo across the top in all caps. I unfold it, shaking the sand from its crevices.

**Are you a thrill seeker? Athletic, tactical, and…single?**
**Defy the odds and test your limits.**
**On a secluded, booby-trapped mountain where two adventurous sin-**
**gles will find love as they become**
**King and Queen of Adventure Mountain.**
**Oh, and did we mention…**
**<u>ONE MILLION DOLLARS</u>**
**RealiTea is seeking twenty contestants ages 18+ for their newest**
**reality show**
**Interested parties are asked to send a video application.**
**Agency Represented Casting Only.**

That's it.

My next adventure. Who better to take on the title of Queen of Adventure Mountain than the queen of adventures herself? My bangles jingle in the wind, and I swear I can hear the unmistakable cackle of the woman from before as the wind howls around me, the rain finally gone and the clouds opening to a tiny sliver of yellow sun.

I yank my phone from the waterproof compartment attached to my skates—something that, yes, money can buy, as it happens—and I snap a quick photo of the casting call. Sending it to my former agent, Tina, I fold the paper into a tiny football and shove it beneath my phone case, returning both to my skate compartment and zipping it closed.

I'm going to apply for this show. And if money has anything to say about it, I'm getting cast too. Throw some cleavage and a couple thousand dollars at a man behind a desk, and you can get just about any gig you want in this city. I learned that in my short stint acting and modeling, quitting after realizing what a sham the whole industry was. At least I got Tina out of it. She may have been a shitty agent, but she's the life of the party, and just what I need to get over the grump I refuse to think about.

I'm sure Papa won't love it, especially when it's not for the benefit of the company...or marriage, something he never forgets to mention when he sees me. I get that he's worried. I haven't found my dream job yet, or man, and despite his attempts to convince me hard work at the family company will satisfy my whims or be *just my thing*, it's not.

And it won't.

Not until it's under *my* control. I can't make change in this place if he keeps insisting we stay in the 1900s with our promotional tactics. I've tried. Working alongside my father is like choosing an A track when the iPhone is right in front of you.

I have plans for this company, but not until he agrees to let me do it my way.

And one day soon, he'll stop letting me gallivant and force me into that box I'm not sure he enjoys, himself, all for the Perkins name.

I feel it coming sooner than I'd like. With each day that nears my thirtieth birthday, his worried eyes scan me, almost diagnostically. Categorically.

Will I settle down?

Get married?

Provide a grandson so his fortune has a proper heir? Stupid patriarchy. That's the first construct I'll be dismantling the moment I have financial power at Perkins Global.

Or perhaps I'll finally take an interest in the company as a good female trustee and roll my ass around in a cubicle and tube skirt with plain black stilettos, possibly with buckles on the ankles.

I shudder at that. Of being glued to screens of arbitrary words, answering foreign rights calls and sitting pretty for press conferences, even though my voice won't ever be heard. It's never been done before for someone like me.

A woman in charge at Perkins Global.

Not with all the Johns and Jims who congest my father's judgement.

A whimsical girl who can't sit still in charge at Perkins Global? They'd never take me seriously.

I'm not serious or still.

And I don't plan on changing that.

So, yeah, I guess I'm gonna climb this mountain and win that competition. Not for a million-dollar prize; Lord knows I don't need it. I'll donate my earnings like always.

No...it's something more.

The power to be unapologetically me.

I can sit still and pretty when I'm dead.

Scrunching my nose, I dial up my bestie. I need to confirm whether I'm justified in today's drama.

"Hey, Jer." I sigh.

"Hey, Lem." He sighs back.

"Am I being a brat?"

"Hmm. I don't know. Probably. Give me the parameters by which I should judge you this time."

"Well, everything was fine until I let Daddy Nashville spank me until he came in his...get this, Jer...fucking gray sweatpants—"

"No!" He groans wistfully. "They were actually gray? Not even ash? He *has* to know."

"Right?" I run my fingers through my tangled mess of hair. "Anyway, he comes faster than a frat boy on a Friday, then gets all 'don't tell your dad' and 'this can't be,' like I'm a child and not a perfectly whole ass woman, and I got mad, Jer, okay? Don't judge, but I used his fancy jacket as a cum rag before I left and threw it at his stupid old man feet."

I take in a breath of air while Jeremy remains silent and the football shaped flier burns a hole through my skate, clouding my mind with my next thrill.

"There's more!" I say, rolling through the plaza, still searching for my psychic. "I met this old witchy woman earlier who charged me six hundred dollars for a dog charm..."

"What?" Jeremy balks.

"It's a long story. But I came back to her stand and found something. A reality show is looking for contestants. There's a mountain and adventures, and it might be a dating show, but who cares. It's a sign, right? I should forget about Daddy Whorebucks and go climb the mountain?"

Jeremy stays silent longer than I'd like.

But I don't want to be wrong this time.

"I'm being a brat, huh?"

"Yes, hon, you are."

"How?" I whine. "I don't see how I was in the wrong when he's the one not man enough to admit he wants me. And even if he does admit it, it wouldn't be forever. He needs like...*a wife*. I think he might have kids. Can you imagine me with a toddler on my hip? Have you seen me? I'm nobody's wife, Jeremy. I'm likely somebody's future mistress, for all we know. Probably multiple somebodies...like mafia brothers or something. I'm that kind of wife. Certainly not a *respectable* one."

"You could be." I hear a smirk, even if I can't see it, and I roll my eyes.

"Okay, sure, Jer. I can see it now, me, the perfect little doting wife. There when he comes home, packing his lunches before he leaves and sucking his big fat cock each night when he's tired from important man work. What the fuck ever."

Jeremy laughs. "You have a very skewed idea of marriage, Lemon. And can I be honest with you without giving offense?"

"Always." If he can't, who will? They're all so baffled by me they'd prefer to wonder rather than ask. I know I'm a lot, but I'm also a little when made to feel that way. I brush that thought back, because in no way, shape, or form will I acknowledge stupid Nash making me feel small.

If anything, I should feel tall and proud, having him squirt like a schoolboy at the sight of my nipples and only one hand on my ass. He's pathetic, really. And I'm lucky that's done.

"Your mom left when you were so little, I don't think you've ever seen two people in love before. Like functioning as a couple."

True. "But I'm supposed to be able to change that because a grumpy old man can't handle his emotions?"

"No," Jeremy chuckles, "you're the only one fixating on the grumpy old man. I was talking about the general population of men at this point."

Fuck. He's right. My thoughts go back to that insufferable grump and his stupid silver beard every time I blink lately.

"I'm saying whether you go on this TV show or not, keep an open mind. You can love adventure and seek passion any way you like, Lem, but there's nothing like finding someone to love forever. Someone who fits that space within you like a puzzle and makes life an adventure just by being near."

A dog barks, and the phone rustles on his end. "Look, I gotta go, Lem, but remember. You are perfect how you are, as wild and free as that may be, but that doesn't mean there isn't someone out there to be your other half. Oh, he's back! Gotta go!"

I shove the phone back into my skate, wondering who *he* is while I try to let Jer's other words marinate.

He's right. I'm the one who can't stop thinking about Nash, even if that's ridiculous. It's not as if I have real feelings for the old asshole.

Lust is a complete biological reaction.

Besides, his intentions with me were made loud and clear. I was simply a toy for him to use and discard.

I'm gonna be on that TV show. I'll win it, too, and I'll write a big fat check to whatever charity the Pine Forest kids have going on this year like usual, grinning ear to ear at Papa's frugal accountant as I do.

The wind whips across my face as I skate back to the bus, and I feel a renewed sense of wonder. My next thrill just around the bend. I'll avoid Daddy Nashville, scoop up my things, and get started on my next adventure.

My heart soars with peace and tranquility, and my body soars with the birds above, carried by the same kiss of wind.

But a scowling figure leaned against the loading bay has me skidding to a halt just before I reach my destination.

My instincts tug me toward him when he lifts his head to meet my eyes, but even those fuckers won't tell me what to do. I skate past without a word and make my way to the VIP lounge where my agent is planning to pick me up and launch my destiny.

# Chapter Five

## OLIVER

Lemon Perkins sits on the far side of the room, legs crossed beneath short, red fabric and plastered to some young roadie's side. My jaw clenches as he envelops her body like plastic wrap, needy and toxic, clung to what was just mine.

There's a gauche tonguing of her neck, and I suppress a groan at his immaturity.

She moans my way, but I maintain her stare with unaffected eyes, until she returns her attention to the accosting of her neck, surrounded by all to see.

It's all fake.

She wants my attention. To punish me for what we didn't do. It's more than apparent when her eyes cut to mine between each breath for reactions, ones I haven't the slightest intention of giving her.

*Not this time, Sour Patch.*

Even if my cock has yet to get the memo, I'm not playing her game. No, in the seclusion of the darkened booth, I slip my hand beneath the table and reposition the perpetual erection she conjures.

She's invited a friend, Tina, auburn curls and legs for days. We've met before, so I'm no stranger to the casting agent whose father *also* owns a production company. She's fierce and promiscuous, like Lemon, and the pair scream two things with their care-free attitude and blatant entitlement. Generational wealth and social privilege.

Is that why she's here? The casting agent?

The word *couch* slams against my skull, and I fight the urge to stomp across the room and tear them apart.

*I want her on nobody's couch.*

But that's not my business.

My phone buzzes in my pocket, and I know without a doubt it's Mrs. Kempling's notice of leave. Another immediate reminder of the boundaries I must respect as an employee of Perkins Global. I'm not part of this world.

Tina? Onyx? They're her world. I'm serving it.

Like Mrs. Kempling, I'm here to do a job. And if I do well enough, Mr. Perkins will ensure my family thrives, eats, and becomes educated.

They will have what I promised Lauren I'd provide for them.

Tina leans across the roadie's lap, whispering to Lemon things I can't make out from our distance.

But I haven't a care what they're up to, so it makes no sense why my eyes can't peel from Lemon's when she and Tina play suck-and-blow across the man's lap.

Her eyes dart to my corner. *What are you gonna do about it?*

I should force my gaze in another direction, any other direction, but I don't. I could get up and walk away, sparing myself whatever debauchery is about to come, but we both know I won't. I would stalk across the room, yank her from the pile of wanting limbs, and take her in front of them all, how I know she wants, if I were a different man.

In a different life.

But I'm not.

So, I watch.

And her eyes stay fixed on mine.

*Your loss*, they say.

Tina pushes the roadie back, tongue tangling with none other than Onyx Barringer's beside her, only Lemon doesn't notice. She's too busy taunting me.

I shouldn't even be looking, yet I can't turn away, not when the man who isn't me spreads her over the table and she meets my gaze the whole way down.

*We can't*, I say with my eyes.

So down she goes, training her focus to my corner as the man she doesn't even know tugs open her dress and moves his mouth across her chest.

She swats him away when he gets too low, and I'm on my feet before I'm self-aware, but he complies, moving his mouth back where she was expecting it. Tina joins, too, licking lines of alcohol off her bare skin.

Her dress is still intact above her waist, but her entire top half is exposed, and even in the privacy of the small VIP group, heads are turning to join the fun, and that's when chaos meets catastrophe.

"Tequila!" the man shouts.

I don't recognize him.

"This is an exclusive event," I warn security through my headset. "Check the lists."

I clench my jaw. Something about the man is familiar. A celebrity, maybe, but I can't concentrate on his identity like I should when I lift my eyes to find Tina using the CEO's only daughter as a human-platform on which to take liquor shots.

Lemon smiles, a satisfied, shimmer of a tease, but it fades when members of the band join in...all but Onyx, who watches like me.

My heart jolts as it unfolds before me.

Her demeanor shifts, brow pinches.

She isn't into this anymore.

It's my job to shut this down. These women are trashed, three bottles of wine between them in less than an hour, and apparently Tina is as reckless as Lem, lime juice dripping from her exposed breasts as partygoers cheer her on in a one-woman wet T-shirt contest.

I'm irritated at Lemon more than anything, but I'm furious with the band. Not only did she tell them their fling was over, but they haven't thought twice about how this could affect the company's investment.

What if the press caught wind? Every one of them is lucky this is private, but a nagging feeling has me searching for the man from before.

"Party is over!" I shove to my feet as Lemon pushes the men away with a swift curse. They comply immediately, offering drunken apologies and stumbling off to corners with groupies on standby.

All but Onyx, who just stares at a half-naked Lemon staring at me.

I've toyed with her feelings just like she's done with his. And still, it's my eyes she seeks, not the successful young rock star with a future and fortune.

Is she testing whether I want her more?

I could pass that test.

But life isn't about wants.

I prepare myself to restore order, the need to cover and lead her to safety overriding the systems in my mind so much that I've nearly forgotten about the strange yet familiar man until his eyes pierce mine.

Eyes I saw...*at last month's press conference.*

The smug man winks, tucking his phone away just as the door to the VIP lounge swings open and a series of bright flashes precedes a painfully smug, "No. Effing. Way," from one person who could mess everything up, Shelia Goldblum of the East Coast Press.

*Fuck.*

# Chapter Six

## OLIVER

Emil Perkins sits across from me this time, but it's not in the VIP lounge. The raised ceilings and gothic chair railing in the boardroom contradict the impossibly intimate feeling that surrounds us.

This could be the swift end of a professional relationship I've spent nearly a decade cultivating.

Because of a woman I should have left alone.

I had one job on this tour.

To maintain order.

Instead, I welcomed chaos in the form of his only daughter sprawled shirtless across a national headline, and this year's hottest punk rock poster boy, Onyx Barringer, staring down her half naked torso.

"You will give no more excuses, Zitrone!" He barks through the phone, leaving no room for argument.

I listen involuntarily, since he chose to take this call during our meeting. The one he called after this morning's press hit his radar.

I run through excuses in my mind while he argues with the only person possibly in worse for this than me.

"I have sacrificed everything to make sure you have the world before you, and you drag my name through the mud like a common *Schlampe*. Are you trying to become your mother, Zitrone?" He quiets, listening.

To her.

I fiddle with a hangnail on my thumb, counting the blue streaks in his paperweight, anything I can to mask the thoughts of his daughter's ripe, red backside beneath my palm.

She only acted out because I rejected her, and that guilt advances upon me as his lecture drags on.

"I love you, Lemondrop. This is why I do this. Why I must send you away. I have friends at Oxford. They have agreed to accelerate an Executive MBA. You will take your place by my side in the company in one year's time."

The air is swept from my lungs with the words *Lemondrop* and *send you away*, but I don't think hers was. The scowl my boss wears as his fist comes down against the table tells me whatever Lemon replied with, was not an amicable agreement.

His eyes widen as his stare meets mine, and even if he isn't addressing me, I pin it to myself. It's my fault she did this. If I hadn't rejected her, she'd have been in my booth, with me.

"*Mein Vater* would have worked me in his steel *Fabrik* had I behaved this way! Enjoy your last night of freedom, *Töchterchen*."

His face hasn't relaxed. He hasn't spoken.

I clench my fists in the silence that follows, rolling through the things I overheard.

Lemon is being sent to Oxford for a master's?

Can he do that?

I guess when you're a billionaire, you can. No mind that there's test scores and hard-working students fighting for a place on waitlists in the very program she'll buy her way into.

What was Lemon's GPA? One look, and you wonder if she finished high school. Probably went to some fancy rich kid Montessori or—

"I do not care what you *want*, Zitrone! Do you hear what I say? You will study hard and work! Or perhaps you wish to have a husband?" He waits, eyes directly glued to mine. "I did not think so," he says.

Somewhere beneath the possibly audible thumping of my heart, I feel an instant relief knowing she won't belong to someone else. Someone who isn't me, even if I shouldn't.

I drop my gaze, Mr. Perkins winning the staring contest neither of us knew we were in. Or maybe he did know. He reminds me of his daughter that way, purple irises that can't be natural yet somehow are, beguiling beauty masking a scorching anger that blazes from nowhere and everywhere all at once, right from their hearts.

He ends the call and slams his phone against the table, heaving a sigh before surprising the hell out of me. Two glasses and a bottle of brandy are brought in from the hall. "A drink."

I eye the glass. Flashes of last night reflect in the amber liquid.

And now he's sending her away.

All for the games I helped her play.

"They drank tequila from her navel," I finally say, eyes widening because I have no idea why that's the first thing that came to my mind in front of her *father*, of all people. "I'm sorry, I didn't mean—"

"*Nicht Schlimm.*" He waves me off. "No worries. Nash—er, Oliver. May I call you that?"

"Of course. And I'm sorry about..." I drop my gaze to the tabloid.

"I have known you for years, Oliver. You are not to blame. *Prost!*" He raises his glass and nods to mine. "My daughter, she is...

"A lot," I offer, understanding his inability to put to words just what Lemon Perkins truly is. So much more than language can comprehend. Abstract enough for art, but so fluid she'd drip right off the canvas if you tried to paint her. She'd never sit long enough, anyhow. "My daughter, Bryar...she's also a lot."

My mind circles to Mrs. Kempling and her imminent termination. I liked her about as much as a fish, but a nanny is hard to come by when you have four children and one of them is terrifying. She can handle my thirteen-year-old no better than the others could. Perhaps no one can, another reason I need this promotion to take me back home.

Mr. Perkins leans in, red cherub cheeks at the ends of his smile, despite the tabloid still sitting at the corner of his desk burning holes in my mind because she's on it. "That is right! I forgot you are a father. Not many men in our industry settle down, you know."

"That's one of the reasons I'm pleased for our meeting. The role of Acquisitions Manager is a shareholding position, is it not?"

He straightens, leaning back in his chair as he assesses me. His nine-thousand-dollar watch shines from the reflection of the lamp above our heads, and I inhale sharply, hoping he can't tell what an imposter I am. That I'm just a widowed father, lucky enough to have made it this far in his company when I had very few credentials for the industry. That the eighteen-carat gold Van Cleef & Arpels on his wrist is worth the next three years of the twins' dance classes or a hundred cases of Poppy's *essential* acrylic paint pens.

"And I suppose you have ideas for this position, should it be offered you?" He narrows his eyes inquisitively. It feels like he's testing me, but something tells me I could pass his test, too.

"I do." I lean closer, heart pounding for other reasons now.

I can lead if given a shot.

It's time to shoot.

"Eight years managing your tours has revealed to me a need for reallocation of budget."

Saying it feels like a mountain has been moved. My thoughts, my plans, my ideas, in the ears of someone who can do something with them.

He raises a brow. "Continue."

"There are things we're spending too much on that are hardly necessities for success, and other areas where spending is so limited we barely meet coding standards. I can help there, if you'll trust me for the job."

I let out the quietest exhale, gripping to maintain the confidence and assuredness he seeks. I can see it in his eyes, the look of a predator, discerning whether I'm a threat or worthy as an adversary.

"Sir, if you'll—"

"I made my decision months ago." He extends his hand. "I'd like to see you by my side, Oliver."

A colossal weight is lifted from me, Atlas shifting entire masses of land from bruised shoulders, held up for too long by strings of a deceased puppeteer. I stand, grinning from ear to ear and gripping his hand in both of mine. "Thank you, Mr. Perkins. You will not regret your decision, I can promise you that. We'll raise company earnings higher than ever before."

"I believe you." He grins, holding up his glass. "To Perkins Global, and a new era of earnings."

"To the future!" I clank my glass to his.

We drink and plot the next quarter's projections with more enthusiasm than I recall feeling in a long time, but his eyes flick to his phone every few seconds, vibrations of incoming texts and calls, all from a flashing yellow screen he switches off.

I need no explanation to know the woman calling him is the same one I can't seem to wipe from my thoughts.

"Your Bryar," he sighs, massaging his brow, "what is she like? I try so hard with my *Zitrone*—eh, sorry, the old tongue slips when I've had a few of these." He shoves his brandy away and shakes his head. "I worry she is like her mother. She will go on her next adventure and never return. Nothing satisfies her."

"I've noticed that about her," I start, but I quickly shut myself up when he studies me. I shouldn't notice anything about his daughter.

"I know you tried to stop the..." he motions to the tabloid, shaking his head, "whatever that was. I have full confidence that you, my most trusted employee, had nothing to do with her...call for help or whatever this newest charade is." He pours another brandy, seemingly no longer concerned with his *Denglisch*, the German English mix I've heard Lemon flit between in the presence of her father.

It's comforting.

Why the hell is it comforting?

Mr. Perkins clears his throat, and my eyes snap to his. It's only then I realize they'd been trained on the tabloid for God knows how long.

On the image of his daughter.

The lamp above reflects on a thin silver band wrapped around his finger. He brushes it with his thumb, and guilt spikes that I no longer wear mine. The truth is, I didn't want to see it shining there when my hand is wrapped around my cock thinking of another.

Of my boss's goddamned daughter.

"Did...did she leave? Your wife?"

He nods to the portrait of the three of them, hung proudly in the boardroom. I've seen it before. It's always been there, but until now I never considered what happened to the rarely mentioned partner of the CEO. "Cordelia, her mother, she was—*is* a free spirit. A hippie, my father called her. And when she told me, swollen with our child, that she could not stay...even when she told me this, I still loved her. I would say to her, 'I do not care, my love, should you wander, so long as you return to me, *du und unser* baby, you and my Lemondrop.'" He exhales, and his eyes darken to a blue-violet, akin to his Lemon's when she's deep in thought.

"Mine's just like her mother, too." I swig the amber liquid. It burns my esophagus derisively—the emotional strife of loss far more devastating than any physical pain could ever be. But the CEO of Perkins Global Records is opening up to me, and I feel an invisible string shorten between us with our shared experience. "My wife passed when Bryar was young. She's the only one of my girls who remembers Lauren. Fitting that she's the most like her of all of them. Her smile, attitude...the way her hair fell to the side on its own, always to left—I'm sorry."

I shake away the memories, where they must stay if I'm to be of use to anyone. Thinking of her too long puts me in a place where I've no business anymore if we're to move on.

"It is fine, my friend. It is what I needed tonight. We understand one another, Oliver. I like you. There are few a man of my wealth can trust. Do you know what I mean?"

"I think I do." I shake his hand. "I assure you, there is nothing you can't trust me with, sir. My family is your family, Mr. Perkins, and I aim to help this company grow alongside you for many years to come."

"It's all set, then. Shall we have cigars brought out to celebrate? Alert the nanny you'll be late, yes?"

The nanny.

"I apologize, Mr. Perkins, but you've just reminded me that my nanny...resigned. Again."

He nods in understanding, and I'll admit it's conflicting to connect with a guy as a parent and want to have that same man's daughter in every position imaginable.

It should drive me away.

To relieve Mrs. Kempling of her failed duties and go home.

But I've never had support from someone who knows the struggles I've yet to face. It's been so long since Lauren was here to share parenting hacks and hiccups. Maybe that's why I accept his cigar on the balcony, to share times our girls pulled a fast one, to feel like I'm not so alone in all of this. But the stories he tells me about Lemon make me grip the edge of my chair, and the possibilities of what Bryar could get into if I don't intervene take ominous form in my head.

"I've got to get a nanny who can handle her immediately," I admit. "I can't have her doing stuff like that when she's finally driving."

"Or worse!" He whistles. "When she has credit cards."

My face pales, and I take a deep drag on the cigar, blowing out a controlled breath. "What did you do when Lemon started this behavior?" I've considered boarding school, but I hate the idea when my gut tells me she needs me to guide her more than anything right now.

"I've been thinking about something, Oliver." Mr. Perkins takes a long drag of the cigar before ashing it from the balcony. "My daughter needs structure, stability, a fast-paced adventure to occupy her impulsivity. And you need someone with stamina to keep up with four girls, and your own delinquent child."

"Bryar is not a—"

His eyes narrow. "Think about this, Oliver. Lemon will be your nanny. There's nothing your daughter could do that mine hasn't tried twice."

"That's what I'm worried about."

"That's how she will keep them from doing it!" He passes the cigar, blowing perfect smoke rings into the sky. "Relax, my friend. They may learn a thing or two. Picking locks, scaling fences, organizing protests on national television...but odds are they will learn how to argue their way out of it if my Lemondrop is involved."

That is not reassuring.

"She will be just what you need."

Neither is that.

Mr. Perkins shrugs like it's done. "Not only would your children have a caretaker, but they are just the wild adventure Lemon needs to keep busy. A challenge of her own shape and form."

"I agree we could both...benefit, but I'm not sure my daughters need Lemon influencing their decisions. No offense."

"*Bitte*," he whispers, ashing the cigar. "Lemon needs to learn responsibility, and Bryar needs to see what happens if she forever lacks it, see?"

"That doesn't make it less of a risk. The two of them together sound like a recipe for a house fire."

Mr. Perkins doesn't deny it, but his eyes widen in thought. "If you work from the Valley office, just outside of your home in Pine Forest, you will be close enough to check in, will you not?"

"You mean, you would pull me from my next three tours, and—"

"Bump your promotion to the present. That is what I am saying, friend. We are the same, you and I. Remember that. I trust you; you trust me."

"Trust?"

"You keep my daughter safe in your home, away from tabloids and these relations of hers." He gestures back to the body shot photo, lingering guilt raining over me as he does. But when he produces a notepad and scribbles a number that makes my eyes pop, guilt is the last thing I feel.

This would make me a millionaire overnight.

"I keep my word, always. This is what I will pay you, Oliver Nashville. Your family will want for nothing ever again. So, what do you say?"

"I can't accept that salary." I stumble over my words. "I mean, I would love to, yes, but Mr. Perkins..."

He waves his hand dismissively. "Oh, come now, you can accept, and you will call me Emil."

"Uh, yes, well...Emil," I say as politely as possible, "that's far too much for an acquisitions rep."

"No price is too high for a friend you can trust, Oliver."

He says my name like I'm an equal, and my chest swells with pride. If I agree to this, my girls will have the world at their fingertips...Oxford, even. Every opportunity Lauren wanted for them will be within their reach.

"Think it over." He stands. "Your whole life could change."

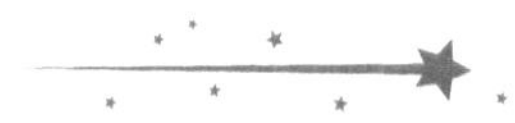

I walk to my car, shut the door, and lean back in my seat, relief a vague simplification of my current state. But it's done. The meeting is over, and the promotion is mine whether I take the CEO up on his crazy plan or not.

"We did it, Lo," I whisper, wondering if she's still around to hear it.

But I feel nothing.

Perhaps that's for the best when I can't stop thinking of what Emil said. Not about the promotion or the trust we now share, but the other part.

The part that has all the blood I possess rushing to the head of my cock and pointing home like the damn north star.

"What do you say, Oliver? I make you a rich man, and you take my daughter."

# Chapter Seven

## LEMON

"This is the most archaic thing I can conceptualize, Papa! It is supremely fucked, and I will not apologize for my un-ladylike language, either." I give a pointed glare to Phillip, Papa's driver, who doesn't even attempt to hide his smirk in the rearview reflection.

"Fuck off, Phil." I flip him the bird because I actually like him, and that's our thing. Still, it's not fair for poor Phillip to endure this.

My father *sold* me.

He is giving me to someone as a live-in fucking sex slave or some cruel and unusual alternative.

Papa sighs, and I swear he must hear my thoughts. "It is simply a nanny position, *Zitrone*. You act as though I have arranged a marriage on your behalf."

"My apologies, Daddy Dearest. I didn't realize this was merely a recruitment endeavor. Can I get my pay in advance, then or do I need to call up whoever Britney hired and cut through the chains of conservatorship while I'm at it?"

I'm fuming, probably as red in the face as I feel in my fiery soul right now, but he only sighs like I've tired him.

How one does around a child, the only thing he will see me as, until I belong to another man.

*Shit.* He really thinks I'll fall into this role of compliant little nanny and emerge a changed woman with a long line of suitors ready to snatch up my winning motherly skills, on recent exhibit as the newest Von-Trappy governess, and all.

"*Mäuschen—*"

"Do not call me pet names, *Vater!* Not when you've just sold me like cattle."

"I did not sell you, *Zitrone. Bitte*! Listen to yourself!" He whips the tabloid from his jacket, the one with Onyx, Tina, and me plastered across the front doing body shots like every other twenty-something I know.

I roll my eyes, but he shakes his head and forces the paper in front of me. "*Bist du blind*? Look at yourself!"

He reaches for my hand, but I yank it away, hundreds of charms clanking together in the wake of my resistance. My father casts his eyes to the ground when I cradle my wrist to silence them.

Phillip's voice cuts through the speakers. "We are here, Mr. Perkins."

"I worry you will become her." My father clasps his hands in his lap. "Beautiful, passionate, proud. And these are such good things to be, *mein Kind*. But you are reckless. Not just with your body, but your heart. Your mind, *Zitrone*. I fear your soul will always wander, and then what?" Hurt and fear cross over his eyes in a flash. "You will become dead in a ditch somewhere like your mother."

Tears fill the space around my father's eyes until the drops threaten to spill free right before me, but my anger flows faster. "You don't know that. You do not know that she is dead, Papa. You do not know!"

"I feel it!"

Silence fills the car, nostrils flared, and lips pressed the same way, as we heave in air but refuse to sound remotely winded. Never rattled by the storm, only ever the cause of it.

I might look like her, but I am him.

Something is silently stated in this moment. I just wish I understood it, the look he gives me as he reaches over my lap and pries the door handle open to urge me away.

"You seek something I cannot teach you, *Zitrone*. I pray this new journey will. I love you, even if you doubt it fiercely."

"Love?" I gasp, tears rolling down my cheeks as the one man I trust breaks every bit of it. "You've cut off my access to banking, despite the fact I'm certain it's not legal, you've contracted me out to a family to...live in their house and...and...serve them. You stripped me of my freedom and my autonomy as a twenty-eight-year-old grown-ass woman and forced me into a prison! And you tell me you *love me*? This is not love. This cage? This is why my mother left."

*"Das reicht!"* His voice blasts against my face before I can take back what I've said. I can feel his anger in the force of his breath against my skin, and it breaks my heart what I've just done to him, the glass walls I shattered because stones were easier to throw with words.

My breath hitches as he wipes his eyes with the back of his ring-fingered hand, a reminder of his unending love for her.

*"Es tut mir leid, Papa.* I did not mean—"

"No! You did not *think*! You have gallivanted far too long, opening your bed and your heart for the thrill of the moment. I have paid for handfuls of degrees and certifications so you can find your peace and live your dreams, Lemondrop, but this..." He waves the tabloid into the air. "This is too far. You will serve this family as if they are your own, as their live-in nanny. You will do an impeccable job caring for my most trusted employee's four children in his country estate—you will keep all rock bands out of it— and you will regain access to your trust accounts when you prove capable of a whole summer with no shenanigans."

"Or what? If I don't go along with this indentured servitude you've conjured up? What will be done to me then? Will you cast me off to a foreign prince with the highest dowry? Perhaps Dubai. I hear the jewelry selection is decent there.”

“Stop this, *Zitrone!* You will act like the adult I should have raised you to be, and you will mind the reputation of Perkins Global while you live in his house, or you will not regain access to your trust. *Ever.* I’ll do what I must to fix the mess I made of you. *Weil ich dich liebe.* Do I make that clear?”

*“Glasklar.”*

I do not blink.

I do not hug my father.

Instead, I slam the door, and it fucking stings, because I love that stupid asshole motherfucker more than anyone on this planet.

“He didn’t sell you, miss, if it pleases you.” Phillip unloads my luggage. “Likely few willing buyers.”

His crow’s foot wink eases my nerves, the banter warming me with familiarity before I’m cast into the unknown, but he frowns just as quickly.

He, too, believes Papa has gone too far.

I know I’ve screwed up a time or two, but he’s completely frozen me out of my accounts. I have zero control over who I am, what I do, or where I go from this point until one of them releases me from shackles.

I stand at the edge of my destiny, a long stone driveway past sky-high, monogrammed gates, no different than the ones I grew up behind.

No wonder these kids need a nanny who can keep up. Bet they’re crawling out their school uniforms to scale these bars if their father is anything like mine.

“Who is this ‘most trusted’ employee?”

A worry line forms across Philip’s brow. I don’t like it.

“What aren’t you telling me?”

He nods to the large French doors, unloading more than luggage at my feet with his final whisper. “This man didn’t pay your father, Miss. Your father paid him. Eight million dollars to keep you busy.”

I’m nobody’s to keep.

# Chapter Eight

## LEMON

S he's breathtaking, the woman in the entryway portrait. Waves of golden hair flow down her right shoulder and complement her amber eyes. The left shoulder remains bare, and her smile tells that it was purposeful. I like her instantly.

My new employer's wife, I suppose.

He did well, I'll give him that. Hot little booty waiting at home and a six-bedroom estate in the fancy part of Pine Forest? Not too bad. Unfortunately, it's nowhere remotely walkable to any of my friends.

I'll have to borrow a car if I want to see Shana or Jeremy, but it could be worse. At least it's close to home.

A weight lifted off my chest when Phillip snuck me the coordinates on the ride over. I'll still be able to manage my properties and check in on things Papa doesn't know about, like the apartments I make available to the women and children's shelter. It's not that I think he'd be angry or be able to stop me, it's just...not how things are done.

*Jeder ist seines Glückes Schmied,* he'd say.

Be the smith of your own luck.

But one man's biases are not another man's truths.

I make a mental note to wire Katie all the funds I have in my backup vault. She can take care of everyone without

Papa's accountant scrutinizing each cent like I fear he's been instructed to start doing.

That's home.

The apartments. The town. Katie and the kids we help. My friends.

This will never be home, even if it does remind me of the mansion I grew up in, a miniature version, which feels elitist to admit.

I've been privileged; it's an inherent knowledge.

When the President sends you a shiny red tricycle for your third birthday, you begin to gather the clues, even if my father did attempt to keep me somewhat humble with public school and sports.

Peers in my tax bracket would have killed for that alternative to their own, prep schools and press galas becoming more important than friends by the time they reached their teens.

At least Papa gave me that.

I hate that I must hate him now.

No one seemed to notice my entry, so I snoop for clues in the expansive foyer. Who am I working for?

And how can I get them on my side sooner than later?

I've met a few of my father's upper crust over the years, but I wasn't exactly briefed on their family lives...not that I cared.

There's only one man on the Perkins payroll I ever wonder about, and it's not the size of his living room I'm pondering when I do.

The decorations are scarce. A few crayon-drawings are Scotch-taped to the walls at average kid-height, telling me it's not the parents choosing décor, and even though I detest children for the most part, I can't help smiling at the artwork, a tall man in an all-black suit holding hands with two little girls. One wears a scribble-scrabbled pink dress and the other purple overalls. Tiny music notes pepper the air, dancing with rainbow butterflies, and I love that.

It's how my mind always feels, swirls of music and nature and life creating movement in my soul.

Cami has signed the picture in the bottom right corner in bright pink pastel, the same shade used for the man's heart eyes.

A man wearing a blue badge.

With red lettering.

Standing in front of a large, black bus.

I know it, even before I hear his clipped vexation or see the glower he reserves exclusively for me. Tragically ironic that it's the same thing about him that makes my muscles clench down low.

"You."

A fact.

Not a question or "Hello, how are you? Oh, your dad paid me, quite literally, millions to imprison you…" Nope.

Just one word.

A finger pointed at a broken doll.

A mess.

And fuck me, but I'm tired of messes being messy just cause men say it's so.

And I hate that I want this grumpy man in front of me even more, because he doesn't want me back. No matter what his body says, he doesn't want the whole of me, not the parts that matter.

But I'm more than the package I come wrapped in.

*"You are…reckless…not just with your body, but your heart."*

I might be this man's new nanny, but I'll be damned if I become his mistress, even if my pussy does part ceremoniously for the rumble of his voice.

If he wants me, he wants all of me. I'll close my legs, chauffer the thumb-suckers to swim practice, and collect my trust when the summer's through, leaving all prospects of Daddy Nashville and his gargantuan sweatpants-clad cock behind me.

Here.

In his house.

Where we will both be sleeping.

I allow my eyes to flick down his body, lingering any-where the fuck I want to make him steam, before leveling them back to his irritated orbs.

He crosses the foyer to stand far enough away that I can't suck his blood, eyeing me wearily, as if my father didn't just pay him entire islands for my captivity.

Smart man.

"You came early," he rasps.

*Don't say it,* I tell myself.

But it's not like me to obey.

"No, Mr. Nashville, you came early. If I remember cor-rectly, I didn't come at all."

He stills, face redder than I've seen, and I delight in that fact. Smirking outright, I stalk forward and straighten his tie, and the horny fucker lets me, because of course he does.

His Adam's apple bobs, and he moves to speak, but nothing comes out, as if every thought he had in that courtly silver head has vanished and been replaced by the shape of my lips.

I run my tongue across them, making certain they're good and wet, and I relish every second of his unease as I march myself up the staircase and make myself at home.

"Don't worry, Daddy," I call down the stairs. "I'll be good if you will."

# Chapter Nine

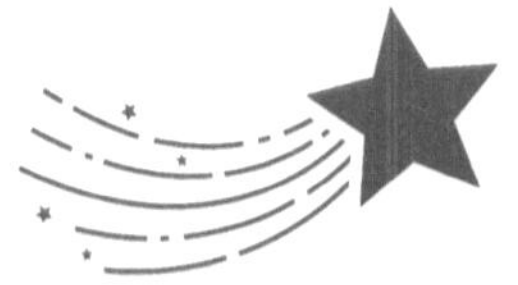

## OLIVER

**"I** still can't believe your father's first name is Oliver. That's the O, so what's the L?" Lemon beams from across my dining room table.

At the head.

Lauren would want that. She wouldn't want me to be weird about her place or request a guest move.

"When Cami was a toddler," Poppy grins, "she swore it was Olive Lover, so that was pretty much all Bry and me called him for months, wasn't it, Dad?" My twelve-year-old stabs her roasted carrots, ignoring the peas altogether.

"Olive Lover?" Lemon teases.

"Yes, Lemonhead?" I imitate, making Poppy spit her soda all over Kimmie and Cami.

"Sorry, Two-Bits." I don't know what came over me.

I shuffle from my seat, but Lemon's up before I can stand, wiping their giggling faces while Poppy replaces their food.

Kimmie says nothing, as usual...but then...

She smiles.

The single act has Poppy and me locking eyes from across the room. Words aren't needed to understand what we're both thinking. Cami stares curiously at her new nanny, who has no idea the walls she's scaled.

"There you go," Lemon pinches the twins' cheeks. "You're a little sticky, but it could be worse. Your name could be Oliver." She dabs a thumb in my direction, enacting more sorcery as my quietest little lilac laughs.

For the first time in what feels like forever.

Cami admitted to hearing her sister speak on rare occasion. Full sentences spoken only to her twin.

A mental block, the therapists said, *selective mutism.* Titles have been thrown around, but they stem down to the same roots. And the knowledge that it's a form of anxiety plaguing my youngest child that I can't quell, is something I live with in my gut every day.

I was convinced I might never hear her speak, and now...right in front of me, before my very eyes and ears, she's laughing.

"Kimmie!" Cami jumps up and down and hugging her sister.

Both girls giggle uncontrollably, like every laugh Kimmie never let out was stored behind a dam that's finally broken. Tears flow down Cami's cheeks as she bounces between Lemon and her twin in awe. "You made her smile. She...she's laughing!" Cami throws her arms around Lemon's neck. "Thank you, Nanny!"

Lemon's eyes widen, shooting me thousands of questions with one glance, but wrapping her arms around a child she's only met moments ago, despite the ongoing war between the two of us.

"Is that hard to do? Make her laugh?" Lemon conjures more laughter with that, even from Kimmie, who I scoop up and kiss on the cheek.

"Yes," I say, looking into my youngest daughter's eyes as she smiles at me.

*Smiles.*

"That is very hard to do, Sour Patch."

"Sour Patch?" Bryar sneers. There's an edge to her voice that bridges argumentative, before anything's even been spoken. She slams the solid oak door behind her, and the ground vibrates to match her energy.

But that's how it is with her these days.

I'm always on the wrong side of anything she wants, needs, or could possibly provoke.

Parenting, they call it.

"You're late."

I release Kimmie and motion for everyone to sit, including Bryar, whose plate is now cold and stale.

She rolls her eyes.

And she does not sit, shooting death glares at Lemon, in her mother's chair.

"What is *that?*"

Lemon's brow lifts to the sky, but I cut in before she can retort. Although, at this point, I think Emil might be right.

Bryar's lip curls up at the sight of Lemon in the very style knee-high boots I forbade her from purchasing for herself last week. The daggers she wields are intentionally sharp as she snaps her eyes back to mine.

"That is your new nanny, Bryar Elaine, which you'd have known, had you been home after school."

She scrunches her nose, holding my gaze in challenge.

"But I suppose you thought Mrs. Kempling was still here. Counting on missing your curfew without me knowing?"

My oldest daughter has taken a vow of silence at this point in the conversation, clenching her fists by her sides with nostrils flared.

But she'll only push it so far. I know about her joyride.

"Sit."

She does.

"After dinner, you will give me your phone, your tablet, and your laptop. This summer, you will help with your siblings and have zero social leniency. For the next week, you will ride the bus to and from school or Ms. Perkins will drive you. Do you understand?"

Bryar's face contorts. "That's not fair! It's the last week of school. It's prom for the high school, and—"

"And you are in middle school, are you not? Do you think I don't know about your high school boyfriend?" My fist makes a solid connection with the table all of its own volition, the sound reverberating through the high-ceilings I never chose. Ceilings that remind me of the distance between me and her mother, who is counting on me to protect her.

"You are a *child*, Bryar! Look at yourself."

Bryar makes a sharp inhale, and from across the table, so does Lemon.

I knit my brow, searching her face for the answers. Am I wrong?

But she just presses her lips together and stands, taking the twins by the hands. "I think it's getting late for the littles. Wanna help me do bath and bed, Pop? You can show me where the good bubbles are." She winks, throwing an inviting smile at my trustworthy middle child, often forgotten on messy nights like this.

"Okay!" Relief floods Poppy's eyes as she throws her napkin to the table. She skips ahead of Lemon, taking the stairs two at a time. "Dad's bathroom has the big jacuzzi. We can use the jets."

I groan internally, but I'm too engaged in a staring contest with the thirteen-year-old clone of a ghost to stop them.

Still, Lemon finds a way to lighten the mood. "I would love to see your dad's bubbles," she says, just loud enough for me to hear.

I run my tongue over my teeth, too stunned to speak at the temptress who snakes throughout my home so casually.

Beautifully.

"You called her Sour Patch," Bryar snaps. "Little young for you if you ask me."

"Little late for your curfew if we're trading opinions. She's here to take care of you."

"I don't need anyone taking care of me. I'm not a child, like Poppy or the twins. Poppy's hardly a child anymore. And she needs a training bra like yesterday, but I guess you haven't noticed. You're the only one who doesn't see her. Even the slutty nanny sees it. That's why she's having her help with grown-up things. Because we are all growing up, whether you're here to see it or not! We should be able to do things like ride with friends for—"

"That's enough!" I shout, louder than I realize. Bryar backs away, eyes wide and lips trembling. "You will watch your mouth, Bryar Elaine, or I will—"

"You'll what? Scream back? You always get the last word, huh? Because you're Dad, and that makes you automatically right, doesn't it? No matter what anyone else's side of the story is, it's just about what you say, and that's all that goes. You might be in charge at work, but you can't manage our whole lives."

"Who were you out riding with?" I run my hand through the air in amazement that she's found a way to turn this around on me. It's then I take in her outfit for what it truly is.

Looks like Lemon's wardrobe.

Ripped tights, short skirt, crop top and...*no*.

"Is that a—how the hell did you get a tattoo? Who gave a thirteen-year-old child a tattoo?!"

"It's henna. Oh, my God, Dad. You don't trust me one single bit, do you?"

"No, I don't."

Bryar steps back.

"I mean, I do, baby. I trust you, but—"

"I am not a baby!"

She swipes her arm across the table, shoving several dishes to the floor, and slams down a card before barreling to her room in tears.

I snatch the envelope with quivering hands.

It's a get-well card.

Across the front is a heart symbol matching the henna on Bryar's midriff, and beneath it, a slew of signatures and a glittering message.

**Coach Jasmine,**
**It took a few days of driving around and stalking the team to get everyone on here, but we wanted you to know that you mean the world to every single one of us.**
**Keep us by you during chemo. We're with you 100%.**
**Kick cancer's butt, or we're gonna do it for you.**
**Love Always,**
**Captain Bryar & The Eighth Grade Cheer Team.**

*Oh.*

# Chapter Ten

## LEMON

### *Twelve Years Ago*

"Papa! I get it, okay? I'll delete it." I swipe my hand across my eyes and sniffle, not even caring how gross I sound as I rush down the staircase after him.

"I said I'm sorry! *Es tut mir leid*, okay?" I grab my MacBook from the window seat in the drawing room and stumble back to the landing to show him my Myspace page. "See, Papa, see? The picture is gone! *Weg*! I deleted it. Only so many people even read the—"

"I do not care who saw this one instance, *Zitrone*!" Father's anger is so potent, I feel it in my soul. "*Das Internet* never forgets. And the things you say about that poor girl...after what she has been through. She may not recover from her wounds, yet you give her more through heartless gossip. I did not raise you this way. Rumors for a worthless crown."

My stomach clenches. *Am I heartless?*

I jingle the charms on my bracelet, the seven colorful crowns marking each pageant I've won hang from the bangle. What words of wisdom might my mother offer if she were here?

But she left us like a used nail file.

If she wanted to say something, she could raise me herself and say it, right?

I don't want to be like her.

To run.

To hurt the ones I love.

I don't want to be heartless.

I pinch the largest of my crown charms in my thumb and forefinger and decide I never want to care for something so deeply that I become even a shred like Cordelia Perkins.

I will never want something so bad that I drag another heart through fire it doesn't need to burn.

Not a title, or a job...or friends.

With confident fingers, I pry the Junior Miss crown from my hair and snap it in half.

*No more.*

No more pageants or skating for the win.

Lemon Perkins will be a vessel for hope and positivity, and there is no room for competition here.

I'll be selfless. I will not be like my mother.

I take one last look online at the girl I used to be, delete my entire profile, and say goodbye to being selfish forever.

Yanking all seven crown charms from my wrist, I find solace in the person I vow to become as they settle at the bottom of my wastebasket.

# Chapter Eleven

## LEMON

"Hey, Em. Hey, Abs! Wow, it's busy this morning." I steady my purse on the Sugar Stable counter and crane my neck in search of my cousin, Katie, Pine Forest's resident social worker.

I pulled out some spending-cash at the credit union, and I have about seventeen thousand left in my side account. I thank the stars for sending me to the longest line of the newest clerk the day I opened it. Her inexperience allowed me to use a school ID with a nickname rather than my driver's license, so our family accountant's been none the wiser.

See, *Zitrone* Perkins is worth billions.

*Lemon* Perkins doesn't exist.

It's wrong, I know.

But it's the only money I have that's really mine.

It should be plenty to cover utilities and food for the families in need while I'm barred from my trust. The debit card in my hand will allow Katie to deduct whatever they need.

"Shana's not here, if that's who you're looking for. She and Jeremy usually grab coffee before her adult barre class."

"She's still teaching this far along?" I'm impressed. "I'll have to swing by before drop-off one of these days and see how big that baby bump's gotten."

I narrow my eyes at the board. The twins probably want sprinkle donuts as an after-school snack, while Poppy and Bryar might enjoy the sophistication of a bear claw. Would Nash...er, *Oliver*...want anything?

I think about how he treated Bryar.

He doesn't really deserve one. I overheard his eldest daughter venting to Poppy late in the night, and while I'm still not sure what Bryar was doing with that boy, Poppy was on her sister's side by the end of it, and I trust that twelve-year-old more than anyone else in this family I now serve. If she thought her sister was in the right, my instincts say she is.

"Did you say drop-off?" Emily zones in on the key to Oliver's Denali, hanging from my thumb. "Oh, my gosh, you did! You got the nanny job for the Nashvilles?"

Her eyes widen when I tuck away the keys.

"You so did. I told y'all Lady Kempling wasn't gonna last a week. Abby's gonna be pissed." She shouts over the coffee grinder, "Hey, Abs, did you hear? Lem's gonna snag your sugar daddy! Guess who got the—"

I stop her, hand on the register as she slides in my crisp dollar bills. I always pay in cash. It gives the illusion that I'm a stripper, and I like that for me. What I don't like is the words *your* and *daddy* coming out of this little girl's mouth in reference to my...employer.

That's all.

Has nothing, whatsoever, to do with how he used my body like a pocket pussy less than a week ago, or that I still haven't gotten the mud off the bottom of my skates from the audacity of his existence.

Abby meanders over, blushing from head toe, so I can't stop myself. I simply can't. "What do you mean, sugar daddy?"

"It's nothing." She cuts her eyes to a giggling Emily. "Em is supposed to keep secrets to herself."

"What secrets do you have with Oliver Nashville? He's double your age." I attempt indifference, but my body doesn't get the memo. My fingers grip the counter awaiting Abby's response.

"Older men have so much rizz." She says it like the interns say his name, breathless.

"He has four children," flies from my lips faster than I'd like.

"Who cares?" Abby grins at Emily. "The way those pants hug his ass...I'll be *mommy*." She winks, and my pinky nail cracks in half against the counter. Shoving away, I curse as my pastries fall to the floor. "Sorry, y'all. I'll pay for more."

"No need." Emily strides over with a broom. "Dustin would kill me if I let you pay twice." Abby scoops up a new bag of goodies and returns to the back. "You're on the list of like three people to call if there's an emergency. Pretty much a VIP here."

"How is Dustin?" I ask. "I haven't seen him here lately, but that's reasonable when your wife is a month away from delivery. Last time I visited, he'd built a Noah's Ark shaped crib from plans he found online and Shana was padding the sharp parts with pool noodles."

"He's the same as always." She laughs. "Just more of a pep in his step. Always humming something I swear Shana hears from across the courtyard." Emily stares out the window. "Sometimes I think she dances in time to it, but..." She shakes her head. "That sort of love is rare, right?"

*Right,* I wish I would say.

"Well, I need to find Katie so I can get back and snoop for diaries and candy stashes. Nanny duties, am I right?" I jiggle the new pastry bag. But something pulls me back before I can reach the patio door, and I hate that it feels a lot like Olive Lover.

"Is Abby involved with Mr. Nashville, Em?" I swallow, giving her a glare most women understand when they receive it.

*He's mine.*

I'll worry about why I feel that stupid shit later, but for now? "I need to know."

"Seriously, don't worry about it." She flicks her eyes to the back. "She thinks he's a zaddy is all."

"A *zaddy*?"

"I swear, millennials are the new boomers." My young friend pinches the bridge of her nose. "A zaddy. A snack."

"She wants to...eat him? Not sure I like that any better."

"She thinks he's a hottie! Ohmygosh, you are so vibing with him, aren't you? Do you know his sun, moon, rising signs?"

"His what?"

"Never mind." She lowers her voice with a knowing smile. "Look, he's been off the market even before his wife died. As far as anyone knows, he was a faithful husband who kept to himself, and now he's a faithful widower who keeps to himself. And apparently you." She smirks when my eyes widen. "If you want my opinion, he's packing." She searches the room and drops to a whisper. "I know the shoe size thing isn't always a good comparison, but have you seen the man in some steel toe boots?" She fans herself.

Unfortunately, I have.

She winks when I can't seem to hide my blush, and on that note, I need to get all thoughts of zaddies out of my brain before I, too, want to eat a snack.

"Thank you, Emily. If Katie comes by, can you send her to the patio?"

"Will do. And hey! If you end up riding the magic carpet, do us fangirls a favor and report back. We're dying to know if it matches the drapes."

Abby bursts into laughter, poking her head from the back. "Don't let us down, Lemmycakes!"

"Or do!" Emily winks. "Let us all the way down. We want to see, too!"

"Goodbye, ladies!" I smile unmanageably.

Their unbridled confidence reminds me of myself at that age. But if that was me then, who am I now? I hold the pastries in one hand and Oliver's keys in the other.

Who do I want to be?

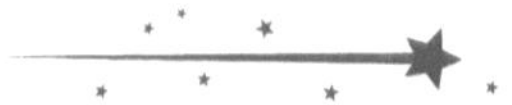

K atie never made it to the patio, and the anxiety has me picking at my gel polish the whole drive home. Oliver's home.

The thought of housing in general forces my mind back to the debit card still burning a hole in my pocket. The underprivileged families of Pine Forest need this money. Ryder has baseball fees, my scholarship is funding parenting classes so Garrison can earn back custody of Jonathan, and the DiFazio twins need formula for another two months before their overworked teen mother—with zero support system—transitions them to whole milk.

These people are my neighbors, and fences may separate us, but basic resources never should.

I'm stopped for construction at Mullins Road when I finally text Katie.

ME:

> Where ARE you?! Answer me, or I'll release the Hannah Montana sleepover photo of 2006

> Posting in 3…2…

KATIE KAT

Sorry! Things got chaotic at the fundraiser. PLEASE don't post Hannah.

The fire department showed up. <Exhausted Emoji>

My heartbeat quickens.

ME:

At the group home?

No response

ME:

Is everyone okay?

No response.

ME:

WHAT HAPPENED?!

Questions spring to my mind faster than my fingers can navigate the keys.

*Fuck it, I'll just call her.*

"Oh, my God, you're certifiable," Katie answers.

"You don't sound very relieved to hear from me."

"Z, I'm never relieved to hear from you. I tend to avoid it."

The road workers wave me through the left lane, and I switch to the car speaker.

"I said the fire department showed up, not that there was a fire."

"Why'd you stand me up then?" Annoying. "You realize I'm under constant watch now, don't you? Delivering secret debit cards has never been more difficult."

"You're a lot," Katie says, "since we were kids. You know that, right?"

"I've heard." My eyes roll. "What I haven't heard is a legit excuse."

"It's a long story, but there's this person," she sighs, "...man. The fire chief to be specific."

"You stood me up for a fire daddy? You little harlot."

"I did not. He was there, yes, but he's infuriating. Hardly responsible enough to be anyone's daddy. You have no idea how much I want to pound him."

"Kit Kat, I can hear how much pounding you want with him."

"I pretend we aren't related, have I told you that?"

"Often." My grin wars between irritation and pride. Even if she doesn't care to admit we're alike, my cousin rarely expresses interest in anyone seriously.

My thoughts immediately shift to the parallels with Oliver. It's genetic, isn't it? This aversion we have to permanency.

So, what makes this man different than the rest?

"He has a big water hose, doesn't he?"

"Zitrone Perkins!"

"Long, hard pole?"

"You're bad."

"Fine, tell me about his schlong when you're ready. In the meantime, you need these funds. I promised Ryder he'd have his name on the back of his jersey this year like the other kids, and I'm not about to be made a liar after he gave me a bubble-gum machine ring and asked me to be his girl."

"Thanks for helping, Z, even when you can't. Are you sure you don't want to pause the funding until you're done with—I'm still not sure what to call this situation Uncle Emil has put you in. I did check, and it's not illegal to halt your trust. The way his lawyers have it laid out, none of it is yours at all until you're a seated partner at Perkins Global."

"I figured as much."

"You're not pissed?"

"Oh, I am, but the problems I have come in much larger forms at present. Grumpy, silver, employer forms, unfortunately. And I'm not sure how much longer I'll behave, cuz."

"Z, listen to me. As your older and incredibly wiser cousin...do not fuck the man your father paid to keep you from fucking men."

"I don't think that's what it is..."

"It is." Her groan fills the silence when I don't reply. "It's already happening, isn't it?"

"Happening feels like a strong word." I flick my blinker.

"What are you wearing?"

"Huh?" A button on the sun visor opens the gate, and I cast a curious glance at my skirt as I turn down the pristinely paved drive. I wonder how smooth he keeps other things. "A black skirt and a red crop top? I don't see how that makes a difference."

"It makes all the difference. It's happening, whether you admit it or not."

Maybe she's right.

I did crop the top.

"What if I don't want it to happen?" The heat between my thighs screams my deceit, surging like a tidal wave when I pull into the garage and his car is already there.

"Then you need to ask yourself why you aren't stopping it. You've had no problem ending every other relationship."

"He spanked me a little," I admit.

"*Jesus, Z.*"

"It was good, too. I'm talking ginormous hand cupping entire cheek level spankage. He didn't even get me off, yet all I can think of is how that same hand might feel holding mine."

"Z?" Her tone softens. "Have you considered you might feel something real for once? Something you could want long term?"

"Have you?"

Neither of us has an answer.

S weat beads across my forehead, but I won't stop. I'm one mile into this run, and if I keep pushing, that second and third will feel like nothing.

Then everything.

Adrenaline. Distraction.

I level my breathing and check my form, pulling my shoulders back, and rolling through the feet.

*Just push.*

Anything to take my mind off Oliver Nashville.

I'm adjusting the ponytail, loose across my back, when I hear the door slam.

Eye-rolling immediately commences.

He didn't have to slam the door.

He didn't have to be in the gym at all.

Okay, so it is in his house, and I might have noted the calendar on his fridge has this time slot marked 'gym,' but that is so far beside the point, it doesn't even matter.

Not when he's standing here shirtless.

His eyes skate down my sweaty form, and I narrow mine directly at him.

In those stupid horny-ass sweatpants, for the love of fuck!

Jer's right. He so knows.

But Oliver is a big boy, right? A powerful man who makes million-dollar business transactions and secures nannies he doesn't fuck.

My jealousy stems from...I don't even know what. My own self? His refusal to see me? The fact I'm in his goddamned house, right under his own roof—

just down the hall from him every night for the foreseeable future, and he has yet to acknowledge the spanking wasn't the end or the beginning of this?

Or was I just a voyeur's secret thrill?

I'm no longer running anymore, but sprinting, jamming the speed up to seven point five and increasing the incline by two...six...ten.

I'm running up the mountain.

And a thought occurs to me as I make my stationary ascent.

I am in control of my own destiny.

If I win the adventure show, I won't need a trust fund to help myself or others. The missing crown charms on my bangles propel me on my run, reminders of who I never want to be.

Selfish.

I don't compete anymore, my number one rule. Do all things from a place of love, not success.

Still, I wouldn't need anyone this way.

And I shouldn't.

Not when I know the last thing they need is me.

Rule number two, you ask? No long term anything. Jobs and relationships alike. And scout's honor, it's for the best. It really is me, not them.

Oliver does reps on one of those frippery total body machines, placing and removing weights in a series of events that I don't pay a lick of attention to, so that's cool. Before I know it, I've hit mile five, all while his ridiculous existence flexes in the mirror behind me.

I towel my face and take a quick selfie for Jeremy. We're accountability buddies, mostly so neither of us slacks off too many days in a row, but also because we're both too full of ourselves not to send pics. I add a few kissy face emojis before I send it, hoping the smug set of eyes and abs attached to the old grump behind me sees it and misreads.

But why?

I don't want to make him jealous.

I certainly don't want to bait him.

Katie's earlier question hangs in my mind, and my stomach flutters.

Something real.

An arrogant grunt sounds from behind me, and I flick my eyes up to the mirror to see his judgmental grimace. Pity it makes me so wet when it's rather unattractive compared to the smile I saw at dinner last night.

Fuck, do I want this asshole.

And that makes me so damn mad that I refuse it to be so. I may be unable to control my fantasies around him, but surely, I can control my actions.

I, Lemon Anne Perkins, will abstain.

I just need to distract myself.

But right now, with untouchable Daddy Nashville in front of me, growing haughtier by the minute, sweating, and dripping, and lips moving because...because he's speaking.

And I have no idea what he said.

I spin away, ignoring him being preferable to admitting I've no idea what he said while I memorized the path of travel his sweat took to his groin.

His eyes burn holes in the back of my head like he knows that anyhow, but I remind myself he rejected me, and I snap one more photo for my bestie before stuffing my phone in my bra.

"Why do millennials do that?"

Despite my very worst efforts, I turn back around. Unwelcome relief surges when our eyes meet. "Do what? Have friends? Text? You should try it. Might help those pants of yours loosen a bit." I kick myself for being this way when his eyes darken, and I love goddamned the shade.

"I don't need friends." He nods to my phone but does not adjust his massive cock that's all I can focus on, quite shamefully I do admit. "I meant selfies." He clears his throat and draws my eyes back to his with a clear as fuck smirk.

*Stupidly huge cock.*

"People your age are always snapping pictures of themselves like anyone cares."

He isn't that much older than me, forty-five to my twenty-eight, but in technological years, that's an era.

I could tell him the truth, that it's to guilt Jeremy into working out today per the blood oath we took over pinkies last month, or for my own health, which is also not a lie.

Either of those answers would be better than pushing my cleavage to smothering heights and licking my lips like I might drop to my knees and blow Oliver Nashville right where we stand. I think he believes it too, as his breath draws in on a swift inhale and steel blue eyes search mine.

I'm baiting him.

And what's worse is Katie's right. I have no desire to stop myself.

"Selfies are for sugar daddies." I snap my thong against my flesh. "The prettier the panties, the sweatier the selfie. Gosh," I towel my brow, "I'm practically drenched today."

Oliver's eyes never leave my body as I strut out of the gym and slam the door behind me.

Whether I like it or not, I'm a hopeless ho.

And I think I'm an olive lover, too.

*Joy.*

# Chapter Twelve

## OLIVER

Twenty-four hours. That's how long it took for me to get comfortable with Lemon in my space.

A single day.

And here she is, only a week later, brightening things.

Even now, she shimmies on a chair to reach the mantel, dusting a portrait of my wife.

It's surreal, to say the least.

The only two women I've ever felt right about, side-by-side in my home, neither attainable.

Somehow, I've never felt more connected to them both. And call me crazy, but when Lemon's near, it's as if Lauren is too, pushing us together, linking our hands.

An overwhelming calm fits over me, and I want desperately to sink into it, but how is that fair?

Leaning into these feelings only gives the girls someone to count on who may very well leave when the summer is through.

The last thing they need is more loss.

And the last thing Lemon needs is me dimming her light.

I promised Mr. Perkins to keep his daughter out of trouble, but I vowed to my wife on her deathbed to keep our own children safe from harm, be that physical or mental.

I achieve both by keeping my feelings for this woman what they are—only feelings.

I pound the tenderizer over the chuck steak, encouraging my thoughts on the task before me and not the coruscating light source that is my new nanny, arranging flowers around Lauren's portrait.

Her spirit mocks me at the sight, laughter practically pouring from the clouds and piercing my heart as we both fixate on the tan legs and tight shorts before me. A slow smile finds a place across my lips at the memory of Lauren and I in our twenties, drunk from the sun and discussing who we'd entertain with a hypothetical hall pass on the beach.

"I'd do her," I can hear her now.

*Fuck.* I miss my wife like I miss breathing once I've let it all out.

And then there's Lemon. *I'd do her, too, Lo.*

I want to, trust me. But how is it fair to be happy? Can I be?

Is it allowed?

The year after Lauren died is when I met her, this anomaly of a woman who seeks attention but detests validation.

I tried to ignore her. It helped I was grieving. An old, depressed widow of a man she hardly noticed. But years of unfiltered light in your eyes will eventually blind you. I fought my entire body to look away. It didn't matter that she was an adrenaline chasing groupie with cartoon hearts for eyes, Lemon Perkins filled some twisted void in my life simply by living her own.

A complete train wreck, she'd have given someone her full social and mother's maiden name had I not stopped her. Become enraptured by her presence in my life.

But Lauren was my first love, my only wife, and no woman could ever come close to what we had. So that was it. I told myself I could watch. I could protect. But I would never touch Lemon Perkins, no matter how much I wanted her.

I didn't count on her wanting me back.

And here she is, the most captivating secret I have, living and breathing in my home.

Laughter pours from the open foyer, and my eyes water at the sound of my usually silent child dancing with her own voice. I poke my head in to see Kimmie and Poppy rearranging the living room with Lemon. True to Bryar's fashion, she's nowhere in sight, and it irks me I can't get through to her. Another problem I can't seem to solve. I wish that kid would participate in the family for once.

It hits me then that the whole family isn't here. Not just Bryar, but...my eyes trail to Kimmie. Alone.

"Where is Cami?" She's fiercely protective of her twin. "She never leaves Kimmie's side in case she needs to speak for her."

"I don't know." Lemon shrugs. "Fifty percent is a great return rate, though."

"Are you joking?" My jaw flexes, and I'm irritated as I've ever been at the way her smile seems to tease and taunt. I'm both attracted and appalled by all it stands for, but I don't have time to play games if my kid is missing. Surely she realizes that.

"Did she get off the bus or not?" I say as calmly as possible, directing my lack of control to the fingerings of Brahms Sonata Number three in D Minor against my palm.

"Wow." She shakes her head as her eyes slide to my silent concerto. "You're serious, aren't you? You think I'd forget a whole-ass kid?" She fumes when I can't meet her stare to confirm, but memories of Cami alone flood my mind. Of the nanny that forgot her, just after Lauren passed. Kimmie cried nonstop for her twin, Poppy said, until a six-year-old Bryar convinced the young sitter there were supposed to be two toddlers, not one. I mean who the hell had I let take care of my children? All while I was away for work. Kimmie stopped making sounds after that. All that crying and then nothing. Cami's never left her side since.

My fingers stop with the memory.

"Seriously, Oliver?" Lemon eyes me quizzically.

But I'm not joking. "Where is she, Lem?" My watered eyes meet her blazing purple ones, but I don't answer the question I see there.

I'm not sure I know how.

"Cam's with me!" Bryar calls from the sitting room where I hurry in to find the same teen I was just judging, painting bright blue polish over her little sister's wiggling toes. A new guilt packs right on top the old that I made assumptions about both Bryar and Lemon just now.

*What is wrong with me? Why am I like this?*

Bryar casts an annoyed glare my way when I rush to kiss them both on the head. But they're here. They're safe. And they'll have no idea the fear that courses through every inch of me at the thought of the alternative until they have their own kids one day.

"For Mom." Cami beams, showing off her polish. "Bry said her favorite flowers were the little blue ones."

"Forget-me-nots." I nod, gesturing to the streamers above the piano. "What's all this?"

"Lemon said we can have a memory day." Cami bounces excitedly. "Isn't that fun? I don't have any memories of Mom, so Bryar and Poppy will have to tell them. I know Kimmie will love it, too."

Bryar scrunches her nose when I turn for confirmation of this and she nods. "A memorial, Dad."

I don't miss how she draws in a trembling breath when she does, as if she thinks I'd forbid such a thing. "Of course," I choke. "You do what you must, and I'll...I'll just go..."

"Hold on, Cam." Bryar stares at the polish for a quick second, looking every bit the like her mother before she leads us to the privacy of the fireplace. "I know you don't like this kind of thing, Dad, but Poppy's been...she's starting to..." She turns her face to the side and sniffles. "She's forgetting Mom."

I can't find the words I need, but I know it's not a day of talking about my dead wife in the presence of my new nanny and my children who need me sturdy and strong in the wake of this life-changing promotion, not withering and depressed.

"I can't do this, Bry. You girls have your event. I'll go to my office, all right?"

"No."

Her brows pull and she takes my hand. Funny how I thought it was smaller. When did it grow so large that it could cradle mine?

"You need to be there, Dad. We want you to be there."

"Baby, please understand it's not that I don't want to remember her, it's—"

"You miss her just as much as I do. But you always act like you don't. You act like nothing ever matters. You have to let yourself feel things, Dad. Mom would—"

"Mom's not here. And you are a child. My child!" It's louder than intended.

*Shit.*

"Bry, I didn't mean—"

"You know what, Dad? You did mean." Tears shine over her eyes. "I can't convince you of anything, not even this. You're always right. About life *and* death."

Cami rears her head our way, and it dawns on me they were having a one-on-one without Kimmie, because Kimmie is with Lemon. This moment is something they've never gotten together before.

Thanks to the woman I just doubted.

"Why are you guys fighting?" Cami's whisper is laced with worry, and I can't bear that.

Not because of me.

"We're not, Cam." Bryar casts sharp daggers at me when I don't respond.

I don't even know how I got to this moment. One where my teenager felt the need to parent *me.*

But if she's right?

"Dad's just getting ready to put the steaks on the grill. That's all." She cuts me one last dismissive glare before returning to her little sister with a pasted smile. "Now, was it pink you wanted on this side? Mom had this bright pink purse. Not sure if you remember it, but Dad hated the thing, and one time..."

I let myself out, the story of Lauren's atrocious purse bringing a smile to my lips even as tears fill my eyes.

Even if I want neither of those things.

I brace myself for the weight that follows her memories. The ones there to slam me against a solid metal wall, pinned by the nothingness of her departure, but when I pass through the living room and find Lemon shining brightly as ever, laughing and dancing with my girls, the pain is somehow lessened.

Kimmie, my most sensitive child, is in full acceptance of someone new.

Poppy has a confidant.

Bryar is spending time with her siblings.

And for the first time ever, Cami is learning who she is apart from her twin.

Is my daughter right?

Is it time to feel?

When everyone's nestled in their respective quarters, I find solace in the one place I'm able these days.

I sink into the hot tub until my neck rests against the rim, water sloshing around me and spilling to the deck below.

The night sky is above, and warmth surrounds me. I wish I could pluck the stars from the sky and replace the light I lost all those years ago.

But life doesn't work that way.

Positioning the headphones over my ears, I lie back and let the melody of Bach's Chaconne, Partita Number Two, become my present. The bow slides back and forth across the strings of the violin, calm and calamity at war.

Fitting.

The tempo rises and falls in waves, and the song becomes a roadmap to my grief that computes for once.

It makes sense in song.

People say Bach wrote it to pay homage to his late wife, which used to bring me comfort. I'd listen to the rise and fall of the sounds, knowing that despite my inability to pick up a violin since my own partner passed, I could play alongside this recording by heart.

In the water, my fingers take on the movements with ease.

Evidence now suggests the tune was composed prior to learning of his wife's passing, but it doesn't mean we're not brothers. I play the water for us, eyes closed, heart heavy, and I pay tribute to my lost love and his.

"Wow. Are you seizing?" Lemon drops her towel to the floor, inspecting my eyes.

Eyes that fall to the curves of her hips in the...

"Oh great, you're back to normal." She puts her finger under my chin and adjusts my focus back to her face.

"Sorry, Sour Patch, you are..."

"Hot as fuck. I'm aware. Still have eyes."

She leans over the tub and flicks her fingers through the water, testing the temperature and studying me. I toss my headphones to a nearby deck chair and sit straighter, making room for her beside me.

"I'm relieved you're not having a medical episode." It's genuine, and it digs at me that I've never paid attention to this side of her before.

I've seen this woman in a lot of ways. Most of them make my cock hard to even consider. But there's more to Lemon Perkins than the party girl or the billionaire's heiress.

There's a selfless side, a caring one. The parts my most untrusting children trust. And even when I lost my mind about Cami, she didn't inflate the issue. She swooped in where she was needed and painted nails with my girls as they celebrated a woman that isn't her.

"I came about Bryar." She lowers into the water, and her foot brushes mine.

Our eyes meet before she moves it away, and that single act twists everything inside of me. The absence of her body when it was just so close is taxing alone, but I inhale a defeated breath at the added mention of my teenage wild child.

"What'd she do now?" I hang my head, already exhausted by the same conversation I have with every nanny. I find a little comfort, knowing this one won't quit like the others, but I'm left wondering how true that is when she lifts a brow and remains silent. "It's bad, isn't it?" I rake my hand through my hair. Lemon watches it fall back over my forehead, every inch.

I don't want her to quit.

"It's because we fought earlier. I'll handle this."

I move to stand, but Lemon shoots up before me and slams me back down, pinning me in place, as she straddles me.

"Absolutely not." Her fingers press into my bare shoulders, her thighs squeezed around me, her center pressed against mine. I clear my throat and concentrate on the conversation at hand, not on how my cock could be inside of her with a single thrust. "You will not handle this. You have no idea what you're walking into."

"Whatever she did, I'll talk to her. I know you don't have much of a choice being here and all, so I'll make sure you don't have to deal with her issues too, while you're here, at least."

She shoves her hands into my chest and presses away from me. "*Her* issues? Wow, Bryar's right. You are delusional. I thought maybe it was just my father with a penchant for misunderstandings, but you, my sir, take the cake with this one. Emil Perkins might have found a way to sell me off with a million-dollar dowery to some old voyeur from his payroll, but you are much worse, Oliver Nashville. You are the type who sees his daughter struggling, has every resource within his power to lift her up, even has the time now that you've been promoted. And she wants to be lifted, for fuck's sake…but you let her sink. All alone."

Lemon springs from my lap and scrambles out of the water, wrapping her shaking body in a towel before lashing back. "You know…" She looks at the stars. "My mother left me. Bryar's died. We aren't the same, and I won't claim we could be, because the difference is, at her age, I took that pain and loss and I harbored it in my soul, tearing others down so I could feel important enough that the thought of someone leaving me would be laughable. Unthinkable. Until the memory of my mother was just a stack of stupid charms." She shakes her wrist, and I look at her bracelets for the first time, considering her past. Like me, she's felt loss and pain. Maybe more than I imagined for the stuck-up heiress I thought I knew.

And maybe like me, she will always feel that pain. Yet here she is, going on. Shaking her wrists at a broken man.

"You jumped to conclusions. The moment you heard your daughter's name, you assumed she did something wrong. You know how many times that happened to me at her age and it *was* my fault? The difference is your daughter wants to cheer others on. She misses her mother, understands the weight of her loss. Of all your losses. She started this memorial to bring awareness and donations to her coach."

She lets that sink, and the silence weighs heavily on my ears, but not as heavy as the rock that settles in my gut when I recall the card Bryar slammed on the table yesterday.

"Coach Jasmine."

"Yep." Lemon whips her hair over one shoulder, dabbing it dry. "Coach Jasmine Montell of Pine Forest High who is currently under treatment for melanoma. You'd know that if you approached your child with an ounce of respect instead of mistrust."

"That's what Lauren had. Melanoma."

"Yeah." She drops her gaze. "Bryar told me. She also told me she worries her sisters won't know what love feels like because you've forgotten, too."

"What?" I move from the tub now, too, whipping my towel around my body in a flash to meet her eyes in earnest. "She said that?"

Lemon nods. "Yeah, she did. And she's known me for only two days, Oliver. You know that actually says a whole lot, right? She is not getting something she needs here. I hate to be the one to tell you, but maybe none of them are."

"Of course I love them. They're my girls. I—"

Lemon puts a hand up. "You don't have to be perfect, Oliver. At work or home. I may have just met your family, but I've known you a very large chunk of my life. You want to act like you're this impenetrable force of protection, but all you've done is paste on Band-Aids and throw up blinders, only ever homing in on what needs fixed. What's broken. But what about what's working?" She gestures into the house where the girls are sleeping. "Look at your daughter, Oliver. You were in the wrong with that grounding. With your refusal to show up for your children at a memorial they are facilitating for their dead mother." She shakes her head. "Do you even hear how shitty that sounds?"

*I do,* I want to say.

But she already said it for me, and I don't know what's worse.

Lemon clicks her tongue. "Bryar was right. And I'm sticking up for her, not as *your* anything. But as *her* nanny. You need to see the strong young woman she is, not the kid you're too damn cowardly to trust."

# Chapter Thirteen

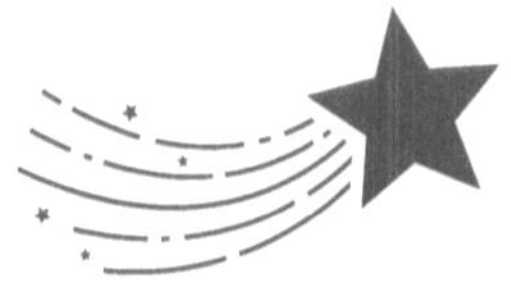

## LEMON

What if you had a chance to do something you've never done before? Something that could change the way you see the world and how the world sees you.

I was mad before. Angry, even. How could Oliver judge his own children the way he does?

One week. And today's their last day at school. I've learned so much about them simply by listening, and it boggles my mind that their father hasn't realized that's all it would take for him.

Poppy is a fantastic photographer and artist. She's got an exhibit on display at the library. She showed Oliver the flier at dinner last night, but he was quieter than Kimmie. Did he even read it?

The twins ate with their fingers half the meal, and while I probably should have helped out and enforced cutlery, I didn't. I let it happen so I could observe.

What I noticed? Oliver Nashville is disassociated. And his children are vying for his approval. Only, Bryar's done waiting around.

If he's not careful, she'll find it somewhere else.

I know this.

I try like hell to let the stress and weight of these new emotions fly behind me with the wind as my roller-blading speed increases. My pulse picks up, and I love every second of it.

I glide in a spread eagle, deepening my stretch into a lunge as I roll down the carefully maintained asphalt in Pine Forest Estates, the gated community with everything in its place, just how Nash wants it. The bushes are all maintained, the fountains all lit and flowing, surrounded by bright, beautiful flowers, and not a single pebble of a walkway is out of place.

I hate it with half of my soul.

The other half of my hate is reserved for the stupid old grump I now live with. I gave him the silent treatment for the way he acted with Bryar, and I know it's not my place, but as the daughter of another rich old prick, I felt it necessary to help another queen, you know what I mean?

Whether she's thirteen or thirty, she was in the right by supporting her sick coach. Should she have let her boyfriend drive her without permission? Probably not. But as the twins informed me, it wasn't even her boyfriend. He's the cheer captain for the high school team Jasmine also coaches. It was just two captains rallying their teams, but would Oliver have trusted that even if she'd been truthful?

The wind howls, an unusually chilly day for the end of May, but it feels renewing, restorative in a way. It's laughable, I know, but I feel something in the wind.

A calling.

No, a legitimate calling.

My foot buzzes at the end of a double lutz, and I realize it's not the pavement, so I skid to a stop and unzip my skate pocket, revealing a screen full of Tina's smiling face.

"Lem! I'm so glad I got you before this next meeting. I'll be tied up for hours." She blows out an audible breath and then howls into the phone. "Girl! You got it! They loved your audition video for Adventure Mountain. You got the callback."

"I did? I got it?" My whole body tingles with excitement. I can make this work. With this million, I can be my own person, my own way.

For the rest of my life.

Maybe one day I'll even take over like Papa wants, but I'll have power and money behind me when I finally make Perkins Global what I know it can be. No more unnecessary spending, no more snail mail...we could be entirely internet based, reduce the fuck out of our global footprint.

"This is incredible." I shake my head at Tina. "When does everything happen? I'm pretty booked up until..." I scrunch my nose as I glide to a stop at the Nashville residence. Nash is shirtless, rolling beneath the Denali.

I clutch the phone tightly, nodding to Tina who goes on about something.

Something that isn't torsos, and oil smudged forearms, and sweat beading and—holy fuck, it's the damn pants again!

"Hellooo, Lemon Perkiiins!" Tina hollers. "Did you hear me? When are you tied up?"

"Hopefully tonight," I mumble as Nash's six-pack glistens in the sunlight. *Fuck!* "Sorry, T, what were you saying?"

"They make final casting decisions at the end of the summer, and the show films in November."

"Perfect!" It all works within my timeline. "What do they want for the callback? I can do some skating or hiking. I could get a GoPro and—"

"There's one thing I forgot to mention about this show, Lem." Tina bites her bottom lip. "It's one of those survival shows. Like, eat bugs from the earth and you don't get to bring anything kind of shows."

"Oh," I say, taken aback, but I'm still not ready to quit. I mean, I've gone camping before. I'm sure with some practice this summer I could learn about berries, and one of my redneck friends could take me hunting, even if the image does shake me up.

The thought of killing an animal makes me want to not kill an animal. You know? But...

"For one million, Tina. We can work with survival." I'm great at things I can learn later. At least it's not one of those shows where you're naked.

"One more thing," Tina chirps. "It's one of those shows where you're naked."

**"T**ake a picture; they last longer." Nash rolls from beneath the SUV, but remains horizontal, which looks ungodly good on him, the sweatpanted fucker.

I roll to a stop with a hand on my hip and pop a large pink bubble as I lift my sunglasses. "Remind me again, who needs to last longer?"

"Very funny." He props himself up on his elbows. His biceps flex beneath him, his body forcing them against the rolling cart that's pinned by his weight.

And now the asshole's got me jealous of inanimate objects, too. I check him out shamelessly as he sweats and simmers just feet from the hem of my skirt. He could reach right up. I want him to reach right...

"Lem, you know we can't. We shouldn't..."

He struggles, but I know what he's going to tell me.

We can't fuck.

He can't be with the nanny.

With me, more specifically.

But I know he wants it. I'd wager hard cash he's inflating like a birthday balloon beneath those cotton monstrosities.

"We can't be a thing, I get it." *Doesn't mean I don't want it.* I blow a raspberry into the air when he just glares at me. I can't read the look in his eyes, so it's a welcome relief when he breaks contact to grab a new filter.

"Why are you changing the oil, anyway? Does your new salary of millions not leave you much wiggle room for a mechanic?"

His jaw ticks.

I hate that I love it.

"You challenge me, Lemon Perkins." He closes in on my space until there's no division between what's his and mine, and I sneak a quick breath, determined not to flat-out pant.

As of now, I hold the cards.

I'm the tease he can't stop thinking about, the one who couldn't care less if it's his dick or someone else's in my bed tonight. That alone might be what's kept him from caving, even if it is a lie.

And there's absolutely no way I can let him know that. He can't fall in love with me.

And I refuse to fall in love with him.

Not with his children depending on him to be their steady force. He's the only one in their corner, and fuck if I don't want to join that corner and brighten it and paint it and make it part mine, but I can't do that to them when I plan to leave.

Because I will leave.

When the sparkle fades and the newness and wonder dims, they'll feel how everyone else does.

I'm simply *too much*.

His gaze fixes on mine, boring into his lips, fantasizing about the ways I could use them despite all my convictions telling me no. I can't even hide the lust I feel anymore; I send fuck-me daggers straight to his cock.

A single beat passes before we both know this is fucked, this wall we're half-assedly erecting, pushing the other away just to tease them right back in.

I'm not sure when we conclude it, but sometime between closing the garage door and untying my halter, my legs wrap around his body, and we say fuck it to avoiding the inevitable.

One arm supports me while the other roams my breasts, pawing the fabric of my blouse. He doesn't handle me with care. It's quite the opposite, and I know with every piece of me it's for the same reason I want to throw caution to the wind myself.

This thing between us is uncontrollable.

He wraps his hand around my throat and pins me to the wall, wetness sliding down my thighs.

And when he pushes his fingers into my panties and finds me soaked for him?

"I'm always wet when I skate." I gasp.

"Liar." He smirks, sliding a finger inside of me and curling, dragging my pleasure out straight from the root of my G-spot and *fuck*, he's good at this. I lift my eyes to his, my head too weak to stay up when all my focus is being sent to my legs to keep curled around him.

He smirks and slides his fingers back out. The sudden loss of his existence within me is assaulting, and I cry out, guiding him back.

"Do not leave me with blue balls again, Oliver Nashville, or I swear to God when I find out what your middle name is, I will post it live on social media." I rock into his fingers until they settle back in where I want. "There's only room for one tease in this house."

"Brat." His amused smile stretches to meet his eyes. I like it, I think.

"I was going to point out that women can't get blue balls, but with the look in your eyes, I'm afraid to do anything but—"

"Make me come?" I tease, moaning in delight when he hits the perfect rhythm, circling his thumb over my pulsing clit. "Oh, fuck, Nash."

The pressure builds to a near explosion, and I rock my hips into his entire hand while I chase my climax. "Fuck me!" I scream, unable to keep the thoughts that race through my mind at bay.

*Oliver. Fingers. Eyes on me.*

"That's it, Sour Patch, squeeze me so I feel how good you'd take me. Naughty nanny, so damn tight around these fingers." He adds a third and stretches me wider, pumping into me, over and over, hand delivering my pleasure directly to the center of my body. I clench around his fingers, so close. "Ohh! Oliver!" I full-on orgasm into his hand, and even though half my body's water supply is now pooling down my thighs, I almost come again when he drags his fingers through it, as I rock my hips forward.

He rubs my arousal in slow, languid circles around my wanton clit, and it suddenly registers that he's been holding me up by one arm this entire time.

"Arms like that aren't fair." I'm horny for this freakishly hard asshole all over again being in them.

He kisses my neck, his groans porn of their own that settle at the tips of my hardened nipples, and I can't help but press my swollen pussy into his hand for more. Our foreheads touch when he lets out a steady exhale.

"You have been so fucking bad, Lem." A chill travels down my spine when he says my nickname. Not Sour Patch, but the one my friends call me.

His erection presses tightly against his sweatpants. "You drive me mad, living in this house. I have ruined every pair of pants I own just breathing the same oxygen as you."

"What does it say about me if I'm proud of that?"

Oliver shakes his head and presses a kiss to my nose. It's intimate.

Too much like something real.

And I have to deflate it.

Remind him I'm just the slut in the nanny costume he thought I was. The bratty billionaire's heiress he can't possibly sate.

"Is that why you're always sporting the crotch-huggers?"

He lowers me to the ground, a serious question in his glare, but I slide my hand between our bodies, driving the moment back to the physical so our emotions can stay the fuck away.

*This is what we can be*, my hand suggests as I wrap around his length. *It doesn't have to be forever.*

My center pulses touching Oliver Nashville, and I'm not sure what this says about me, but the fact I can't wrap my fingers around it seems to be the cause.

"Please tell me crotch huggers aren't anything like casting couches," he sucks in a breath when I stroke his shaft, "because I had to delete my search history on your father's server, of all places."

A laugh jumps from my throat at that image. Nash and his perfectly horrified face illuminated by a Perkins Global computer glow as some actress is railed by three dudes with shaky cameras.

I smile, stroking Oliver behind the Denali. As kinky as it is, it feels like our own little porn video. The nanny behind the car in the garage.

I used to think he had this thing to keep up with the Jones's my father has working for him, but it seems to match the joystick for Nash, here.

*Just fucking huge.*

I think about Emily's request to know if the curtains match the drapes and can't help how eager I must look when I stare up at this beautifully broken man I've been handling and practically beg him to throw two sheets to the wind.

"Can I put this in my mouth, Oliver?"

His cock juts forward in my grip as I say his name.

"Oliver," I tease again, stroking harder and longer, lowering to my knees—which is honestly a skill in rollerblades—and wrapping my lips around his leaking tip before I suck him down to the base.

I take him all the way in, tongue tracing ridges, spit spilling from my lips, and hollowed cheeks puckering as I suck him down. His head hangs back, resting against the metal of the car as praises mix with his moans. I maneuver my tongue out flat until I'm painting it with his cock. I love every second of the sloppy mess I make between us, and it's not even for him anymore. This is me, take it or fucking leave it, Daddy.

I lift my eyes to his, still gagging on his length, slurping it up like it's me on the casting couch. He's my director and I'm his actress, his sounds of pleasure my critique, as I find the exact rhythm and tempo that makes his hips pump and hands tighten on my head, my freshly fingered pussy dripping for more when he does.

"Jesus fucking Christ, Sour Patch. I'm gonna—"

"Knew you couldn't last longer." I tease the words around his cock, and he lets out an exasperated laugh, licking his bottom teeth, studying me as our eyes remain locked in challenge.

One last flick of my tongue across his swollen tip is all it takes before he finally gives in. I know it the moment his fingers thread my hair and tug.

*Yes!* This is the Nash I want.

The one who fucking feels something.

"Do you know how long I've dreamed about putting my cock in the back of this throat?"

His reckless abandon feels powerful. The growling, the face fucking, the loss of control.

This is what I do to him.

And I can't help but spur him on even more, popping his swollen length from my mouth so the spit trickles down my chin. "I know how many men you've watched fuck it for you."

"Brat." He chuckles, growls? All I know is it's raw, and it's reckless, and it's all the fuck for me. He lowers my head back down, slamming his cock into my mouth, full force, thick quads tightening around my neck with each thrust, and I'm here for it.

He's seen what makes me come, and that thought has me even hornier, every goddamned second of his fingers tightening against my scalp and the taste of him on my tongue are fuel for my aching clit. I gag, opening my throat and allowing the space he needs to fill me. To take my mouth and make it his.

I only wish it were the rest of me he'd take.

*Fuck!*

What am I thinking?

This was supposed to be to fuck him out of my system, but my conversation with Katie forces its way to the front of my mind.

*Something long term?*

Fuck. That.

I swirl my tongue around his tip, taking back the control I've just lost and marveling at the pleasured sounds he makes as I stroke him with both hands, basting the underside of his shaft and balls with my spit until he tenses.

"Fuck, Lem."

*Lem.*

His hands tighten in my hair, twisting through the start of his orgasm, and I'm there, mouth slabbing back over top of his length, sheathing my way down until my lips are flush to the hilt. My lips tremble as he pushes into my mouth one last time before I taste his explosion across my tongue.

I suck him clean, swallowing every bit of what just occurred like a crime to be covered, then I lick my lips and lift to my feet, steadying on my skates as my chest rises and falls in heavy waves.

"Lem," he breathes, wild eyes still searching mine for answers I don't have. Not the ones he wants anyway.

"Sour Patch," I correct.

His lip quirks. "So, you do like your nickname."

"I didn't say that." I twist my hair around my finger, skating around the Denali and eyeing the duffle bags and fishing gear he's piled beside it.

What I don't tell him is that he's right.

I like my nickname. But even more so, I like my own name.

Especially the way it sounds falling from Oliver Nashville's mouth. And that is a big no.

I don't do forevers. I don't do homewrecking.

And I certainly don't do grumpy, widowed, millionaires my dad paid to keep me busy.

Only I just fucking did.

"You have a huge ding-a-ling." I sigh, still unsure what to do about the colossal phallus I now want inside of me in every way. "For an old dude."

Nash's sapphire eyes meet his smile. "You know I'm not that much older than you."

"That's funny. You're fifteen years older than me. You have a whole-ass child the same difference in age, just the opposite direction."

"Don't say that." He pinches the bridge of his nose, but he knows how long he's stared at me, doesn't he?

I know how long he's looked.

"Right," he hisses at his already hardening cock, and he clears his throat, eyes scraping my body as he decides something he doesn't make me privy to. I see it flash across his features before he shakes it away. "Well, I think we can agree that this was a one-time thing. We can't do this again."

"That's fine," I lie. "I don't double dip."

Truthfully, it's not fine, and I don't normally come back for seconds, but I would come back for thirds and fourths and seventeenths for this man. I would come undone for him. But what he needs is forever, and...

"I'm not a permanent person."

He stares at me for a long time, until my phone buzzes, and he breaks away.





I groan, typing and deleting words I'm not sure I should send. I decide the x in the word sucks annoys me more than anything else. Like, why sub a letter when all it does is shorten the word by one? It shows his age. I think that's what bothers me most.

He's sickeningly cute, and I hate every second of it, because I am not the obsessed fangirl he needs rushing to his side to inflate his ego. I don't want a boy who needs me to stroke his growing feathers, I need the whole damn peacock. Preferably the aging silver one.

But Nash knows where I stand. He knows nothing would be serious between us.

And he just told me to keep my crotch away from him, right? Maybe this is the distraction we both need for me to continue with this obligation all summer.

But as hard as I try, I can't hit send. It feels wrong to send Onyx texts when I'm still dripping from Nash, so I don't.

It's the first time I've left anyone on read.

I shove my phone in my skate holder and lift my eyes to Nash's hardening stare just before he turns away. He sorts through bungee cables, avoiding my eyes.

"Why are you packing this stuff, anyway?" I trail over the tents and fishing gear.

His arms flex when he coils the cables, and the way he swings back around to meet my eyes and blows out a conceding breath...it has me. "Family camping trip. We go to the mountains every summer. Forage, hunt, cook."

"I'm sorry, what? You go to the mountains with four children and survive off the land like that show on television?"

"The one where everyone's naked? God, no. But I suppose the surviving part is similar."

"This is it!" I skate to Nash's side.

I tell myself I'm not upset when I see his erection has deflated since our awkward moment with Onyx's text, but I so the fuck am.

None of my feelings change that he's still my father's employee, he's still being paid to hang out with me, and I am not fit to be a wife and mother of four, most importantly.

This type of kismet means only one thing.

"You can help me prep for the competition!"

"What competition?"

"I'm sort of slated to star in this show. It films in the fall, and my father knows nothing about it, so please don't breathe a word. I'll know if you do and tell him about the fantastical girth of your cock."

He bursts out laughing. "Okay, I promise I won't tell him." His eyes crinkle, and I believe him, my handsome silver asshole.

"It's a survival show."

"You're naked, aren't you?"

"Yeah." I bite my teeth together and backward skate around the garage to distract myself from the weirdness. "So, anyway, I'm pretty good at the naked part." I meet his eyes again and blush when his lip curves up just the tiniest bit. "I just don't know much about the survival part."

"Wait." He drops the remaining cables. "You're going on a survival show, and you don't know the first thing about surviving?"

I blink.

"Well, when you put it like that, it sounds kind of stupid."

"Kind of? I have heard a lot of crazy stuff in the music industry, but the television world must be batshit if they think they can drop off a trust fund debutante in the woods for the night and expect her to survive."

"It's a month. And I'm not a debutante, anyway. I never finished that stupid course. White gloves are patriarchal and so last century, don't you think?"

"A *month*?" His face turns serious. "Lem."

"I told you not to call me that."

We tense, silence separating our unity.

"Sorry," I finally say.

I truly don't know why I snapped like that. Maybe because he's acting like I couldn't possibly survive or win a game show if it means I have to get down and dirty, like he thinks all I'm worth is the billions of dollars that have been written in my stars before I even knew you could wish on them.

What the fuck is there to wish for anyway, when you're the girl who has it all?

And yet I did.

I wished for my mother to come back and be with us and kiss my father once more, to wipe his tears and pick up the shattered pieces of his heart that she trampled upon all those years ago.

To glue them back with love.

With home.

But people leave.

They grow and they change.

Or they die, like Randall Holiday.

And worst of all, I don't want Nash to stop calling me by the name he's used since I was nineteen.

Because that *is* change.

"You remind me of Bryar sometimes. Is that weird for me to say?" He winces, like he knows it is, and I'm not sugar coating that shit, either.

"Yeah, it's fuckin' weird." But I skate to his side and give him a hip bump, so he knows I'm toying. He's a sensitive soul, even if he acts hard and rough to his colleagues and children. I think deep down he's just scared.

Of everything.

"You know what I mean." He nudges my hip back. "I don't intend to upset you sometimes. I just don't know what you want, or what I want, or where either of us stands. Ever." He lets out a breathy laugh and meets my gaze with sheepish eyes. "At least with my own kids, I can ground them when it's confusing."

"See, that right here is why you're sucking at this whole parenting thing."

His brows hit the ceiling. "I'm not sucking. Am I sucking?"

I scrunch my nose. "Sorry, but you have two choices, the way I see it. Get to know your girls on their own level, in their own ways, and appreciate them for who they are, or keep doing what you're doing with this whole authoritarian, 'what dad says goes' bullshit and see how long it takes before your sweet little baby is sneaking from her window onto some senior's Harley and getting a tattoo that says Bone Me, in Latin, above her ass."

"Lemon, what the hell?"

"Sorry, too personal?"

"Do you have a tattoo that says—"

"That is neither here nor there, Nash. Look, the point is, your children need you to stop and smell the roses, okay? Maybe on this camping trip you can, yeah?"

"I wasn't going to take you with us."

My heart sinks.

I don't know why. I'm cool with that. I mean, I didn't think I was going just because I'm the nanny and I sucked his big, fat cock or anything like that, but I mean...

"Why not?"

"Honestly?" His lips curve. "I think you'd break a nail, babe."

"Oh, fuck you! I'm coming! I'll make you a deal. You to teach me to forage, and I'll teach you to do all sorts of things."

He snorts. "You really think you have what it takes to survive off the wilderness for thirty-one days?"

"Thirty," I correct. "It's filming in November." I shrug when he just gapes at me. "Might as well get the facts straight."

"You are genuinely petulant, you know that?"

"Nice vocab, Professor Pedantic. Use those big fancy words on all your girls?" I cross my arms, skating figure eights between his two vehicles as he unnecessarily flexes his biceps with some under-the-hood wrench action. It's not even notable how stupidly fucking ripped it is.

"Are you saying you're my girl, Sour Patch?"

He licks his top teeth with the tongue I wish was inside me, and we share that same fucked up look again.

*I won't push if you don't pull.*

"No," I say, deflating both of us. "More like your concubine. I get what we can't do and why, okay? I understand you need this thing you have going on with my father to work out." I wave my hand, dismissing the thought of being his girl from the conversation, entirely, and begin practicing smaller turns, but I stop when I hear that growl again.

Slow.

Organic.

*So. Fucking. Hot.*

"Concubine?"

I suck in a breath, the muscles in my pussy squeezed so tightly I fear I may fall over on my wheels at his gravelly vibrato.

I nod, casting my eyes down to my skates. If I avoid his gaze, maybe my clit will stop pulsing long enough for me to think.

His voice softens. "You think your father sent you here to be some...what, mail-order sex nanny?"

I blink through my squinted lashes, because...*sorta*, and when he scowls like this, he has no idea how much I wouldn't mind if that were true.

"For Christ's sake, I do not understand women. Not teenagers nor grown up...whatever you are."

"Nice."

"I'm sorry." He sighs, grabbing my hand and guiding us to the plastic folding chairs by a large blue toolbox. A crinkled crayon drawing taped to the side presents two stick figures on a boat with fishing poles. My heart tugs when I see Bryar's name scribbled in the bottom corner. She must have been very young.

"Your father didn't send you here to do that, Lemon. You know that deep down."

"Well, so far, nothing has been deep down in me since the tour bus, so—"

His lip twitches. "I'm serious. Take it from another struggling father. It stings the most when he thinks you hate him, and like my own daughter, you use that power like a sword. Don't you see how deep it cuts him?"

"Well, like my own father, you seem to know it all. And I hardly think he notices the cuts beneath diamond set bandages."

But Papa's tearful eyes when I did not return his I love you take form in my head and cut just as deep.

The warmth from Oliver's hand is almost too much to handle. It feels safe, and before I know it, the only man besides Jeremy who peers through my bullshit has me doing the near impossible and listening.

Can you believe that?

Me. *Listening.*

"If you were supposed to be my...plaything—" He pauses at his word choice and clears his throat when I twist my lips, repositioning his cock in that thinly woven penis-display he calls pants and rolling his eyes when I can't stop my chortle. "Well, anyway, a man would have had to pay for that type of...service, right?"

"Presumably." I snort. "Let me call up my girl Jasmine and see what her take is. She has tons of experience, what with the whole Jafaar debacle and all."

"You are one dramatic woman, you know that? Your father paid *me*. He just wants you safe. Out of trouble."

"Like that's his business."

I stand, but Nash keeps hold of my wrist, his body hanging from my limb like a shiny, new charm.

*My silver fox.*

He lifts a brow. "Is his only daughter and legacy to all he is and has ever accomplished not his business?"

"Fuck. I know, okay? I know. But it doesn't make it any easier that all he sees in me is a mess. Not the girl who has four degrees he paid for and should be very well privy to. Not the girl with all the crowns and plaques and ribbons. Not the crazy girl who made silly little videos and grew the label's social following by thousands in less than a year. Should those things not earn me worth?"

"He's beyond proud of you, Lem. I can assure you of that. Have you seen how many awards and pictures of you are hung in his office? You're his world."

"Really?" I spit, unsure why I'm so worked up by this, but I am. A scab has been ripped from my skin, fresh blood spilling free without recourse. "Is that how you feel about Bryar? Because the last time I checked, you trust her so little you grounded her for organizing a cancer card for her coach, assumed she was off fornicating or whatnot, and then rejected her when she sought the comfort of her goddamned father. You said no to a memorial for your dead fucking wife! What the *fuck,* Oliver. I mean, I love you, but what the actual fuck?"

I stop.

The world stops.

"You love me?"

I leave without another word.

And I've never skated faster.

# *Chapter Fourteen*

## OLIVER

She loves me? She loves...a lot of things, but me? I've never been one of them.

Fast cars, rockstars, shots of Patron from stiletto shaped goblets...that's the kind of stuff Lemon loves.

At least I thought it was, until this week.In this seven-day stretch of madness—half of which I'm shoving my cock to the side of my leg to avoid her mocking smiles—I've learned things about her I never noticed under the hazy lights of my tour bus.

First, she takes seven-and-a-half-minute showers. It's the same every time. Yeah, it's fucked up that I know that, but she times it down to the half second. What is that? And how does she do that? Suspiciously fast for how good she smells.

She's also a workout junkie. She's always skated around, literally, but she also runs and does yoga.

Right below my window.

When she isn't off teaching my girls some new way to make the house even messier, or texting God knows who in that phone, she's up and moving.

Lemon Perkins never sits still.

And those bracelets of hers...those, I haven't figured out. She's always had them. You can't know her and not notice, but she's been worrying her fingers over one of the charms all week, some silver thing I can't get close enough to see.

I increase my speed to eight-point-two. It's faster than I normally run, but it feels good to push my muscles. To feel something other than the gutting jealousy that rakes me when I think of who she's texting. I see the way Onyx Barringer looks at her. Hell, it's plastered across the tabloids and newsstands in that photo I can't wipe from my mind.

She doesn't double-dip.

But will she with him?

My feet pound the treadmill with the thought.

For six days on that tour bus, I watched him tongue her body. I'll admit I thought about it, got myself off to the image of her screams, and I'd do it again, because watching Lemon Perkins drives me mad. Pain and loss can't coexist with her pleasure.

Seeing her come undone is worth gold.

But before, I could leave the bus. Shut the door. I hadn't touched her. Hadn't tasted her fucking come on my tongue, so damn sweet for the sour mouth.

I want all of her, and I should have known not to take it this far. That I would be the one unable to keep it together once we finally did.

But that was when I thought it was one-sided. Just another scuff on her skates, that's all I ever was to her, but now...she loves me.

My heart thuds against my chest. I slow to a walking pace, but there is no cooling down when he comes back to my mind. I don't know if she responded to the string of texts she's been sent, but I suddenly can't bear the thought of it. Will she text him back under my roof? Touch herself to another man's pictures in one of my beds?

And if it's Onyx?

Her father paid me millions to prevent this exact damn thing. I could tell Emil he's involved, but what would that prove to Lem? That I'm just as untrusting as she says I am?

Involving her father isn't right, and I know that.

And if it isn't Onyx, it will be another. The sugar daddy she mentioned with the panties...who the hell was he?

If she was trying to get a rise out of me, it worked, and now all I can think about anytime I run on this god dammed treadmill is the way her eyes looked when she snapped that photo of her sweaty, pushed up tits and claimed it wasn't for me.

"What do I do, Lo? You always knew what to do when things got messy, but here I am with the biggest mess of them all, and I—"

*I love her too.*

Whatever comes over me next is wrong. I know it with all my being, but here I am anyway, a jealous, angry, widowed, old fool, fallen for the most wildly inappropriate woman anyone could have picked, and I know she can't be mine, but I'll be damned if she'll be someone else's while she lives with me.

I tell myself it's for the band.

For the deal with her father.

It's for Lemon's own good because her inheritance rests on this, does it not?

"Barringer," I clip. There's some shuffling and zipping on the other end of the phone before he clears his throat.

"Hey! Boss man. What's up? We miss you on tour, but they got this sexy little number working as your replacement, so don't rush back from desk duty, all right?" He snickers, like we're buddies.

We are not.

"Good to hear." I grind out, choosing my next words carefully. "Look, there's some important people on this stop of the tour, and between us, they're looking at what you guys can do with more set-time."

"No shit?" Onyx whispers something to the girl in the background, who giggles as his bed creaks, and I know Lemon is open with her partners, but something about Onyx texting her and sleeping with the new tour manager at the same time leaves me with zero remorse for what I say next.

"Yes, shit. So, play it cool and maintain that nice boy image, got it? We already have four other band members claiming the bad boy territory, and Perkins wants you to be the face of this next generation of listeners."

"Straight up?" I can feel his ambition through the phone. Good.

"All the way up, kid. I know you'll do us proud. Now, enjoy the rest of Europe, and one last thing."

"Anything, man."

"Stop texting Emil's daughter."

"Lem?" The line goes quiet, and I try not to bristle at the nickname he's allowed to call her. "Is this about the tabloid? Because I told the label it would never happen again. We were all drunk and careless that night. I know it."

"Don't text her."

The line goes quiet with the possessiveness of my growl, surprising us both.

*She's mine*, it screams.

"Enjoy the tour, Onyx."

"Yes, Mr. Nashville."

*Click.*

Silence can be extremely loud.

I know what I've just done is wrong. I knew it the whole time I did it.

And what's worse is Lemon's right. What I say does go. But this is different.

She sees me.

She calls me out for things nobody has ever dared before. I'm ashamed to admit that when Lauren died, we weren't on the best of terms.

Cancer is hard.

I was angry when she stopped fighting, even if the chances were next to nothing, it was enough for me to hope.

That hope was all I fucking had.

So, when she looked at me, a wisp of what she once was, and the smile couldn't even form for pretend, for the kids...I shut myself away, a concrete pillar wedged between what we were and what we became.

Until death do us part.

But did it? Part of her is with me every time I breathe.

And then there's Lemon.

She treats me like any other man, one who isn't on a pedestal bridled with the responsibilities or expectations that come with management of a company and a family. She doesn't fawn over me like the doe-eyed interns who whisper as I enter a room.

She encourages porn, wipes her cum on my jacket, and points out when I'm being a shitty father.

I'm present because of her.

Kimmie laughs because of her.

Bryar has an ally I didn't know she needed.

And Poppy...what does Poppy do? I don't know, but I do know Lemon bought her a training bra I failed to supply.

She may be new to my family, but this wonder of a woman has been taking up space in my heart for almost a decade, hasn't she?

And I'll be damned if I don't love her, too.

My phone rings, a number I don't know. "Perkins Global, Nashville speaking."

"Okayyy, now, that's hot," a male I don't recognize sings into the phone. "Lem, he sounds so much grumblier than you said."

"Lemon?" I rasp. "She's with you? Is she all right? She skated off so fast, I..."

I know she can take care of herself, but she's gorgeous, and alone, and wearing hardly anything but leggings. I'm relieved her friend has called me.

Her male friend.

A storm of jealousy I haven't felt in all the years I played voyeur to this woman boils from within me and erupts into the phone. "Who am I speaking with?"

"Possessive, too?" he coos. "I think he wants to fight me for you, baby cakes. Love that."

*Baby cakes?*

"If you are another one of her flings, like that idiot drummer, just know she's occupied from now for the rest of the summer. Employed by me."

"Oh, gosh, yeah." He sighs. "I heard all about him tonight, too. My honest best friend opinion, hon? He is so last week. Single dads with tented sweatpants are the new in, if you catch my balls."

"Izz'e talking about Onyx? I knew he saw my text! Gi-iimmie the phone, Jer!"

"Is she drinking?" I rub my forehead.

"That's why I called you. She skated to Cowboy's Paradise, like the whole way here, and she was pretty much drenched in sweat and teary-eyed mascara lines when I gave her the first shot, but I'll be honest, I can't stop her once she starts a quest. Nobody can. She's a whole vibe, ya know?"

"I know."

"Yeah. Well, I still have three hours before my shift is up, and homegirl is welcome to stay with me until she's done loathing you, but she wants to fuck your brains out and kill you at the same time, and I reckon she can't do either of those things from here."

"What're you saying to him? Tell'm I lied. His ding-a-ling is smaaall!"

"So, yeah," he says.

"I'll be there in fifteen."

# Chapter Fifteen

## OLIVER

Jeremy becomes my favorite of Lemon's friends as he helps us to the car. She yawns when he buckles her into my passenger seat.

"I know, Jer. I promizzz I'll behave." Lemon hiccups, swatting her best friend's hand as he pads her makeup clean. "I don't liiike that brand. They aren't cruelty-free!"

"Stop it," Jeremy scolds, "you can resume political activism when you're sober. Now, hold still or you'll look ugly next to the small ding-a-ling the whole ride home."

"I lied," she sobs. "It's huuuge. Couldn't even hold the thing!"

"Shh, I know. It's okay, babe." He brushes sticky strands away from her face and raises a smug eyebrow my way.

He's right; it is tear streaked. And she is into an old guy with pants tented for her.

Jeremy makes her laugh, dabbing beneath her eyes with the morally questionable compact, and I think back to the conversations we've had after being intimate.

*This is a one-time thing.*
*You can't tell your father.*
They all have one theme in common.
*We can't be.*

Jeremy pats the hood of my car. "Thanks, Mr. Nashville." He winks. "Now, get my girl home and fill her up with something."

"What?"

"Food." He winks, returning to the bar.

"Don't you jus' love him?" Lemon smiles. "He told me I loved you back at the stuuupid market!" She flips the sun-visor, meeting her reflection in the mirror. "I shouldn't 'ave gone back to the bus that day. Felt your hands on my skin."

It grows quiet as that settles.

I say nothing more, and she says nothing less. We enter and exit the highway before she finally breaks the silence

"You!" She twists, as if she's only just seen me. Is she so drunk she already forgot Jeremy putting her in the car? "Youuu have some nerve, makin' me fall in love with your stupid face and your dumb stubble-beard jusssta act like you don't have *feelings!* Well, *I* have 'em! And even if you *don't* want me—"

I stop the car.

"I want you, Lem."

She freezes, glassy eyes searching mine. "You do?"

I nod.

"I want to keep you, Lemon Perkins."

"Fucking keep me, then." She moves across the console, swinging her leg over my waist, straddling me and casting a spell with those fiercely violet eyes.

"You're drunk," I say, as her mouth meets mine. Her hips rock into me and our centers press together as knowledge builds that it's just clothing between my cock and her willing cunt.

But the unmistakable tinge of the tequila she just consumed zings across my tongue when she kisses me, and I am many things I'm not proud of, but I am not that kind of man.

"You're drunk, Lem. We can't do this."

"We can't do this! You alwayssayyy that. I feel fine." She slumps into her seat with lips pressed in a pout that would drive any man mad. She knows it, too. "I want this, Mr. Nashville." She bats her lashes. "I want it so bad, I—"

"You are intoxicated." It isn't just her I'm reminding. "I will not take advantage of you under the influence. That's final."

"Okay, *Dad*."

"I can't believe I'm having this conversation with a grown adult." I grip the wheel tighter.

"Oh, sorry," She bats her lashes. "I mean, *Daddy*. You like it when I call you that, don't you, Daddy?"

"Lemon, stop it. I'm not playing games tonight."

"Or what? You gonna spank me, *Daddy?*"

"I swear to God."

"Oooh, take me to church. I looove a *sky daddy!*"

"Enough!" I slam my hands over the steering wheel. "We haven't even made it halfway home, you're about six shots of tequila deep, wearing nothing but fucking roller skates and a...what the fuck is that thing, a corset tucked into pantyhose? I don't even know! And I want—more than anything right now—to bend you over my lap and take my hand across your bratty ass until it glows so red it lights up the night when I bury my cock inside it, but *you* are under influence!"

Silence overtakes the rest of our drive.

I find I like it less than anger.

We drive in a state of nothingness for a few side roads before a sniffle to my right pinches my heart.

She wipes her tears with the hoodie Jeremy gave her, and even though he seemed supportive of whatever Lemon and I are to each other, it still bothers me it's not *my* hoodie.

It's reassuring to know she has loyal friends. It's all Flinger models and sugar daddies with how she talks, but I'm beginning to wonder which parts of Lemon have been a guise this whole time I've known her. Jeremy seems like one of the real parts, the one I find myself increasingly curious about.

What are her dreams? Her greatest fears? What kind of man could earn her heart?

My eyes pull her way to find her asleep against the window. It settles my nerves to have her near me. My girl, safely curled beside me.

But she's not mine.

And the silence is annihilated as my phone rings through the car speakers. I shoot a glance at Lemon as I lower the volume.

"Mr. Perkins."

"*Bitte*, Olly. You know it is Emil to you, my friend."

"Sorry, Emil. How's the European tour looking for numbers? I talked to some of the guys earlier today, they're on their best behavior with that new hire you sent."

"Yes, it does sound like she runs a tight ship."

*Tight something,* I mumble beneath my breath.

"Oliver," his voice cracks, "I aim to check in on my daughter. She won't answer my calls, but I didn't think she would. She's good on a grudge, you know."

"Oh, I know." I look at the sleeping woman beside me, and I admire her forwardness earlier. I wish I wasn't the cause of her tears, but I can't have sex with a woman who could barely get herself to the car, let alone buckle herself in. "She's been a huge help, sir. My girls really respond to her."

"She is not giving you a hard time, then?"

"Not at all," I rush out. "My littlest, she sees the world differently, but she's taken to Lem like nothing I've ever seen. Bryar is helping with chores again. She's even put me in my place a time or two." My smile fades when I think of how many times she's propositioned me over the years, and how very many times I've rejected her. "I deserve it."

Emil chuckles. "I'll bet she does, *Lem*." He pauses on the nickname I just used. "She loves just as deep as she should be loved back," he says. "But look at me, taking up your Saturday night. I'll leave you to it. I trust I will see you at the charity event tomorrow evening?"

The charity? I'd nearly forgotten with setting up for next week's camping trip and Lemon involved in my entire everything lately.

"Of course. Looking forward to it," I lie.

The very least I can do is sneak in a quick appearance for the man who just made me a millionaire.

"With a plus one, yes? Appearances must be impeccable. Miss Shaylyn Tryst will be in attendance."

I jerk the car. "Shaylyn Tryst?"

He chuckles. "You've heard of her."

"The same Shaylyn Tryst whose posters are plastered over my daughters' bedroom walls? Sir...signing with her could mean..."

"Yes, Olly. And I aim to make American Sounds look like the lesser choice at this event. We already have the upper hand with Darkpath's success this year."

I scrub my hand down my face. This will be huge for Perkins Global. But I stall on the thing he said before. "You mentioned a plus one."

I steal a glance at the girl in my passenger seat, curled up with dried tears on her cheeks. I care whether she sleeps or wakes, if she's rested or well.

She is my plus one.

When did that happen?

But I can't tell her father that.

"I admit," Emil lowers his voice. "My request that you bring a date is shamefully one-sided. I have a lady friend joining, too," he clears his throat, "and it would ease my mind to have a...eh, what *ist das Wort?* A wingman."

"A date?" Lemon shoots up in her seat.

"*Zitrone,* is that you?"

"Yes, *Vater,* whom I am not speaking with 'cause you sssold me, it is *I*, your precious bargaining chip, fresh off the bottle in a strange man's car, just like you predicted."

"I'm sorry, Mr. Perkins, you weren't supposed to know she was in here...like this." I shoot Lemon a desperate look. "Please," I mouth across the seat.

*Please don't tell your father I can still taste your pussy on my tongue.*

His relieved sigh travels candidly through the speakers. "You see, Zitrone? *Das ist* why I have placed you in the care of my—"

"Most trussssted employee, yadda yadda yadda. You gave him millions for his loyalty, but you should have given him a medal, too, for his unwavering goddamned abstinence." She sticks her tongue out.

*I want to cover it with my cock.*

"Zitrone, *bitte*! Stop this nonsense."

"No, you stop it, Papa!" Her voice slices through the car. "You lost faith in me. Called me a mess." Tears streak from a storming violet glare. "And *you* cockblocked me."

I hardly breathe as my eyes work on a plea with hers. If she reveals to her father the things we've done, or the way we've been, I lose the promotion...the raise...the job...my girls' future. I lose everything. She knows this, flaring her nostrils in that way she and Emil both do, challenging anyone brave enough to step any closer should they dare.

I do not.

And I lower my eyes, conceding to her, whatever that means. I swear, I hear her sigh of disappointment as I pull into the driveway, past the unforgiving metal gates that cage me to sameness. Even as my heart bangs against the bars to take a risk, for the kids...Lemon, I'm still here on the inside, behind painted glass I'm afraid to shatter.

"Yes, Papa. He cockblocked me, then drove me back to his..." She chews her lip. "Very safe home." Her eyes never leave mine. "A home where I'll be tucked away in a room, blocked by any and all cocks," she rolls her eyes, "how everyone here seems to want it."

"Sir, I—"

"Thank you, Oliver. I'll see you, tomorrow."

"Sure," I start, but he cuts me off, addressing his daughter. And once again, I'm reminded of who she is. An heiress. *His* heiress.

"You will be there, too, Zitrone."

"What?" She sits up straighter. "I don't want to go to that money-floundering event. It isn't feasible, anyway. Who will watch the Nashlings?"

"Nashlings?" My heart warms.

"Kimmie coined it."

Kimmie doesn't talk, but I file that away for later because she makes a fair point. "Sir, she's right. Who will watch my children? I don't have a backup for Lem."

And I won't allow myself to linger on why I couldn't possibly ever want one.

"It does pose a problem," Emil sighs, "yet I feel strongly that our *Lem,*" he pauses on the nickname I've let slip again as sweat drenches my brow, "she needs to be at the table more if she's to run part of the company one day."

"Part?" She moves to the edge of her seat. "What do you mean, part, Papa? I would run it all, would I not? That's what you've always said. I have plans for the future of Perkins Global."

"Plans?" He chuckles.

It scathes even me that he dismisses her so quickly. What if she does have plans? I've seen her plan plenty—dinners, picnics, even a birthday party for Poppy's guinea pig, but it doesn't seem Emil has noticed those attributes. Her ability to take a scene before her and re-write it, make it her own, finding all the best parts and enhancing their greatness on a whim.

Chaotic poise, like a symphony. Sharp staccato just before a smooth bridge. My fingers play against the seams of the leather seat as they argue.

"Plans to what?" Her father scoffs. "Make videos on the social medias and hope they sell records? It is about business, networking, presence."

"I've watched you run this company my whole life, *Vater.* I know it from the ground up. Anything you can do for Perkins Global, *I* can do better—from my phone, with my *social medias.* I promise you that. In faaaact," she hiccups, "I bet half my shares on it."

"Whoa! Lem, that's a bit much." I put my hand on her leg, and it all but burns there in her stare. I yank it back as she eyes me with purple venom. "You're drunk," I whisper. "Is it wise to be making this kind of deal under the influence?"

"Tell me, Olly, do you think *Lem* can secure a deal with Miss Tryst before I do?"

"Uh..." I drag my eyes to Lemon's.

"Yeah, what'll it be, *Olly Boy*?" She lowers her eyes to my bulge then raises a brow.

"It doesn't matter," I remind them. "I don't have a backup nanny, and you can't trust just anyone to babysit your kids."

"Yet you trust my daughter?"

"You told me to trust her!" I gape at the speaker. "You trust me, I trust you, remember?" I rake my hair as Lemon presses back a smile, clearly loving this exchange between her father and me. They're two peas in a provoking little pod.

"What about Bryar?" she asks.

"Bryar babysit? You're kidding. She's—"

"Thirteen. Fourteen soon. *Ninth grade in a few short months.*"

"Perfect!" Emil rejoices. "Bryar will watch the little ones while you both attend the charity, and then, my little Lemondrop, you will see what it means to be...as you say, cockblocked. I will win this game of ours."

"Oh...sir, that's..."

Lemon's adorable tipsy giggles have me struggling not to laugh, too. She's uncontrollable.

Messy.

*I fucking love her.*

"That's not what cockblocked means," I finally manage as Lemon snorts, and it's all I can do not to erupt with laughter, mouthing *stop* as an uninvited smile skates across my face accompanied by a flutter in my chest I haven't felt since Lauren.

"Is it not a poker term? You block me with...*dem* Joker...*Ja?*

"N-No. It's—"

Lemon slaps her hand over my mouth.

"Yep! That's *exaaactly* what cockblocked means, Papa. *Benutze* with all your poker buddies, so they know you're hip." A wild gleam lights her eyes that has my mouth tugging at the edges.

Jesus, what have I gotten myself into? A pissing match between the woman I want to fuck and the man who could damn well fuck me in a very different way. Still, there is something endearing about their relationship, as toxic as it may seem on the outside. I hope my daughters will want to call me every week, make bets and play pranks. To know they would meddle in my affairs is to know they still care, is it not?

She may be pissed at him, but I can see the part of her smile that betrays her in the safety of her father's voice.

On the other hand...

"Bye, now, Daddy Dearest. Rest up for your cockblocking!"

*Click.*

"Holy shit, Sour Patch, you did not just make me part of that." I scrub my hand over my face, as if I could wring the remaining laughter out of it.

Lemon Perkins has me tickled. My lip quirks my once clean passenger seat, covered in mud from the skates she slung off, and I should be bothered by that, but I don't mind. The weight of the world seems gone around her. Nothing is serious anymore. And even when it is, she finds the light.

"He's gonna go tell all the guys at work he cockblocked his daughter. You know that, right?"

"I know!" She steadies her laughter. "I can't think about it without combusting. That was the best!"

I laugh too. I can't help it when the light pours from her soul like a song I haven't played on my violin in eight years.

"Do you do that often?"

"Drink and gamble millions with my father? Or take advantage of his language barrier so he says funny things?"

"Your grin tells me you're proud of doing both." I nudge her shoulder, and her eyes fall to our connection, as if summoned.

The question in her gaze nearly knocks the wind out of me, even if I do know the answer. "Olive Lover, can I ask you something super-duper real right now?"

"Keeping in mind you are still, in fact, drunk, and apparently have no mute button..."

She swats me. "I'm serious."

"Would you kiss me if I weren't drunk?" Her eyes scrape mine, searching. A real, honest-to-God question.

So, I give her a real, honest-to-God answer.

"Yes."

My symphony continues against the car's interior, fingers fiddling to stay grounded through her next admission.

"What I said before I skated away...when I said I love y—"

"Yes," I repeat.

"But I haven't finished the question." She worries her lips, ones I'd kiss if the moment weren't what it is, and we were who we aren't.

But it is.

And we are.

So, I lift her chin instead, until our eyes do what our lips won't dare.

"And yet my answer's still <u>yes</u>."

Even if it can't be.

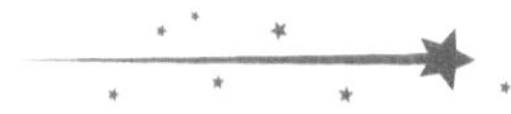

It's only after the woman of my dreams peels her way out of the car and stumbles down the entryway that I hear the buzz of an incoming message, only it's not from my phone.

The hot pink, heart covered rectangle lighting up the seat next to me isn't my business, and guilt already stains my thoughts at the way I shouldn't have spoken to Onyx Barringer. So when I scoop her phone up, I have no intention of seeing the unlocked home screen.

Until I do.

New Message from<br>LIL' DRUMMER BOY

I don't click it.

I won't invade her privacy any more than I have.

Even if all I want right now is to swipe open the message and delete the whole thread, the entire history of a relationship that existed before me, gone in a single tap...

She isn't mine.

I have no claim or say or right to be that person for her. I don't even have her consent to be that man.

Just her confession that she loves me and the pull when I'm in her orbit. Every sense I have claws at me to be her person. But this is her life, and if she's still texting Onyx Barringer, that's her own decision.

But she can't be angry at me for protecting my family. My daughters have hearts, too. Ones she could break just as easily as mine.

She said herself; she won't stay.

So is it Onyx she's toying with or me and the four biggest parts of my world?

Does she love me, or love me not?

# Chapter Sixteen

## LEMON

Oliver's finger jams down the coffee bean grinder, the clanking and tumbling abrasive to my ears. My head pulses, but I did this to myself.

A gnarly hangover.

Normally, when this happens, I roll my merry ass over to my bedside table, pop a pain killer, and chug some electrolytes before drifting back to an additional five hours of sleep. Only after this intense period of metamorphosis would I emerge, a renewed woman.

But this?

"Lemon, why did your parents name you Lemon?" Cami smacks her Corn Pops in my ear. The kind with red dye that makes kids hyper. The milk turns a swirling shade of pink as it gets soggy.

I eye my keeper suspiciously, rubbing my forehead as sounds seep into the crevices of my brain and dance around, banging and clanging like the damn chimney sweeps in *Mary Poppins*. All the while, the apple charm burns against my wrist, the past pulling me backward. But it isn't lost on me how she, too, was an eccentric nanny with a bag of secrets.

Miss Poppins and Miss Perkins.

*Hm.*

I drop my arm to my side, the bangles clanking just as the metal chair scrapes across the floor, pulled by a scowling Oliver to the breakfast nook behind us.

I turn and raise a brow, but he dismisses me, eyes darting down as his newspaper unfolds.

Is he doing this on purpose? Red dye...loud ass coffee and scraping chairs.

Dismissive looks.

If I didn't know any better, I'd say he was trying to piss me off.

But it's Oliver. I shake the thought away. He can barely laugh, let alone meddle. Although now that I'm meandering on that thought, a vivid image of that same grumpy man sitting beside me in a car doing just that pops into my head.

Oliver Nashville was laughing.

It hits me then, all that happened last night, a visual rollercoaster shoots zero to sixty as the images flash across my mind.

*Would you kiss me right now, if I weren't drunk?*

*And yet my answer's still yes.*

I widen my eyes at Oliver, but he's not paying any attention to me or Cami. He's intentionally paying no attention, to be precise. But what happened last night to shift us from laughter and love declarations to this?

There was the call with Papa...

*Oh fuck.*

I hang my head. "I made a bet last night, didn't I?" I peer at Oliver, but all he offers is grumbly condescension.

"Nash," I groan, ignoring Cami's question. But kids don't let you forget.

Or have a moment of silence, it seems.

"What bet? Who's Nash? Why is your name Lemon?" Cami smacks into my ear.

He lowers his paper long enough to twist his lips at me, his darkened scowl far sexier than I think he intends. "Yeah, *Lem*, is it Nash or Oliver?"

I ignore his blatant use of my nickname, the one I told him not to call me before I professed my dumbass love for the geriatric jerk, and I focus on the present issue here. The big, billion-dollar one.

"I can't believe you let me bet my shares while I was drunk."

"Me?" He slams his paper down. "I tried to stop you."

"Well Superman, if I had been at the bar where I skated myself instead of on the way home, I wouldn't have been privy to your little chum sesh in the first place. And what gives with that, anyway? Are you like besties now?"

I don't acknowledge that I just called it my home.

Neither does he, and I'm not sure why that stings.

"Yeah, Dad, how could you?" Cami pipes in, spoon held proudly in the air. She's a girl's girl.

But I scold myself in the moment that follows, because that's not right. As their nanny, and for no other maternal reasons whatsoever, I want them to see the importance in accepting your faults. And more than anything, I want to prove to the stick way up Nash's grumpy ass that a good role model isn't always the same thing as a boring, sad, Stepford one.

"Thanks, Cam. You're my ride or die," Nash rolls his eyes when Cami lights up, "but a big girl accepts her consequences with grace. I made the bet, now I must lie in it...or something like that."

Nash snorts from across the room, but he doesn't show his face, and unless I forgot some major part of last night, I'm still not sure why he's so irritable with me.

I raise a brow his way, an olive branch of sorts. "Your dad's a good man. It's not his fault I'm better at winning arguments. Sorry, Oliver." I flick my eyes to him. He keeps them there, but only for a second before I'm both discarded and deflated.

"Ride or...what?" Cami scrunches her face. I boop her stupid-cute nose, and she giggles before I turn back to face my captor.

This beautiful man who is suddenly mad at me.

And I suddenly care?

My phone, left dead on the counter, buzzes with notifications the minute I plug it into the charging station. I scan through them, finding little of importance, but there is a text from Onyx.

I hover over it, but my stomach pinches when I think about texting him back. Messaging Onyx feels wrong after everything with Oliver.

I peek over my chair and admire the furrow of his brow as he reads the paper, the crinkle of his eyes when he squints, and the way each of his girls wear that same intimidating scowl when they concentrate. I imagine the portrait above his mantel and ache for the possibility of another beside it.

Before my next heartbeat, I hold my thumb over Onyx's name and hit delete.

*"I want to keep you, Lem."*

Warmth spreads inside me, whether I want the shit to do that or not, taking up the spaces that pinched within my gut and replacing the pain with something stronger when I think of what we could be.

Together? Maybe.

But forever?

How easily could it come unraveled? Like my mom...Randall Holiday...*Lauren.*

"My mother chose Lemon," I tell Cami, forcing the pain back to the holes it seeped from. "You'd have to ask her."

I slide my phone back on the counter and pour myself a bowl of the toxic red puffs, shoving a hasty spoonful into my mouth.

Cami snickers. "Kimmie does that when she doesn't want to talk, too."

I roll my eyes. "Smartass. Kimmie doesn't talk." I mouth around the cereal.

"She does with her eyes. And you said a bad word!" Her giggle is infectious, and I realize in our heart-to-heart over breakfast cereal, that this Nashville child is the most empathetic of them all. She feels what others need and sacrifices her emotions to lift them.

Admiring Poppy's drawings, speaking up for Kimmie, reminiscing about Lauren with Bryar...even joining her father in the breakfast nook...none of that was for her own benefit.

I hope her selflessness never gets swept away. As much as Oliver wants to think he's a shit father, Cami was a baby when Lauren passed away. The intuitive, thoughtful soul she has become is a direct reflection of his parenting, and I will not for a continued second think about the pulsing of my ovaries with that realization.

"Dad's like that, too," Cami tells me as her voice drops to a serious whisper. "That line between his forehead gets all crinkly, but he doesn't cry. Why do grownups do that?"

"Do what?"

"Pretend," she says thoughtfully. "They tell us not to lie, but they do it all the time. You do it, too."

"I do not. I'm as open as they come."

"I'll say," Nash mumbles across his newspaper.

I ignore the comment that doesn't even sting and give Cami my full attention. "Explain it to me, then. What do I do that you see as a lie?"

"Kind of the same as Dad, just upside down." She slurps the pink milk from across the table and wipes her face on her sleeve just as her father's eyes meet mine. "He pretends not to be sad, but you pretend to be happy."

*Wow.*

"Where is your mom? The lady who named you Lemon?"

I break away from Oliver's gaze and pinch my apple charm. I think back to what Papa said in the car. I think about Cami and her empathy. Mostly, for the first time in forever, I think about the example I set with my convictions. With the lies I tell myself.

"Probably with yours."

"Dead, then."

She says it with such finality, I almost break. For her and me, two daughters left too young.

Oliver's hands tighten around his paper, his face still hidden from our view. The tips of his fingers grow white from his grip but hiding it won't stop him from feeling. And he isn't the only one who feels it, not by a long shot.

His daughter feels it enough to bring it up right now.

We all feel grief at some point.

For Randall Holiday, the old man who used to be my everyday job. Reading him stories, checking his meds...he was there, then he was gone. One last beep to follow his last whispering breath.

And even if we don't know her fate, even if we never will, even if I hate her just as much as I miss her...I feel it for my mother.

Truth is, I grieved for her a long time ago.

"Dead," I agree.

When Cami squeezes my hand, my heart jumps to my throat. I don't know when I pull her into my body, at what point I wrap my arms around her in a restorative embrace, I just know we both need it.

A rustling sounds behind us, and when Cami slips from her stool and skips up the stairs, I spin to find the newspaper facedown at the breakfast nook and Oliver Nashville nowhere to be found.

# Chapter Seventeen

## LEMON

"What the fuck gives, Nash?" I throw open his bedroom door, taking up the space he felt he needed.

Screw that.

You don't get space when your child is grieving.

"I get that you might be mad at me for having actual feelings. You know, those things you're terrified of showing? But pull your head out of your planner for once and open your eyes to what your family feels. Bryar, Poppy, now Cami. They are grappling with something big, Oliver. And I have to wonder how long they've been struggling. How long it went unnoticed."

"So, it's Oliver again, not Nash?"

"Are you kidding me? I have been wracking my brain trying to figure out why you suddenly loathe me again, and it's about nicknames?"

"Well, you might not want me to call you Lem, but I like Oliver. Nash was just a friend."

"You were never just a friend."

He swallows, and I want to kiss those pouting lips. To smooth the furrowed edges of his heart. But none of that changes what's happening here.

"Look, neither of us know what we want, and it's incredibly hard most days, pun intended, but you can't sulk about labels and nicknames. We are what we are. Besides, none of those things are as important as your other name."

He pushes off the dresser and stalks to the closet as his fingers tug at his silver hair, but I follow him there. He doesn't get to walk away from this. Nobody stuck up for me when I needed someone to explain loss, and my father stuffed it so deep inside I believed it was wrong to feel anything at all.

I won't let that happen to these girls.

I study the beautiful fool who's lived a whole lifetime and died before his death, but it's far from over.

Lauren is gone, like my mother, like Randall Holiday.

But O.L. Nashville lives on, and so does she, through the four beautiful brats that are starting to feel like mine.

"Dad," I tell him. "The only name you should worry about. Because you know what sucks for them, more than you? You chose that love before you lost it. They had no option but to love her, no say about their family. And the cold, hard truth is only one of their parents is dead, but the other, Oliver? He just refuses to live."

He stiffens, hand on the closet door, hinged on the choice to walk into the storm or out of it.

*Walk the fuck in,* I plead with my eyes.

One step. Then two.

And when he's facing me again, his forehead creasing in the center, tugged as tightly as my heart, I reach out and press my thumbs to it, smoothing it back down. "You have it inside of you; can't you feel it? Something like...*starlight.* Brightness worth chasing."

I slide my hand to his chest, where the beat of his heart meshes with my pulse. I could kiss him now, but I fear our games are becoming more than that. "Your girls shine for you, Oliver. Don't let them burn out because you refuse to look at the sky."

# Chapter Eighteen

## OLIVER

"Dad. What are you *wearing*?"

I look at my tux then back at my mortified oldest child. "It was the only thing appropriate I had." As a tour manager, I wore the usual black on black button up. I didn't need a tie or tux.

"I wore this to your Aunt Posey's wedding twelve years ago. I can't believe it still fits."

"It does?"

I straighten my arms and the fabric pulls at my shoulders. My kid might be right.

"So, you don't think I should wear it tonight? The big boss will be there. That singer you girls like, Shannon Tryst? We might sign her tonight."

"Dad! Shut up! Shaylyn Tryst?"

"Yeah, that's the one. I have got to write that down. Shaylyn not Shannon."

Bryar tosses a pillow at me. "One does not need to write down the name of Shaylyn Tryst, her lady and majesty of all that is pop, Dad!" Her mouth hangs open when I have no response. "Oh, my gosh. You're going to blow this." She paces the living room, stopping to tug at my sleeves. "It's okay, we can figure this out. You have to sign Shaylyn, so you just have to not be you for one night. That's all."

I balk at my firstborn, who used to see me as the coolest guy around. The one who rushed to hug me before my foot stepped over the threshold at the end of a day's work.

Guess I'm basic now. She circles me.

"Bry? What are you doing?"

"Figuring out a plan for all of—"

"That!" Lemon shrieks when she sees me from the landing. "What is that, Oliver?"

"See?" Bryar goads in triumph. "I told you it was a problem."

"A huge problem." Lemon bounds down the staircase. "You think Shaylyn Tryst is going to promenade around on your arm like that? You shouldn't even let your *arm* wear that."

"Poor arm," Bryar agrees.

"Enough!" I throw my arms—which are apparently a hot topic—in the air, yanking off the ruffled suit jacket and tossing it. "What am I supposed to wear, then?"

Lemon rubs her temples. "You are the worst millionaire I've ever met. Have you even begun to conceptualize how much money you have at your disposal?"

"We're millionaires?" Bryar gasps.

"Thanks." I hang my head. "I wasn't going to tell the girls quite like that."

"Sorry." She clicks her teeth together. "But better to rip the bandage off with news like this." She kneels in front of my oldest. "Bryar, honey, you are fucking rich now, okay? How did Papa put this when I was little? Ah, yes! With great richness comes great...opportunity! Yeah, that's about it." She shrugs. "See, she's fine. Oh, and we need you to babysit while we sign the most famous singer of all time. Can you do that?" She nudges me with a wink. "Only for a couple hours until my besties get here. Shana and Dustin texted me earlier. They're excited to practice parenting, if that's all right with you."

She knew I was worried about tonight and had it covered without question, by my girls' dance teacher, no less, someone I already know and trust. It's both pleasant and unnatural to have someone else be the planner for once.

"We're...millionaires?" Bryar's eyes remain wide, and I'm finding it hard to tell the difference between her and the broken record player in the corner of the foyer. "Sh...Shaylyn Tryst?"

Lemon nods. "The culture shock can be a lot for noobs." She ushers her up the stairs. "It'll be all right, sweetie. Let's order something nonsensical on your dad's card, and it will all be fine."

"Hey! That's horrible advice."

"Excuse me, are you now, or were you ever a millionaire's teenage daughter?" Lemon scoffs, waving me off. "Just like a man to explain water to a river. Let me handle this. I'll give her the babysitting rundown while I'm at it."

Just as she reaches the top of the stairs, she spins around and steals my eyes. "I'll sort out your fashion deficiencies next, Mr. Nashville."

Now, why the Hell does that turn me on?

"You're saying, your father is the billionaire who my father works for, and he made you come here because you basically got grounded? He can do that at your age?"

I hear Bryar and Lemon laughing as I come up the stairs.

"Well, he certainly thinks he can, but men think lots of things. Your most powerful weapon as a woman in this world is your own mind. Anyway, your father is not like that, trust me. My father and I have bigger fish to fry than a grounding."

I'm on my way to my room when I'm stopped by Bryar's response.

"Me and my dad have bigger fish to fry, too. He never trusts me. I bet this babysitting idea was yours and not even his, wasn't it?"

She doesn't answer, but my daughter's smart enough to know that's still an answer. It chips at my heart that she feels I'll never trust her.

"So, what's it like growing up rich?"

Lemon hums beneath her breath, twisting my daughter's hair in a French braid. My heart feels heavy and light in one instance. Lauren knew how to do those fancy braids I could never master, and Lemon executes them so effortlessly.

And I'll be damned if I believe in this stuff...

But Lauren did.

*Coincidence,* I'd say.

But she'd shake her head.

*There is no such thing as a coincidence.*

My arms tingle, a chill passing over my skin when I manage to sneak past without ruining their moment. I duck into my room, unseen, and as I click my door shut, I hear the final arrow to Cupid's godforsaken bow.

"Lonely." Lemon sighs. "It was lonely growing up like me. But it won't be like that for you and your sisters. I won't let it."

"Promise?" my baby asks.

The words Lemon pierced through my heart only hours earlier now brand the inside of my mind while I listen.

*I'm not a permanent person.*

So, is what she tells my daughter next a lie or the truth?

"I promise."

# Chapter Nineteen

## OLIVER

"It feels good to be confided in again. I feel like I'm really breaking ground with Bryar. I missed that since leaving my last job with Randall." Lemon chokes up when she says the old man's name. Shana's father. It's clear to me they grew close, and it only fascinates me further that she manages her sparkle, despite the grief.

She wipes a tear from the corner of her eye and focuses instead on fastening the ankle straps on her heels. A deflection I know well, and my heart aches for the pain I know she feels.

She scrunches her face in concentration, and it has my jaw twitching to smile. The black dress, with chrome sequins and a long slit, bunches around her hitched up thigh as she struggles with the shoe strap, and before I can stop myself, I'm on my knees for this woman, and my hands are there.

Lemon inhales sharply, but holds my gaze while our hearts pound.

"Let me." I lace the strap around her ankle, and every brush to her skin feels electric. "You're the only one that's ever made any ground with Bry. You're good with people, kids, surprisingly."

"Thanks." She releases a weighted breath.

"Are...are we all right, Oliver?"

It's only then I realize my hands are still around her ankle.

I like them wrapped around her.

"Oliver?"

"Sorry." I finish the strap. "We're swell.

"Swell? You're older than I thought."

I huff a laugh. "Well, you're complicated."

"And it's your job to uncomplicate me? Because I hate to assure you that many have tried and none have prevailed."

I finish her other shoe and meet her amused glare. "I like you complicated."

"I thought everything about me bothered you. The chaotic mess you kicked off tour?"

"Do you genuinely think I kicked you off tour because you're a mess, Lemon?"

"That is exactly what you led me to think."

"I kicked you off to focus."

"Yeah," she rolls her eyes, "the band needed to focus on their music."

"Not the band, Lem. *I* needed a break from you. I needed to focus on the tour, not on the off-limits daughter of my boss that I wanted for my own."

"Your own?" She raises a brow. "You're the one who likes watching. If it weren't me, it'd be some other girl they were railing and you could watch her, too. I don't buy it."

Yet her body says she does, eyes begging for the answer that makes it so, nipples pebbled beneath her dress. She wants it just as bad, and the hardest part about that is she's already told me so.

"Do you think I do that on all the tours? Even the ones you aren't attached to? You know me better than that... I didn't even know what casting couches were before you told me."

A genuine, beautiful goddamned laugh bursts from her mouth at that, and I shake my head unable to stop the smile that breaks over my still mortified face.

"I still wish I didn't," I add.

She presses her tongue to the inside of her cheek, pleased with that, no doubt, and I have to tell her more. The urge to assure her she's been the only one since Lauren claws from inside out.

To see her smile and keep it there becomes my all-encompassing need.

"After parties aren't in my contract, Sour Patch. They have assistants and security detail for that. I never had to go."

"Then why did you?" She steps closer, amethyst eyes reflecting the sun from open windows, sealed shut for half a lifetime.

She opened them for me.

"Because I can't take my eyes off you."

Lemon Perkins does not kiss me. Our faces rest centimeters apart, but she does not advance.

Nor does she retreat.

I blink. She blinks. We just goddamn blink until the grandfather clock chimes and she clears her throat.

"We don't have much time if we plan to get you a new suit, and I delight in telling you that Bryar is right." She inspects her nails against the suit and shakes her head as I bow mine. "What are you doing?"

"Between you and Bryar, I'm praying," I tease.

She pats my shoulder. "Miley did say, only God can judge us."

"That's the Bible, Sour Patch."

"No, I don't think so." She scrunches her face. "Pretty sure it was Miley. Either way, your outfit requires divine intervention. Leave it to me. Well, leave it to my decisions, but your credit cards. Does that work? Although I do have a thick wad of ones, I still can't access my account for my non-stripper money."

"You were never a stripper." I grin at her games. "You can't prove that." She grins back, and I know we're okay then. We might be in the strangest arrangement of all time and have irreconcilable feelings, but we are still okay.

"So, what do you say? Shopping trip?"

"Doesn't feel like I have a choice," I concede.

"You don't." Her phone buzzes. "Shana and Dustin are locking up to get here. Let's get you looking like a billionaire, Daddy Nashville."

"Don't call me that."

"Don't tell me what to do unless you're gonna spank me for not doing it."

My cock hardens at the thought of doing just that, but I go back to the bet she made with her father last night. She won't say it, I know she's worried. I don't know what she uses her money for, but it's not clubbing and chaos like she wants us to believe.

It's something more important than that, and even if she won't tell me, I'll do what I can to help, just like she's helped my girls.

Lemon's eyes narrow on the keys to the commuter car hanging from my thumb, and she chews her bottom lip. "We can't take that to the charity, Oliver. I'm no fan of elitism, but I have been forced into extreme wealth from a young age, and—"

"Forced?" I laugh. "You seem to thrive in it."

She raises a brow. "I'll ignore that. Now, why are we not taking the Denali instead of..." She huffs a genuine breath of frustration at not knowing the brand of one of the most common cars among lower to middle class families, worrying her lip.

"It's a station wagon." I take her hand before I realize my actions, and the way she calms with my touch feels like...

There's no such thing as coincidence.

"Sore subject?" I ask.

"I never want to make anyone feel less than, but I didn't...I didn't grow up with cars like this, which is exactly why we need to act the part to impress Shaylyn's team. They're like me...only not. They are the parts of me I hate."

For a long steady moment, we breathe that in, having shared something silent but loud at all once.

"Well, anyway." She slips her hand from mine so effortlessly it pains me, and I have to wonder if that's how it will be, losing her at the end of the summer.

"At the risk of sounding like someone who thrives on wealth, which okay, maybe I do, but at that risk...do you really think the record label who signs Shaylyn Tryst, the biggest singer of our generation—well," she tussles my grey strands, "*my* generation, at least...do you think they should show up in *Chitty Chitty Bang Bang*?" She jabs a thumb at my car. "And that's like *before* the dad pimped the ride."

She's right.

"But the Denali is all roped up and ready for camping Monday." I could take the stuff off, but then we'd have to transport the kayaks back to the shed or tarp them down. "We don't have time for that on top of shopping."

"Shit."

"Yeah...shit."

"Oliver L. Nashville. Did you just cuss arbitrarily?"

"What are you talking about? I cuss."

"Sure, you do." Lemon eyes my mouth like a snack. "You should know, it turns me on. It sounds so forced coming from your wholesome dad mouth, and I want to corrupt you every time. Climb your face and make you sin a little longer."

My cock felt every syllable of that.

"That does nothing to help me see you as a nanny and not..."

"Whatever we are?" She finishes my sentence, getting in the passenger seat and clicking the door shut.

I'm the one holding back.

Not her.

Me.

She's willing to see where it goes. Live by the moment. But the fear I'll lose it all again and be forced to shove it in boxes just to manage is crippling. Being with her goes against the very promise I made myself when I held Lauren's body as her soul left my arms.

I buried it with my memories, the good and the bad, just like my violin, because my song was always for her, and those memories were better off gone than roaming as ghosts in my head, and heart, and home, reminding me that we would never again be whole.

Because she would never be whole.

Never to see, to hear, to touch...

I swore I'd never love again.

Now here's this...this *starlight,* and I never want to lose sight of her.

The horn blares in my ear, crumbling my mental fortress, and she's there when I get in the car, feet propped on the dash, right where her muddy skates were last night.

And even if I don't want to see or feel or hear her, she brightens my space.

"I don't know what we are," I say, "but I know tonight you're my date, and if you'll let me, I'd like to kiss you."

Her eyes soften. "You can kiss me, but only when you're thinking about me. It's not fair to either of us if your wife is where your head will be."

"Why would you think that?"

"Because you fiddle your fingers along the side of your clothes when you talk about her, or any time one of the kids brings her up." She lifts a brow. "You're doing it now."

My hand stops.

She deserves to be made first, if I'm to make her anything, and that slices me up and down, because I fear she's becoming everything.

"You read people extraordinarily well."

"Tell my father. I'm sure it would be useful in negotiation meetings...if he'd ever let me in." Her nostrils flare. "He pawns me off to the social media and event planning departments every time. He doesn't think women belong on the financial side of things. I know it, even if he won't say it."

"I don't think your father feels that way," I start, but she cuts me off with a sharp look.

"I see you, letting him line your pockets with his decisions, just like the rest of them. It won't be long before he throws you another bonus at that rate. Maybe even a vacation castle...Bavaria, perhaps? I've been there, you know." She holds my stare. "They make world-renowned violins."

I don't miss the accusatory lilt in her tone.

"I saw your abandoned instruments in the closet. Do the kids know you play?"

"Played," I correct.

"Unsurprising. Another thing you're scared of loving."

"Lemon, can we—"

"No." She frowns. "We have less than three hours to get you better clothes and ditch this ride before the charity. I have a car we can take, but we will literally need to take it. From my father."

"I don't like the sound of that."

"It'll be fine." She waves me off, like I'm the crazy one. Maybe I am.

There's more to say, but we don't have time for that now, so I comply without another word, but as we're backing out, my eyes fix on the third story window of our home.

"You think Bryar will be all right babysitting until they get here?"

"I've been around her plenty. My personal assessment? You're a worrywart, and she's perfectly capable of it."

"Capable isn't the same thing as responsible." I sigh, as my house gets farther away in the rear-view reflection. But it's possible Lemon and Emil are right; it's time for her to be given the independence she's so intent on taking.

Still, a worry lingers in the back of my mind.

"Trust me." Lemon squeezes my arm.

"Your father told me something similar before he sent me you."

"And you're saying he was wrong?" She waits less than a second before issuing a smug grin and clicking on the radio, and as *Lovefool,* by the Cardigans blasts through the speakers, I see my girls in that top left window, waving and smiling.

Even Kimmie.

"He wasn't wrong." I offer her my hand, and every prayer in my head comes true when she takes it. "Wrong doesn't feel this right."

# Chapter Twenty

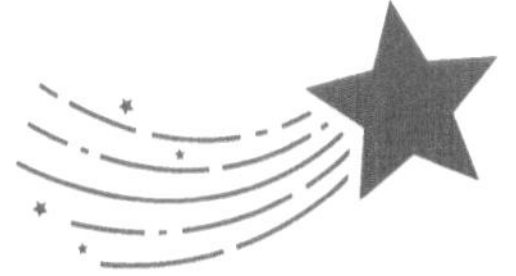

## LEMON

"Oliver Lowell Nashville," I try. "Oliver *Lionel* Nashville. Lafayette? No, doesn't suit you."

"Hey," he protests. "I'm one-sixteenth French, if you care to know."

"Sure, and I'm one-tenth Kardashian. Lester?"

He rolls his eyes.

I can't decide what his middle name could possibly be, and I've gone through most of the options, trying like crazy to center my thoughts on anything other than the way our hand holding activates every bit of my core.

"For the love of God, Oliver, I give up. What is your middle name?"

He snickers beneath a dark, recently groomed beard, aftershave scenting the air in the tiny car. Not sure what they put in that stuff, but I inhale it and instantly liquify, the all-consuming smell of him everywhere inside me, except where I wish he'd be.

"And what if I don't ever tell you?" He smirks as my legs cross tightly. "I might not. I like you flustered."

"It *is* Lester, isn't it?" I ignore his come-on, and damn was it a good one, my legs shifting of their own volition in the seat. But I won't back down on what I decided.

*He* must make the next move, decide he's okay with the unknown.

When he only smirks in response, I bring my hand to my heart. "I swear on all that is holy, I will spread Lester rumors if you don't correct me."

"Sure, you will."

"Don't test, Lest. It will start slowly, but you'll be surprised how quickly gossip trickles through the circuits once the girls in marketing get hold of the information."

"It's Love."

My cheeks heat. "What?"

"Love. My middle name."

Now I'm the one with nothing to say.

"Come on." He shuts his door, going around the side to open mine. "Let's go shopping."

He drops his head in defeat when I beam at the word *shopping,* and he produces a platinum card at my disposal. His signature half-smile is something I'm growing to love.

*Love.*

Now it's my turn to smile. Maybe.

"Is this my father's Perkins Global card or yours?"

"Mine, of course. I'd never use his funds for a personal purchase."

"C'mon, it's for a company event. You can even write this off on your taxes." I hold out my hand. "Give me the card. He won't even know. He's a billionaire."

I start the test before I even realize what I'm doing, the one only my two closest friends have passed.

When people see the gold in your tears, they will stop at nothing to make you cry.

So, I wonder, how far will this man go?

Can my father trust his 'most trusted' employee?

Can I?

"You can do anything you want, Nash. It's just not always legal. But even that's kind of bendy sometimes, too, ya know?" I bite my lip to hide the smirk I get from fucking with him, my favorite pastime, and when his eyes bug from his head, it takes every ounce of energy to hold in my laugh.

He really is one of the good ones.

"Legalities are not bendy, Lemon." He stares at me incredulously, flustered at the mere thought of slighting someone.

It's nerdy and righteous and vanilla as fuck, but it's Oliver Love Nashville, a man I can trust.

"You're failing at this whole greedy millionaire thing. Whatever the opposite of corrupt is...well, that's you."

"I won't use your father's card, Sour patch. It's just what's right."

Right.

That word alone transports me to a time I gave a different man this test, a man I almost loved.

*"You'll be a billionaire too, one day, right?"*

But he could ignore my father's wealth no easier than I could the apple blossom perfume on his collar that wasn't mine.

"You okay, Lem?" Oliver's voice breaks through my sullen memory, and I love him for that.

"Love," I say, testing his name on my tongue. "What a coincidence."

Oliver stills, our eyes meeting just before our lips. "There's no such thing as coincidence."

F our stupidly attractive suits and about a million smoldering glances later, and I'm melting into the private changing room chaise, all of my existence centered on the flexing of his arms as he rolls each cuff.

"Miss? Did you all decide about the navy jacket?"

The woman's face comes into view, as she's forced it between me and the flexing. I suppress a whine along with my libido, crossing one leg over the other.

"He won't be needing a jacket," I decide. "And we'll need all the items steamed, to be worn at checkout, please."

The apprentice, wearing the tag Lydia, has yet to introduce herself by name. She can't be more than twenty, and she can't control her resting bitch face either. She presses her lips together. "We don't really do that at this kind of establishment." She gives us a once over.

It annoys me.

I realize Oliver looks like a freak in the flouncy old groomsmen's jacket he insisted on wearing, but you can't judge by so little. People are more than their clothes or money or circumstance, so I glare back until she saunters off...to gather the manager, I'm sure, which is lucky for me.

"Lemon!" Anastasia Matisse pulls me in to kiss each cheek. The longtime family friend marvels at my gown, her eyes sparkling in delight. "*Magnifique*! It is an Oscar De La Renta?" She twirls me for the full scope.

"Ahhh, but I miss making your gowns, *mon petit citron!* Tell me, I do not see your father much these days." She raises an accusatory brow. "Is he having his suits made by someone else? Please tell me it isn't so."

"I don't answer incriminating questions." I smirk.

"Oh, did I teach you well." She pulls me down to sit. "I was so happy when you texted me. It is always a pleasure to serve your family."

Lydia slides her eyes between Annie and me as we discuss my father's newfound love of golf pants for formal occasions, and I take a shameful amount of pride in teaching her you can't judge a book by its bindings.

"Lydia, meet Lemon Perkins of Perkins Global Enterprises. She's putting together an outfit for the right-hand-man of Emil Perkins himself...a very good looking man if you ask me." She winks. I try not to smile at that but fail horribly. "They will be meeting The Shaylyn Tryst tonight. They must make a good impression, so let's get them anything at all, yes?"

Lydia has fewer words now, so I offer my own.

"Nice to meet you, Lydia."

She lets out a quick breath when Annie leaves us. "Thanks for not telling Anastasia I was...well, rude."

"It's okay." I level with her. I've been her before, striving for social status in circles where wealth defines your worth. I was Lydia. "I know we didn't seem like a sophisticated couple, looking for expensive suits on an hour's notice, but it never hurts to treat everyone as if they are worth millions, whether they look like my father or..." I scrunch my nose at the brown, woolen wedding suit Oliver wore over here, "that."

She lets out a defeated laugh.

"Money means nothing when respect can never be bought. Anastasia has gotten where she is today because she never forgot that. She helped teach me."

Lydia's cheeks flush a deep red. "He looked the best in the Armani."

"I agree. He'll take flat front, black Armani seersuckers and the plain white button up from the Dior collection earlier."

Lydia nods and makes her way back to the sales floor, just as Oliver's gravelly voice teases me from the dressing room opening.

"He will, will he?"

"Um..." I manage as he approaches me shirtless. "Yes."

"Why don't I need a jacket?" He stops in front of me on the chaise, re-belting his pants, and it's all I can do not to tell him to stop.

*Take them off.*

Yank the belt back through those loops super-fast like those thirst traps and snap it against my...

"Lem? Jacket?"

He puts the metal rod of his belt through the hole and tightens the leather around his body, and I know he's just said my name, but all I can do is wet my lips and wish to God he'd put a rod through *my* hole.

"Sorry." I cast my eyes back to his face. "My mind was in the gutter."

"Put it back there." He drops to his knees between my legs, and his lips crash into mine, hot and wet, and smelling like the aftershave I crave. He covers my entire mouth with his own, tonguing the soft skin until he's all I can sense.

My heart beats a rhythm it sends to my pussy, heightened when strong hands grab my thighs and part them more.

"You're dripping." He licks a solid line down my neck and eases me back as his fingers brush my pussy. The bare, naked one.

Also, the only one I have.

"No panties?" he growls.

I whimper at the erotic language, words I never imagined being used by him.

On me.

Having Oliver Nashville do things I never thought he'd do.

I can't get enough of his hand between my legs, drawing circles over the source of the wet, pooling desire I feel for him.

"They don't go with this gown," I manage to whimper.

His eyes glimmer as he looks at me.

Touches me and commands my gaze.

"Fuck, Nash!"

"Not Nash." He rubs my clit in treacherous circles. "Say my name, Lem. Say what we are." His hand stops when I don't respond, and my body seizes from the lack of pressure. "Say it," he commands.

"Love." I gasp.

"That's right, Love." He hums, rubbing me again furiously, until I have to hold my own hand over my lips to silence myself.

"You sure you want to do this? Even though I can't promise forever?" I force out the words on a strained whimper, my body screaming profanities at my mind for questioning this man when he's busy fingering it to ecstasy, but he cups my pussy, kneading my swollen bud, and

I almost cry out before I remember where we are…in a private suite, yes, but a dressing room nonetheless.

He shushes me with a kiss and a shit-eating grin I'd like to ride all the way to the charity. And as if he knows what I'm thinking, Oliver Love shoves my dress above my waist and wraps my legs around his neck.

The ho inside of me sings when his beard brushes my folds. I feel it all the way in my nipples. I rock into his face, pussy aching as I brace my arms against the wall and let him feast.

I'm grinding.

*Moaning.*

Until the pressure releases in an explosive wave, and he lifts his eyes to mine as he lowers my dress back down. "Think I'll get you a little uniform skirt I can flip up and taste whenever I want."

My heart is still pounding as he laps up the rest of my desire and licks his lips with a grin. "You taste like your personality."

"Are you saying it's sour?" I grimace. "My taste?"

"No. It's sweet."

I roll my eyes as I tug my dress back into place. Nobody sees me as sweet. I'm Lemon. Sour Priss, Sour Pants, Sour Patch…I've heard it so long I own it.

"I'm not," I assure him.

But the smug asshole just licks his lips and leans back in. "Better let me taste again to be sure."

His lips brush against mine effortlessly, perfectly. Like they belong there forever.

"Tastes sweet to me."

"One freshly steamed outfit, ready to wear," Lydia calls as she swings open the door to the suite. She startles when we share a hushed laugh and make space between our bodies on the chaise. "Oh! I'm sorry. Should I come back in a moment?"

"That won't be necessary." Oliver stands. "We were just discussing a difference in tastes, weren't we, sweetheart?"

My lips twist at his innuendo. "Sweetheart?"

His face darkens. "That's only the start of what I'll be calling you tonight."

Lydia's eyebrows hit the ceiling, and she quickly excuses herself from the dressing area, leaving us dangerously alone again. He takes his outfit into the dressing room, sliding the latch with a click, and just when I think he's done teasing, his earlier shirt comes flying over the stall, landing in my lap.

My fingers rub the cotton fabric, my smile reaching my eyes when I inhale and it's all fucking him. "Am I the maid now?"

"Do I get to taste the maid, too?" He opens the door to reveal the million-dollar version of himself. The back of his button-up is untucked, and it makes me smile as I eat him up with my eyes.

"You can taste whatever you want if you look this good."

Placing my hands on his chest, I feel the strong beat of his heart, steady, like him. And still, when I run my hands down his body and around his waist, the loose hanging fabric is there. Even on the most confident of men, there's still a flaw.

"And they say I'm a mess," I joke.

My fingers take hold of the fabric, and he inhales when I slip beneath his belt to tuck the rogue shirttail back in.

Once I've settled his bottom half, I straighten the collar at the top, ignoring all thoughts of doing this for him on a daily basis, because he'd be mine in that thought, and he's not mine forever...just for now. My eyes shoot to his with my thoughts, praying he can't read them.

Energy moves between our bodies.

"You're not a mess, Lem. Anyone who only sees the crazy side of you hasn't watched you long enough to see the rest."

His words skate through my soul and rest on my heart.

"And you've watched enough?" I reach up on my toes, nose to nose with the same shattered crystal eyes I search for in every dream I've had all week.

He nods, curving his lips with a hungry growl.

"I will never have enough of you." He roams my body, lingering on the fabric stretching over my pebbling nipples, slowing over the slit down the side of my gown as goosebumps break over my skin in the wake of his stare.

With one look alone, this man owns me. I know it. He knows it. And we both fucking want it.

"You know," I breathe, "it's rude to look if you're not gonna touch."

He presses his lips together in a grin. "That so?"

"Mhm…" I bite my bottom lip, eyelids fluttering. "It is very so."

"Did Miley say that, too?"

I swat him in the shoulder just as Anastasia swings back into the dressing area, Lydia scurrying behind her with a clipboard and tape measure.

"Just look at that. You look like a million bucks." Annie beams. "Go ahead and run, Mr.…" She looks him over once more before shooting me a look.

"Nashville," I tell her.

"Yes, Mr. Nashville. Lydia, run Mr. Nashville's card so they can get to their event on time. And Lemmy Cakes, please tell your father I can fit him for golf pants, too, and don't let me find out he has Claudette Charbonneau working on his wardrobe, or I'll die."

"Don't die," I say, earning a gasp before she exits the alcove with Lydia on her coattails.

"You made me sound important, calling me Mr. Nashville."

"You are."

"Really? Your father built an empire. I'm not important like that. I'm just someone working to get by. A sad, grieving father, who, as you so graciously pointed out, is sucking at even doing that."

"No, my father was a sad, grieving parent, too. He built that empire to bring back a queen who never cared about a castle. You're a good man who still has the world ahead of you. You have the chance to be different with your wealth, and you can take it from me, firsthand, growing up a princess has its advantages, but growing up with a present father? Well, let's just say I might not have that Bone Me tattoo if things had gone differently."

"You do have one, don't you? Let me see." He grabs for the fabric of my dress, but I slap his hand away, giggling when he tickles my sides.

"You have to earn that. You had so many times to see it, but you were too busy being all grumpy and sexually repressed."

My phone buzzes, the alarm ringing to alert me it's time for us to head to Papa's.

"I'll see it soon enough."

It's a promise I feel all the way to my core.

"So sure of yourself in your new suit," I tease. "You might be getting the hang of this cocky millionaire thing, after all."

"That's because I was assured I get to sample the nanny *and* the maid if I pull this off." His smile stretches wide. It's usually reserved for his children.

But this one is for me.

We walk to the car, hand-in-hand, and I ruffle the sleeves of his old brown jacket, draped neatly over his arm. Everything tidy and true with this man, yet somehow, I fit with him, messy and free and loud.

"We're a yin yang," I say, swinging open his car door. "Balanced opposites."

He grins, pausing to meet my eyes so we can stand here awkwardly smiling at each other, I guess.

I crack first, the laugh slipping free from my lips in a bubbling flutter. Then he's laughing. We use the car to prop ourselves up as we full-on roar into the most absurd fit of laughter over nothing but a look.

Nothing but everything I've never had with someone else.

I clear my throat as we right ourselves, wiping tears from our laughing eyes and nod to the car.

"I'm supposed to open the door for you, not the other way around."

I get in my own side and click the door shut. "I'm treating you to a night of luxury, Oliver. Let me be your guide to the world of the unfathomably rich, and mediocrely palatable, Elites of the East."

"Treating me with my own card? That's new."

"Get used to it. You're a wealthy man now, so everyone only wants you for your cash. It's a whole thing." I wave off his new money stupidity and continue. "Anyway, The Elites—"

He rolls his eyes. "That's not what they're called."

"Maybe not." I squint. "But I call them that because it's always the same people at these things, the richest families and business owners in the east coast, all coming together for another fundraiser that pours money back into the pockets of their target demographic, just so they can spend it again on those same products." I stare out the window wistfully, wishing I could change about half the snobs I've met at these things into frogs with my mind, but that's sadly not a real thing.

"You, uh...really have opinions about this, don't you?"

I tense with his admission, joke or not, and I don't mean to be a bitch when I take offense, but it's that mentality right there that keeps me in the social media cube at Papa's office. "Yeah, well, trust fund debutantes have brains, too you know. I have degrees in technology, marketing, finance, and business management. I graduated high school online at seventeen. I won a national debate once, but those awards aren't as tall or shiny as the skating and pageantry ones, so..."

"Why don't you tell Emil how you feel?"

"Emil, is it?" I tease. "Big important man now. I forgot."

"Stop, Lem. Don't do the goofy thing."

I have no idea what he means.

"You have every idea what I mean."

I gape. "Did you just read my mind?"

*Yes*, his mind says back. Well, his eyes do.

Fuck if I don't want to keep the way they look at me branded in my mind for all of time. I want to close my eyes and see his as the lock screen, boring right into my very soul.

"What the fuck is wrong with us?" I mutter, blue irises still suspending me in time.

"Everything." He brushes his thumb across my lips. "But I don't think I ever want to be right."

Our lips speak their own language, our tongues forging pacts, and the car fogs completely before we finally stop to breathe.

"We should get going." I gasp, prying my lips from his teeth. It almost feels too good to care when I imagine how that same toothy kiss could feel in my lower hemisphere. We could skip the..." *Fuck,* I check the time. "Charity's in a few hours."

"Fine," a shit-eating grin stretches his face, "but we're not done being wrong."

I giggle, moving back to my seat and buckling the belt.

"I'm serious, Sour Patch." He starts the car. "We are going to get so wrong later it'll turn right."

"Too many puns." I scrunch my nose. "Just leave the funny stuff to me. You're hotter quiet."

"Brat." He grins.

And fuck does my pussy feel it. I clench my thighs together and melt beneath his smile. And when his hand wraps around mine and he tugs it to his lap, I drift to sleep, and I've never felt more at home.

# Chapter Twenty-One

## OLIVER

Wrought iron gates, at least eight feet tall, swing open when I enter the code.

I steal a glance at the usually eccentric woman asleep in my car. I've never seen her still, cheek smushed against the window, bare legs tucked and curled under a hiked-up thousand-dollar gown she doesn't give a damn about.

Two nights in a row she's fallen asleep in that seat beside me, and I'm beginning to like the view, even as my stomach tightens.

Her father trusted me to keep her out of trouble, and I have.

He needn't know I also dream about the way her dripping cunt would feel wrapped around my cock, or how torturous it is that I could have her in an instant, a single wall in my home being the only barrier between her and the desires I'm finding it impossible not to chase.

And when I do, because it's not an *if* anymore, when we concede to this, it could all come crumbling down.

His trust in me would be tarnished.

I could lose my job.

And his serendipitous daughter can act like she doesn't care about her status or her stake in the company to piss him off, but I have a rebellious daughter of my own. I see the fear beneath her unending confidence.

She cares about earning his trust, just as much as I do. I'm still curious about the ideas she has. Could there be changes we implement together as a team?

For now, we keep this between us.

*For* us.

We'll have to tell him eventually, if it...doesn't end. If it could be more than temporary. A hollow feeling unsettles me when I think about the end of this summer.

Of her leaving.

And damn it, I wring my fingers through my hair and tug. It's barely even begun.

The dusk approaches, orange and yellow light streaming in from the window and casting a heavenly hue across her body.

*"Love again, Oliver. You have so much of it to give. Promise when I'm gone it won't die with me."*

*"No, Lo. I won't talk like that. You're getting the next treatment. This is the best facility."*

*"Promise, Oliver. Promise you'll live."*

Is this what Lauren meant?

Lemon is beautiful and brilliant. I think about what she said to Lydia at the shop. She stood up for me, but more notably, she helped that seamstress gain a valuable lesson on kindness, regardless of status or wealth.

Now, why would a billionaire's heiress even care about that?

Another one of her surprises.

She stirs, smiling when her eyes flutter open to mine staring back. "We're at your place."

"The apartment?" She sits up quickly, assessing the paved drive that surrounds a large, marble fountain in the center of the parking loop. She sighs a breath of what seems like relief, but it's so quick I almost miss it.

*Apartment?*

"Phillip's car is gone, which means Father's already left. We can get the car without having to explain this." She pats my shirt collar and draws my attention to the lipstick smudges she put there somewhere between the dressing room and the car. "We can bump a Tide pen from the maids."

"The maids, huh?" I tease her with my nose in the air.

"You know what I mean." She chews her lip. "I can't help if my father has maids. And maids need jobs, too, ya know? Our maids have families. They get bonuses and healthcare and…"

"Sour Patch?" I meet her glossy eyes. "I'm not judging you."

"Promise?" Her breath staggers, one hand poised on the door handle and the other reaching for mine, so I squeeze it.

"Promise." My lips meet hers. "Only Miley can do that."

"Ass." She swats my shoulder and curves her lips. "Let's go before I change my mind about the Tide pen. We could let me loose on your body instead and the whole shirt can have little kissy prints."

"You know, I've never really liked Tide. More of a Gain guy."

"You don't say." She laughs.

Holding her hand felt so natural in the car that I almost reach for it again, but the door swings open first. An elderly woman in all white comes out to greet us with an apron secured around her waist. Her eyes crinkle when she yanks Lemon through the foyer. "Lemon Cake! I've missed you!"

Their reunion strikes me as odd. She hasn't been living with me that long, but there was the tour before this, I suppose.

The grandmotherly woman fawns over Lemon's hair, then her dress, before finally appraising me.

"This is Amelia," Lemon says, as her eyes flick between the two of us.

"Hi, Amelia. I'm Oliver. It's a pleasure." I shake her hand, careful not to squeeze. She reminds me of my grandmother before she passed. Her body was frail, but her mind was keen.

Amelia uses hers to read me.

"I like him." She winks, offering me a smile.

We're ushered to a small sitting room with leather sofas and a round glass table in the center. An obscure black sculpture sits in the middle, a figure screaming from inside a cage.

Lemon snatches it up with a dramatic eyeroll, shoving it in a side-table cabinet as soon as she sees it.

"I made that shit in like tenth grade and Papa still displays it like actual decor. It gets old, that's all."

"He loves you." I smile, taking the sculpture back out before she can stop me.

She gives up easily, waving her hand at the piece like it's nothing, but I don't miss the way her eyes flick to mine each millisecond I inspect her work.

"The person screaming, that's you?"

She nods.

"And the cage? It's..." I gesture around the room, "this mansion?"

"No. Good try, though." She smiles, reaching over to strum her fingers across its tiny clay bars. Her bracelets jingle from her wrist, and I wonder what those represent, too.

Amelia returns from the kitchen smelling like cookie dough and coffee, and my stomach grumbles on cue. "Your father and Ms. Clements left for their cocktail reservation earlier. Should I whip something up for you two? Coffee or tea? The event starts in just a few hours, you know."

Lemon retracts her hand from the sculpture and cocks her head. "Did you say Ms. Clements?"

Amelia's face pales. "Oh, dear. I was probably not meant to tell you that, was I?"

"Is he seeing her again? Sylvia Clements of Clements Music? She's his competition!"

Lemon storms up the stairs, shouting German phrases I'm glad I can't translate. All I can do is shove my face full of the warm, gooey cookies while Amelia wrings her hands against her apron.

"Well, don't just stand there, young man. Run up there and make her feel validated. Come on, now!"

I laugh through a mouthful of cookie. "I am not a young man." I gesture to the silver that started in my beard years ago, but she bellows, slapping my shoulder with a dish-towel.

"Everyone is young when you're my age, dear. Even you. Now, go help. And make sure she doesn't make a scene at that charity event. For the love of tabloids, we do not need another press frenzy. It requires me to feed quite a lot of mouths, and my old hands just can't keep up with it these days."

"I hear what you're saying, Amelia. I won't take my eyes off her."

I'm not sure it's in my realm of possibilities, anyhow.

"Good." Amelia exhales at my assurance, but there's the other issue I'm not so sure about.

"How am I supposed to help her?"

The things she's struggling with and the things I'm working through are two very different things. There are entire layers to that woman I'm not sure I'll ever uncover, if I'm honest with myself.

I eye the sculpture, the pain a teenage Lemon must have felt as she carved her own bars and shoved herself inside them to scream from that stone for eternity.

"Do you care about her?"

I place the sculpture back in the cabinet where Lemon wanted it and close its door. "I'm worried I might care too much."

Amelia's smile almost reaches her eyes. "Then show her. Not many have."

"Who could possibly *not* care for her? She's magical."

"Not everyone believes in that sort of thing." She winks. "Do you?"

"Which one's her room?"

"Her *room* room is in Pine Forest Apartments above the bar. Drives her father crazy, you know. She does have a horrendously pink princess suite up the stairs that I assume you were referring to, however. Looks the same as the day she moved out ten years ago."

Amelia smirks at my surprise.

She moved out of this into low-income housing?

"You're not talking about the ones above Cowboys Paradise, are you?"

"I sure am. Clever décor. Those Isaac and Campbell boys do handy work when they get together." She picks up the empty cookie tray and wipes the table. "You know," she studies me, "Lemmy would kill me if she knew I spilled her beans...maniacal about her reputation." She rolls her eyes dramatically, and I see where Lemon gets it now. "You seem like a man trying to figure her out, and I like you, Oliver."

"Thank you, Amelia. I like you, too." She makes great cookies. Most importantly, she cares about Lemon. And aside from Jeremy and Emil, she's the only other person I've met who knows the real Lemon Perkins.

Amelia must feel the same about me. She leans closer, her voice a hushed whisper. "Lemon doesn't just live in those apartments, dear. Her father doesn't know. She owns them. All of them. She used some of her trust money years ago when she turned eighteen, and she rents them free to youngsters who age out of her cousin, Katie's, group home, provided they work and open a savings account. She even maps out the financial planning services."

"She does this for free?"

Amelia nods, tears springing to the corners of her eyes, sharing this secret with me.

But why is she concerned with financial independence from her father if she has properties of her own? She must file as a non-profit to have that sort of program moving, so why play by her father's rules at all? *Furthermore...*

"Why would she agree to be my nanny for the sake of an inheritance if she's got the funds and skills to go at it on her own?"

"If she doesn't inherit her father's money, she can't spend her father's money, don't you see? She wants to make change where she sees it needed, from inside of the broken machine. Why should a woman play by the rules of men who wrote the game?"

I look at the staircase, one I imagined her striding down each morning for freshly prepared breakfast with servants and scones.

It feels shameful to have considered, now I know she lives in a one-bedroom flat above a bar.

Or she lends it to those in need.

It's not at all what I expected from the adventure-seeking, rich girl I thought I knew.

Nothing has been expected with her since we started this arrangement. All the things that persuaded me to keep a distance from her, the risks, the sugar daddies, the status and behavior, all of them were a façade.

And if she lives above the bar, why did Jeremy call me last night? She could have walked up to her room and slept safely there. I would have worried about her all night, sure, but what did she have to gain by calling me?

Unless she asked for me.

Her friend's words from last night replay in my head. *Silver hair dads with tented sweatpants are the new in.*

And her own words.

*I love you.*

"She is more than meets the eye," Amelia finally says. "She sparkles."

"I know," I admit.

And I'm finding it harder to look away.

Papers rain over the luxurious office space of Perkins Manor, and a crumpled notepad hurls past my face on the tail end of Lemon's curses.

I follow her madness over the threshold but stop in my tracks. This is no ordinary office. I stand with my jaw hung beneath thousands of books that line the neatly organized walls. "What is this place?"

"The library," she teases. "Is this your first time being in one?"

"The first one in someone's house, brat." I grin when she hears that word and twists her lips. I shouldn't love it, and neither should my cock.

She leans against the wall, crossing her arms over her chest and blowing a strand of hair away from storming purple orbs. "I'm looking for a note. A love letter, if you can even call it that, from years ago."

My throat tightens at her desire to read letters I didn't write her, and the need to ask her if she still plans to leave after the summer is through drops like an anchor in my gut.

"You look like I just slapped you in the face, Oliver. It's not my love letter; it's Papa's...from Sylvia." She pretends to gag on her finger before a spontaneous giggle. "Just think, if it was yours, it could be called *Love's* letter."

I shake my head. "Already wish you didn't know my middle name."

"Don't wish that! I love knowing it's Love." She kisses my cheek. "Anyway, it's better than Lester."

One of the notebooks from earlier crunches beneath my feet. I pick it up by the binding.

*Generational Wealth and the Duplicity of Giving by Lemon Anne Perkins, 15.*

Stacks of essays are scribbled on crinkled, college-ruled pages. I trace the bubble letters on the bright yellow cover, Valley High School.

Fascinated, I flip through the headstrong ideals of an angsty teen Lemon, turning the page to realize those include taxing the rich and re-allocation of federal funding to community gardens and affordable childcare centers. "I didn't peg you as a public-school kid," I say.

"You didn't peg me at all. *Yet.*"

She pries the old schoolwork from my grasp while I'm busy imagining that scenario and shoves it into a filing cabinet beneath the desk, another door she closes to shield me from the layers of her life I long to peel away.

"Look for something on parchment from the Hotel De Lutz in Centerville. The woman he's with tonight, they met there years ago. She's done this dance with him before, Oliver, and her recording studio has been trying to ride on the backs of Perkins for years, poaching popstar after popstar from us as soon as they hit the top charts. I don't know what she offers them to move over their contracts, but she always gets her way in the end. She only wants him for his money or his connections. Those are the only reasons she'd come crawling back to his favor."

"You don't think it could be that she likes his personality? He's a fun guy. Good taste in...cigars."

Lemon quirks a brow. "Right. So, you agree she's using him."

"You can't know that." I struggle not to side with her father. I understand him in many ways she couldn't know. "Maybe you should trust his judgement."

As a father myself, I don't know what to think. But Lemon's not wrong. I'm privy to the Clements name. The record label has been poaching our artists for years. Could it be a lapse in her father's judgement?

An idea suddenly lights her eyes that has her crossing the room and getting to her knees, counting books from left to right.

When she's counted all the way to twelve, her finger catches something on the shelf and a book slips out. "Got it!"

A door opens from the wall of the library that exists in this woman's home. I thought I knew how the other half lived, but I only saw a fraction of this luxury on the road with musicians. Penthouse hotel suites and five-star dining, sure, but this...

"This is—"

"Completely over-the-top consumerism at its finest?" She shakes her head in agreement as she stands in the center of floor-to-ceiling signed records and a fully operational recording studio.

Behind a bookshelf.

"I realize it's a lot to take in." She winces, a pink blush spreading across her cheeks. She pulls at a strand of her hair, that nervousness again. I only ever see it around topics like this. "It's a rich people thing, but just ignore that and help me look, okay?"

Pink turns red as she waits for my answer.

"Okay." What else do I say?

No, I won't explore a musical treasure trove with the woman I think I love?

Deep inside, my fingers stir, raw energy igniting from some force I cannot see. But I never could see it with music. Sometimes you can't see what you're meant to feel.

Lemon rummages through papers and files behind the mix table, and I run my hand over the glass screen that separates us from the microphone and instruments. My eyes catch on one, and I squint, rubbing them in fascination at what I'm certain I can't be seeing.

The violin in the corner of the room.

"Is that a Stradivari?" My hand slaps against the glass, the slice of transparency separating me from a dream.

"A what?" She looks up from her pile of papers, dumbfounded as I trip over my feet to get a closer look.

"The violin over there." I tap the glass. "That's a...*Lemon!* That's a three-million-dollar instrument! How do you not know that?"

She shrugs, impervious to my fanatics. "I stopped lessons when I was like ten. Way more boring than piano or chess, if you ask me. I think Papa just forgot it was there all these years."

"That was your *practice violin*? For a ten-year-old? And here I bought the twins the pink ones with the plastic strings."

"Take a breath, Mr. Perfectionist. The twins don't care. I've seen. They use them like guitars and pretend they're at a Shaylyn concert, so don't get your new seersuckers in a twist about it. My father had stupid amounts of money to spend on his only daughter's first musical instrument. Literally, anything I did was celebrated by a team of maids and nannies with savings bonds or diamond jewelry waiting in Papa's hand at the end of the line. It was showmanship."

She trots to my side, placing her hand over mine, still sprawled on the plexiglass in amazement.

If I hold it there long enough, perhaps the glass will disappear.

"I knew you missed it." She smirks. "Come on." She drags me past the glass just like I wished.

*Magic.*

"This is called the live room," she says. "The music is played in here and fed through the equipment over there so the sound technicians can make it all cool and such."

"I know how it works, Sour Patch." I flick her hair. "Remember I work for your father?"

"Then act like you know a thing or two about music, Beethoven."

"Beethoven's favorite instrument was the piano. He also found it *way less boring*. Did you know that?"

"I do now." She pretends to check her nails to fuck with me, but I grin when she flicks her eyes back up and they seem to be smiling, too. "But I didn't come for a history lesson, I came for a symphony. Now get on with it!"

"Concerto," I tease back. "That's what they call a soloist in the orchestra."

"Whatever, old man. Are you gonna play the three-million-dollar practice violin or not?"

"Jesus, I can't believe you just said that sentence. I'm beginning to see what you mean when you say I'm a lousy millionaire."

She hops merrily onto a side table, swinging her legs while I tune the violin, and it reminds me of the way she sits on her tour bunk, bubbly and bright, annoying as can be and coaxing me on while I ready the bands for their schedule.

It occurs to me, I've known this side of her for years. Not just the surface parts I thought I knew, but the caring, intuitive side I've seen since she joined my home.

I felt guilty before now. I made a promise to her father, after all, but my feelings preceded that promise, didn't they? My eyes were so fixed on the chaos, I couldn't see the strength beneath it.

Intriguing, how it all began with our eyes.

And now, I close mine, wrapping my hand around an instrument I haven't played since Lauren passed. The smooth spruce and willow finishings shake my hand like an old friend, and for an entire breath, my body tenses.

But when I open my eyes again, and I see the woman I love smiling so wide it nearly touches her ears, I release it all, fingers gliding the strings.

I bow harder, faster, climbing and falling over riffs I'm not entirely sure mesh with the tune I began. My song takes flight, soaring atop crescendos, scaling over bridges, and a climax so tempestuous it feels like Lemon Anne Perkins herself.

It's a new song. One I'm writing as I go. The chaotic sharps and flats blend with the classical stroke of my bow in a way I never imagined.

My heart beats faster as her eyes sparkle so bright they may burst into the very starlight she chases, and just when I think we couldn't fly any higher—

*Snap!*

A string slaps against my wrist.

"I'm so sorry! I—"

"Don't be." Lemon beams. "Never be sorry for living."

*"Promise me you'll live,"* a voice whispers in the wind.

My eyes fix on the wild woman before me, dangling from her whims, and offering me the world in a smile, and I finally see.

*I am. I promise.*

# Chapter Twenty-Two

## LEMON

Annoyance is what I feel right now. At Papa.

How dare he send me off to live with another family to save his company's reputation when he's singlehandedly destroying it for the sake of a love affair with his competition?

I knew I sensed a snake in the grass the first time she slid into our lives, but coming back after breaking his heart and taking the summer chart-toppers with her?

My fingers curl into my fists. She's taking advantage of him. Nobody loves people like us for anything but money. Hasn't he learned this by now?

My hair hangs around my face, the loose bun I fashioned disheveled from the car ride, the library search, or maybe the way I shook it in time to Oliver's song.

Oliver Love Nashville and those motherfucking fingers. I stare him up and down just before Amelia breaks our privacy.

"Sorry to interrupt, dears, but it is within the hour of the event. If you plan to be punctual, you need to be leaving shortly." She taps her glasses back up her nose and scuttles away with what looks very much like a smirk.

As much as I want to find the love note that proves to Papa how persuasive she can be, to remind him how easily she lied to him last time, we have a tight schedule to keep.

And I have a bet that a lot of Pine Forest families are counting on me to win, whether they know it or not. I've been careless, and I won't let them down because I was drunk and competitive. *See what competition does?*

"I'll circle back to this when I have more time." I flick my eyes down his body, the abs I know to be solid and cut beneath his shirt an insane distraction. "Jacket." I remind myself. "You need the jacket."

I shake my head, and all images of his naked shirtless body away as I lead us to my bedroom. "Don't laugh. Nothing has changed in there since I was a teenager, okay?"

"You don't live here anymore."

It's a question, I think, but he says it like he already knows the answer.

I study him, the bad liar that he is, but I trust him, so I throw open the door and close my eyes to avoid his reaction to the—

"Chandelier? In your bedroom? Sour Patch, I had ideas, but...is that a three-panel mirror? And a *stage*?"

I deflate, meandering past him to hide in the closet until he's done marveling. You get used to reactions. It's the judgement that truly stings.

The assumptions.

My heart sits lodged in the back of my throat, waiting for his, only they don't come. Instead, I meet the eyes of a man who understands me on a level nobody tried to reach me on before.

"Your father did all this, didn't he?"

I could kiss this man right now.

Our eyes dance together briefly, and I have to remind mine not to send fuck-me signals to his because, despite the way I want to hold him inside me more than anything right now, we're on a schedule.

"I want to give you something."

He grins. "I don't think we have time for that."

"A jacket." I swat him, smiling, too. "We can get Amelia to steam it up real fast while we scarf down some sandwiches."

"Sandwiches? Isn't there food at the event?"

He has so much to learn. "You don't have time to eat the food if you're working the floor."

"I'm not gonna like you working the floor any more than casting couches, am I?" I think he's serious at first, but as my eyes meet his, I see a spark lighting them, one that doesn't come out often with this curious old grump.

I like it.

"Usually, you can't take your eyes off me while I work a floor."

He looks like he may kiss me again, but his eyes drop to the jacket and widen. "This is too nice." He thumbs the fabric, handstitched by the best in the industry.

"It's not too nice. It will fit you flawlessly, I know."

He raises a brow, and I shift from heel to heel uncomfortably.

"It was meant for someone a long time ago who is very similar to your build, and it was custom fit, so you know, I thought you might want the super expensive, never-worn, one-of-a-kind, designer suit jacket I have no use for. Any more questions, or do you want ham or turkey? I'm gonna let Amelia know."

I pick up the intercom, no longer making eye contact because I'd rather not discuss ex boyfriends. If I get a choice on the matter, it feels like a later kind of conversation.

Or never.

The jacket is a flawless fit. He moves toward me, every bit as rich in personality as he always has been, but now his wrappings match. It's sexy sure, but I never understood the hype of class. He could be naked before me, and I'd prefer the wealth of his mind and his actions more than any of the physical attributes he has to offer. He could be in nothing more than a plain black Perkins Global tee and a pair of jeans, yesterday's five-o'clock shadow darkening his chin, and *fuck,* I think I'd prefer that man to this thousand-dollar version before me.

Doesn't mean my mouth doesn't water as he approaches.

He gets close.

Then closer.

Until we're flush, my body pressing into his, pinned between two sets of wood, the closet door and the one growing harder under my wandering hand. I want to curse at his ignorance in himself, how he has no idea what he looks like right now. How I'd drop to my knees for so little as the way he narrows his eyes.

As if he reads my mind, he works his fingers, the ones I became mesmerized by only moments ago, wrapping them around my neck, a warm cradling of my flesh beneath his, and I catch my breath under the pressure as his lips brush mine.

"Tell me," he whispers against them. "Tell me what I did to earn another man's jacket."

My eyes lower.

"You don't have to explain why he left. Just tell me what I need to keep doing so he never earns it back."

I blush at his honesty.

"You remember Andrew?"

He thinks for a moment, then cocks his head with a wry smile. "No. You don't mean that med student who came on tour with his uncle...who was that?" "The drummer from Stereo Vine."

"That's it!" He wags his finger in the air. "That kid was a piece of something."

"Yeah." I wrinkle my nose, less impressed with past Lemon than I remember. "Well, I almost married that piece of something. I can't even believe I'm saying that sentence."

"And this was his?" He starts to remove it.

"No." I hold my hands over his shoulders, preventing him from removing the stupid expensive garment I wish I never even purchased. Just think of all the charities I could have boosted instead of that asshole's vanity. "It was never his."

I hold my breath inside my lungs before professing the rest of that secret to Oliver.

The one where my eyes searched for his at every VIP party that same summer Andrew joined us on tour.

The one where I couldn't even orgasm unless I closed those same fucked-up eyes and imagined Oliver pounding into me instead of the man I was to marry in a few short months.

The one where my infatuation with teasing him became more than a habit, but a need.

Over a man I never thought unattainable until now.

"Andrew was a douche," I say. "Point blank. And this was the jacket he wanted. I bought it as an engagement gift." I pause to meet his eyes, relieved that I only see support there and not anger or jealousy. "But he was a shit, as you pretty much stated, and I knew it. Too bad the other girl didn't, because now he's shit at the bottom of her shoe instead of mine."

He laughs when I shake off the heebie-jeebies lingering in the air from discussing my past. But I ease when his arm wraps around my waist, letting me know he's still here.

I run my hand over the jacket, perfectly fit to Oliver's chest, and I throw him a wink in the three-panel mirror. "It's ironic how much I want to rip this right back off you. It was made for your body type."

"I do look regal." He wiggles his eyebrows in the most dad way possible, and we both laugh. "Still sort of thrown off that you're out here dating guys with the same body type."

"Are we dating?"

"I don't think we're not." I bite my lip as he kisses me, and it soothes every nerve I had about sharing this part of my past with someone I'd very much like to see in my future.

"Thank you for not freaking out. You can donate it later if you want, I don't care, but please wear it tonight. It looks amazing on you, and it saved you from needing to buy one for all the events that come with your important new promotion."

He quirks a brow. "I could have bought twenty for the price of this one at the outlet mall."

"You're probably right, but keep in mind that you wouldn't look near as fuckable to trust fund debutantes."

"I didn't mean what that sounded like, Lem. When I said that before, I didn't know...well..."

"You didn't know I was a good person," I finish. "Just a slut worth millions."

"You're not, you know. A slut. Women can fuck whomever and whenever they please, you know. At least, someone sexy and citrusy told me that." He cups my cheek with his hand. "And as for worth, Lemon Perkins, you'll always be one in a million to me."

O liver follows me out of my frilly pink nightmare of a past and into the oak shading of my father's master suite, stopping just before he toes the threshold.

"What are you doing? C'mon."

"It's not professional for me to enter your father's room without his permission. It crosses a line."

"And?" I yank him into the room. "I cross those little shits all the time. Makes life more sparkly."

"Yeah, well, *I* don't," he hisses, and it's so cute to see him tiptoeing around as if someone who is clearly not home would ever catch him. "I'm gonna go back to the hallway until you find what you need."

"I'm looking for keys, and so are you," I inform him. It's good for his character. "Rules are meant to be misinterpreted occasionally, Oliver. Stop being a baby. You're sweating worse than when you work out."

"You would know," he quips. "You stalk my workouts."

A laugh bubble from my throat. "Touché." I like this spicy side of him that bites back.

I pull open Papa's side drawer after having checked every other possible spot in the room. It's the last place I want to go wandering, but he knows it's the one place I won't look.

"Fuck it." I yank it open. He can take my money, but he can't take my freedom. My chest rises with triumph when my 'Stang keys are right there where I suspected, but my eyes snag on something else while I'm there.

Something sealed with a red, lipstick kiss.

A note from the heartbreaker herself.

Only it's not what I expected.

*Emil,*
*I'm glad we finally did this.*
*Retirement has felt empty without you in my inbox.*
*Now that our interests don't conflict, I hope for more use of*
*this shade of red on my lips...and hopefully yours, too.*
*-Slyvie*

In her inbox? *His lips, too?*

If that isn't kinky old people sexting, I don't know what is. *Gross, gross, gross!* It's Papa.

And yet, it's Papa. I want him to have love.

Could Sylvia be truthful?

I glance at Oliver Love Nashville, this man I never imagined I'd be involving myself with seriously. Maybe it already is serious.

Maybe it is with Papa and Sylvia, too.

"She's retired." I scan the lipstick line with confusion. "I was wrong."

I slam the drawer shut, grabbing my keys and turning to face him for the embarrassment that will be his I-told-you-so. I completely spiraled over this thing that wasn't even a thing. But he doesn't say I told you so; he takes my hand and squeezes it instead.

"I guess you can trust your father's judgement, after all. That's a relief to know because I was beginning to wonder, on my account with you and all," he teases, dragging me along with zero mention of how crazy I became in my moment of need to prove something—

how I jumped to the negative on instinct. He winks when all I can do is stare unfaltering beams of swoon into his eyes.

"Come on, Nancy Drew, you have a bet to lie in, remember?"

"How could I forget." I click open the garage door and nod my head to the rows of sports cars lining the expanse. "I'm the billionaire, after all." I puff my chest out and drag my fake cigar, waving it in the air at Oliver's shocked face. "Just get in and look pretty for me while I do important man stuff, won't ya, babe?"

He laughs. "You do that really well."

"You don't live this life as long as I have and not learn from the worst." I shrug, beeping my baby alive. The lights flash on my bright yellow, 1967 Shelby GT500, and his jaw drops.

"That's your ride?" He shakes his head, descending the steps into the six-car garage and circling the body, running his hand over the exterior as he kneels to check out the custom, spinning rims. "Amelia made it seem like you don't spend your money, but I see what this is here. You do have your vices."

I gasp. "That old narc told you about my apartment, didn't she?" I shake my head in disbelief. "You can't get good secret keepers these days. I could tell you knew, you know. When you asked if I still lived in the princess palace from hell. You're a bad liar." He rolls his eyes, and I mimic his movement until we're laughing again. "Papa was going to get me a much more expensive car. You have no idea how much negotiating I did for anything less than a jewel-encrusted one of a kind."

"I guess I'm not upset about that." He clicks his jaw, still staring at me like that same puzzle he pulled out and started several weeks ago, the pieces scattered to different corners now, like he might pick me up and turn me all the way upside down to get perspective.

I want to let him. That's the scarier part.

The part where I gave him that jacket, one I thought symbolized the solitude I'd always feel.

The fact I'm falling for his kids, living beings I said I'd never want or have.

Or that I care what he knows and thinks about me, and what he thinks about that same stuff once he knows.

The fact I *love* him.

And it's the most terrifying adventure I've ever had.

"I suppose we should be going, then," Oliver says, opening the passenger door.

"What are you doing? You're driving. I have six-inch heels on."

"You chose them. And I don't feel comfortable driving a car that costs more than my house."

"It's probably only a third of your house."

"Sour Patch! I can't drive this."

"Yes," I shove into the passenger seat and hand him the keys, "you can. Stop being a scaredy-cat and live a little."

# Chapter Twenty-Three

## OLIVER

*C*<sup></sup>*lunk!*

"What was that?" Lemon turns in her seat, eyes wide and nostrils flared. Wish I could say it wasn't sexy as Hell, but it's sexy as— "Hello! You act like you don't know how to drive a manual."

My hand curls around the gearshift, moving from fourth to third, and I swipe my eyes to Lemon's when it feels like the bottom of the car drops out with my driving.

She is fuming.

I should have stuck to my instincts, stuck to what I know. I was attempting to be adventurous. Live free.

"I thought it would be like the one I learned on. It seems there's a difference between a rusted old farm truck and a hundred-thousand-dollar sports car."

"Two-hundred-twenty thousand."

"Fudge! That much?" My hands sweat against the leather steering wheel.

"It's a custom paint job. And I'm sorry, can we circle back to *fudge*? What are you, sixty?"

"I have kids. I can't exactly walk around saying the f-word."

"I say it around your kids all the fuckin' time."

I press my lips together but fail to hold back my smile. "Don't tell me that." The way she makes me laugh about things most people hide is just another reason to want her near.

"Jesus!" She yelps as we soar over a pothole. She's clearly had enough when her hand covers mine on the gearshift, and while I recognize it's usually the other way around, the man teaching the woman to drive a stick, I have no problems challenging the norm on this one.

In fact, I want her to boss more.

"Clutch and decrease speed," she commands, moving us to second. "Guess we can add sportscars to the list of your Not Hobbies," she teases. "So far, it's that and porn."

"I should have told you I'm not used to handling a stick."

"Oh, I am very privy to how long it's been since your stick has been handled." She rolls her eyes. "It's the talk of the coffee shop, if you didn't know. You and your very large shoe size."

"Is Lemon Perkins jealous?" A grin forces across my face, and I'm not sure how it's possible, but I fall for her more. "Think I'll have my nanny make my coffee from now on. She has the best tasting cream."

She blushes, squeezing my hand with each come on, and coaxing me through until I'm transitioning smoothly. Eventually, the practiced movements of her driving lesson click, and I can confidently switch from one gear to the next. Her praise helps, gentle nudges and satisfied grins—things I didn't realize felt so warm.

When did I become so used to the cold?

"You're getting better with direction. Super coachable." She winks. "It's a promising indicator of good...oral skills. Good for you *and* me, I guess."

I break into laughter. "Are you still playing the role of self-assured billionaire right now?"

"Guess you'll have to find out, won't you, Mr. Nashville?" She leans over the console, heating the skin beneath my ear. "Now, be a good boy and clutch in before you move us back to—"

*Clunk!*

"What the hell was that?" Lemon swats my shoulder.

"Ow!"

"You were doing so well."

"It wasn't me," I say, scanning the rearview mirror. I pull to the shoulder. "We ran over something. It felt..." I blow out a breath, anxious to even say it, "big."

"An animal?" She gasps. "Did we kill an innocent animal? Oh, my God!"

"I don't know." My chest tightens. "I don't know, damn it. I don't know. Let's just..."

She closes her hand over mine and squeezes. "Let's just look."

I wipe my forehead, exiting my side of the vehicle, and Lemon does the same on hers, until we're walking along the edge of the road.

"I see it!" She runs ahead. The sun is setting, but orange and pink still paint the sky behind her when she bends down. My breath instantly releases on an exhale, noting the heap in her arms too jagged to be a cat or dog.

Or worse.

It's just a hunk of rubber.

We relax our shoulders at the same time. "It's part of a tire, I think."

We inspect it, exchanging a worried look.

"This tire has blown to pieces."

Several feet up the road, more vehicle debris reflects beneath the glow of Lemon's headlights. We don't have to speak the same words to share the same fear that the person this happened to might still need help.

We hurry back to the Mustang, and Lemon clears her throat. "Not to crush the fragile shell of masculinity or anything, but are you insistent on driving?"

"Enough said." I toss her the keys.

"I'll just be faster." She crosses to the driver's side. "Probably safer if there's debris in the road, too, and someone could need our help."

She wears a hard shell, but deep down, she cares about people. Not just some people, but every person she meets. All bark with nothing but puppy love underneath.

"I'm man enough to admit when my woman is better at something than I am," I say, putting my hand beneath hers on the gearshift. The whimper she lets out is damn near ecstasy.

"Teach me?"

The engine roars to life, her unnatural violet eyes following suit, flaring so brightly I could find them among the stars.

"First I'm your baby, now I'm your woman?"

We say nothing more, but the smile stretches over her pressed lips, and she turns to the road, refusing to meet my eyes as she drives forward.

Seconds go by, and with them, piece after piece of the tire, until the hazard lights of a disabled stretch limo flash in the distance, the frame of the tire flush with gravel and dirt.

Burning rubber pervades the air as we exit the car.

A scream from inside the vehicle rings through the night, and we both pause. Lemon shoots me a single glance before jetting to the driver's side door. "Are you all right?" She bangs on the window. "Do you need help?"

"This side," a shaky voice calls. He's young, maybe a teenager. My parental instincts kick in, and I rush to the passenger side on Lemon's tail to see a scrawny boy—no older than twenty, at the wheel, drowning in what appears to be a chauffeur's uniform, but with bright red cheeks and mussed hair, he looks like a child playing dress-up in his father's suit.

The driver?

He sifts his fingers through his hair, pinning me with his helpless stare and immediately connecting me to his salvation. It's unsurprising, in a way, a weight I'm used to feeling. For the girls, Lauren, the company and the bands I tour with...Lemon's different, though.

She takes care of herself.

Of me and the kids, too.

Teaching me to drive a manual? Who the hell knew that was in my cards tonight? Things are spontaneous and new with her, every single day. Showing me how to walk and talk like a million bucks, even if that's the kind of man she says hates.

And she takes care of things now.

I might be what this kid thinks a hero looks like, but she's so much more than that, an everyday savior who doesn't even bother with a cape. She just follows her heart.

The driver whispers a prayer under his breath and hangs his head. "She hit her head when the tire blew out, because I slammed on the brakes. I didn't know what to do. I didn't mean to hurt anyone."

"It's okay, Benji," an even younger voice says over a wince of pain. This one is female, and when I see who emerges from the back, I think I may have hit my head, too.

"Shaylyn?" I stumble over the name. "I mean...Miss Tryst. Please forgive my familiarity."

"Call me Shaylyn." She giggles, but then sucks in on another pained wince as her hand shoots to her bleeding head.

"Talk about a coincidence," Lemon whispers.

"No such thing," I mumble back.

Lemon procures a first aid kit from her glove compartment. "Here, honey. Let me clean you up. I'm certified in first aid. Is that okay?"

Shaylyn nods with a relieved sigh, and it's only then I see the fear in her eyes. The blood beads atop her forehead, and she shivers. "Thank you. I feel wobbly right now, and my head has been pounding for a few minutes. It didn't happen right away, but it keeps getting worse the longer we wait here."

I swipe at my phone, but nothing dials out. "I've got no signal."

Shaylyn nods, frustrated. "The road assistance signal is jammed or something. It isn't sending messages from the limo's Bluetooth, and neither my phone nor Benji's has signal. We've been stuck for a bit." Her glamor-painted lips tremble. "I'm supposed to be at an event any minute."

Lemon smiles softly, wiping the blood away with anti-septic. I'm captivated watching her work, the same tongue that was sliding over mine earlier is now poking from the side of her mouth as she concentrates on cleaning the wound. She places a clear, gummy strip over it and inspects her work. "I applied a liquid bandage. It's like superglue. You almost needed a stitch for that. Look to the side, up, and down while I hold this light up, all right, Shay?"

"How did you know that was my nickname?" The pop-star shoots me a quick look, but I can only shrug. I don't get it either.

"Lemon is full of surprises."

"My best friend goes by Shay, too." She rolls her eyes at me. "Remember, the one watching your children?" She winks at Shaylyn then. "I can just feel the connection to the name. She's talented like you."

She's not just talking, I realize when she winks at me, too. She's distracting Shaylyn from the exam, making her concussion screening a normal conversation.

"She's a dancer," Lemon goes on, holding up fingers for Shaylyn's eyes to follow. "Owns her own ballet studio, super preggers right now, and I cannot wait to meet the little lady she's going to raise."

"That's so sweet. My friend is pregnant, too," Shaylyn whispers, "but she's a few years younger than me..." She bites her lip as she meets Lemon's nurturing stare. "The guy who...well, the father, he's complicated. He hasn't helped her."

Lemon nods. "Keep her close. I knew a girl who had a hard time once, too, and I wish I'd realized sooner how much she needed a friend, not another set of eyes to judge her. She can't go backward, you know? Sometimes you must lie in the bed you made and hope there's someone there beside you when it's all said and done. The great thing about beds is they can always be remade, no matter how mussed they get."

"Hm." Shaylyn bites her bottom lip. "Thank you. I hadn't thought about it like that."

"Anytime." She smiles. "Now, I know you were planning to attend that event, but I think you've got a concussion, baby doll. It's my duty to advise you to seek emergency care...and have them run an MRI to check for internal damage, okay?"

"It can do that?" Shaylyn's eyes go round.

"You hit your head." Lemon holds Shaylyn's hand. "Even whiplash can cause a concussion. I think you're fine, but you have a big old contusion forming. You should see a doctor."

"Isn't that what you are?"

"No. I wish I was that smart. I'm just a chick with a lot of certifications and no direction. But I also happen to know you need medical care. Do not sleep anytime soon, and you should get lots of fluids because it can make you—"

Vomit erupts out of nowhere from the popstar's mouth all over us, chunks of stuff I don't want to identify, spattering the pavement at our feet.

"I'm so sorry!" Shaylyn sobs, hair sticking to her still-glamorous face.

If my daughters only knew what I was up to right now.

It's gross, I won't sugar coat it, but just when I think Lemon could finally show that true billionaire entitlement I keep holding my breath over, she wraps Shaylyn in a hug, unfazed by the bodily fluids or the chaos, and lets the popstar rest her snot-bubbling nose on her shoulder to cry.

"It's okay. We got you. I was about to explain how a concussion can make you throw up. It's normal. Nothing to be worried about." She rubs her back, like I've seen her do with my girls, and I can't take my eyes off her. It's not the first time the thought of Lemon raising my children crossed my mind.

But it's an unfair expectation if it's not what she wants. "Shh, it will all be all right."

"It might not," Benji says after his third attempt to dial roadside. "I can't get signal, and we can't go to the event, let alone the hospital, which is ten miles farther, without a tire."

Lemon's brow pinches. "Just change it to the spare."

I chuckle at the irony of it all. The juxtaposition of the spoiled rich girl being the one to think about changing her own tire. Here we all were waiting for roadside assistance or goddamned Batman to swoop in and save us, and she's already rolled up her puke covered sleeves.

Benji frowns. "I'm sorry, Miss Tryst. My dad owns this company, but he's always giving me the dumbest tasks. I wanted to prove I'm worthy of our last name, but I didn't expect a tire to blow, or to be this underprepared when it did." He shakes his head. "I can't even change it for you. I don't remember the first step." He sits on the curb and hangs his head.

"Hey...chin up. I get it." Lemon pats his shoulder. "I have a difficult father, too. Sometimes dads can really fuel your fire. Cause a chain reaction, can't they?" Lemon swipes her eyes my way with a sly smile. "Let me teach you how to change this thing, and then you're going to get my bestie here to the hospital and show your dad how responsible you were in an emergency."

"Really?" He perks up.

"Really." Lemon nods to the limo. "Do you have a jack, at least?" I almost laugh aloud when he winces at the question and her nostrils barely flare. She masks her annoyance but shoots me a look that says it all.

It's not lost on me how we can speak entire sentences with our eyes.

"You know what, don't worry about it," Lemon says. "I have one." She retrieves it and heads to the back of the limo, throwing a wink over her shoulder. "You just gonna stand there and watch, Mr. Nashville?"

"You know what I like," I tease as she bends over the trunk.

"Nashhole," she mumbles, hefting the tire out and lowering it to the ground on a perfectly formed squat I wish I could sit beneath.

*Who am I?*

She turns back, like she can hear my earlier thoughts, and I get a front-row view of my girl, sexy as hell in an evening gown with a slit up to her thigh, kneeling by a jacked-up, two-ton vehicle, changing the tire like a professional.

"Full of surprises." I shake my head. "I can't look away."

"Be careful," she teases. "Remember it's rude to look if you're not gonna..."

Our eyes dance beneath the stars.

"It's past dark. We're late for the event."

"No, I think we're right on time." Lemon angles her head to Shaylyn, searching for a phone signal.

"I can't reach my agent," she huffs. "I was supposed to meet him at the venue. Almost insisted on riding with me and hiring a whole-ass bodyguard, but I said it'd be fine." Worry glosses her eyes. "We had a fight before this at the hotel. I just needed to feel normal for little. Not just a popstar with entourage. But now, he'll think I stood him up. That I don't want this record deal. He set this up specially for me to meet the head of the label. It could launch my career to the next level, and I blew it. I completely blew it!"

"But you didn't blow it." Lemon smiles. "Accidents happen. And your health is more important than a record deal, because you are a normal person, Shay, not just a popstar." Lemon braids the young woman's hair off her face, and warmth spreads over me, remembering how she did that with Bryar. "Now," she says, in a motherly way I can't seem to stop noticing, "who did your agent want you to meet that can't wait until your head's done oozing?"

"Emil Perkins." She sighs. "Do you know Perkins Global Records?"

Lemon kicks my butt from behind, and I squeeze hers back.

"It's the biggest label on the East Coast," Shaylyn continues, "and now he'll think I'm not serious."

Lemon smiles, shooting me a look, and then I'm smiling, too. The irony of being in the middle of the mess but exactly where we need to be is almost too clandestine, and before we know it, we're laughing.

"What's funny?" Shaylyn's gaze bounces between us as we struggle to compose ourselves.

"You're right," Lemon whispers, "no way this is a coincidence."

We all jump when a loud clap booms from above, cool summer rain spilling from the clouds.

I search the sky, Lemon's infectious spirit altering my senses, connecting the time we share like constellations in the stars.

Brightness worth chasing.

"Shaylyn?" Lemon grins as water droplets hit her face. "What if you could sign with Perkins Global from the convenience of your puke-covered limo?"

Amelia was right; she sparkles in every sense of the word. But this time, it's me grinning wildly.

And that's no coincidence.

# Chapter Twenty-Four

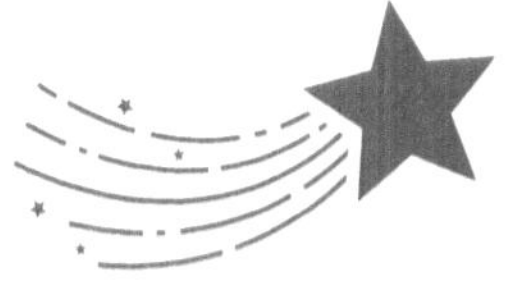

## LEMON

"That was incredible," Oliver marvels for the quintillionth time in my passenger seat.

Pretty sure I could pluck the stars right from his eyes if I wanted.

"I could get used to this enchantable side of you."

"Me too." He squeezes my knee as I drive, catching my eyes for permission to do more.

I nod as goosebumps overtake me, promises of the places his hands will go if we continue down this path.

I release a desperate moan when those places become my upper thigh, his pinky finding me soaking beneath the slit of sparkling fabric, that single connection drenching my pussy with urgency.

Shifting my weight to trap him between my quads seems dangerous behind the wheel, so I don't rock my body into his hand.

I let him play.

It's absolute torture, and the smug Nashhole knows it. He curls the edge of his lip, moving his fingers through my arousal with each frustrated breath I exhale, until I'm swatting him away.

"I can't drive if you distract me!"

"That's what she said." He snickers, and I roll my eyes.

"That is, without a doubt, the last thing she said."

He crosses his toned arms over his chest with a pout I'd like to taste, and I roll my eyes at myself this time.

Even my mind has dirtier jokes.

"If someone would have bet me a year ago I'd be sitting here having this conversation with you of all people—"

"You'd what?"

The cold river air promises adventure against my cheek, just as his fingers brush the other, two sides of me calling the same soul, but his call is the loudest.

"You scare the hell out of me, to be honest, Lem. You are fearless in the craziest possible ways. Brave enough to travel the world, smart enough to earn accolades and degrees, with wit enough to talk your way in or out of any situation. Rules and reason mean nothing when it comes to you. I mean, look at this thing!"

He waves around the contract I drew up for Shaylyn, purple gel pen on a Sugar Stable napkin I found in the glove box, and I blush.

"This is genius. But who else but you would have thought of it? That makes you special. That's what makes you who you are. It's also what terrifies me, because you are the whole package, Lemon Anne Perkins. And that's so damn much to lose."

Tears roll down my cheeks with the admission of his love. That what he sees as strengths are the very things I believe to be my flaws. I brush away teardrops and blow out a grateful breath.

"Napkin contracts are sort of my specialty." I sniffle. "A story for another day."

"I'd like to hear you tell it."

"I bet you would."

"That's what she sai—"

"No, Nash." I hold up my hand. "She did not say that, either, sadly. I think maybe you should just stick to stuff she didn't say."

"Brat." He slaps his hand back over my thigh, and my eyes drop to meet it there, every pussy muscle I possess tensing involuntarily before I force my gaze back to the road.

"I want to do all the things with you, pretty much all at once when your hand is there," I tell him. "Just so we're clear."

"Is *that* what she said?"

"Okay," I take in his shit-eating grin, "I'll give you that one if you stop trying."

"Noted." He smiles brighter than the moon, and I can't take my eyes off the view.

Oliver Nashville at peace.

I pull us over to bask in this light he rarely lets shine, just a bit longer, but his smile falters when we lean into one another, and both of our lips curl.

"Uh, Sour Patch, I want to do all the things, too…to be clear, but we smell ungodly." He sniffs his jacket and gags.

I smell my own clothes and just about retch. "There might be some weirdos out there willing to pay for this popstar puke."

Oliver gapes. "That's—"

"Awful? I know. Jeremy says I make jokes when I'm in tense situations. It's something I'm not working on, as you can see."

"I was going to say genius."

We fall over with laughter, our foreheads finding rest against the other, until our breathing slows as one.

"I'm going to kiss you," I tell him.

So, I do.

But it tastes like fucking puke. "Gross!" I spit out the window.

Oliver wipes his mouth on the back of his hand. "Let's go home and shower."

Our silent breath fogs the car before either of us says more. I don't acknowledge that it isn't my home, nor do I acknowledge to myself why. Instead, I find ways to avoid the word altogether.

"We could take a swim." I slip a shoulder out of my gown, my eyes lingering on his pants before exiting the car.

His jaw drops, but I don't look back to see if he's gathered it from the floor. You can lead your whore to water, or something like that.

As predicted, he follows frantically behind me. "It's after dark, Sour Patch. You can't go in there."

He whips out his phone, to google it, maybe. Who knows? But there's a reason Shaylyn couldn't call out for help. The cell towers don't make it this far in Pine Forest. *We're in God's land now*, as the locals say. And by locals, I mean me and Jeremy when we're tipsy at line-dancing night.

He groans, pacing on the other side of the unhooked chain. "Don't."

But I do.

And I relish teasing him from the other side. He doesn't dare cross it, the invisible line in the dirt.

It seems Daddy Nash has returned, and the adventurous man-child I pulled free is back in his little hidey-hole.

He refastens the chain. "Lem, it's trespassing." He holds out his hand for me to join him on the safe side, but I'm not budging. He needs this.

For sanity *and* sanitization.

I narrow my eyes. "You're doing this, Oliver. It's part of healing. Be free and live in the moment. You were on such a good streak there for a bit, so what happened?"

"This happened. It's one thing to gamble with your father, but you're asking me to break the law."

"Laws are flexible, like I said. You can't be broken if you bend. It's the circle of law."

"That doesn't even mean anything! You're just saying a bunch of words."

"Look, it's land, Nash." I peel my dress off so I'm down to just my bra. His eyes roam every spot they can before finding mine. "Nobody can own land, can they?"

"Of course they can. That's like...that's the whole point of wars and nations and... It's a national park," he argues. "It is literally the nation's park; don't you get that? *They* own this land!"

"And we are the people of the nation," I quip, my nipples pressed tightly against my cups with the chill of the wind. I'm Lady Liberty, standing tall on her island, ushering the freedom of this one single man. "And in order to form a more perfect union, we have to establish some...just us, if you will." My bra drops to the ground. "Ensure *dom*-estic tranquility, perhaps?"

I slap my naked ass as a nod to the moment he lost control in that bus. "I can flex the law for you all night long if that's what you want, but guess what?"

He groans, and I love it entirely.

"You'll have to catch me first."

# Chapter Twenty-Five

## OLIVER

"Come get me." Lemon's voice bounces off the trees. "Better hope a river monster doesn't find me first. I've read some good books that start that way!"

*Brat!*

I can be fun. Spontaneous, or what have you.

I can break rules and do dangerous, exciting things.

But this is beyond my comfort zone.

"You've had your fun. Let's go back," I whisper shout. "This whole forest could be under surveillance."

"You're paranoid."

The moon lights her entire body against the dark water behind her. It's slow, a steady spot with little to no current, and the way she runs her fingers through her hair before it falls over her bare shoulder drives me primitive.

Growling. Craving.

Breaking rules.

Thinking and doing things I've never dared to say aloud.

*I want to taste you again.*

"You're breathtaking," I say instead.

She parts her lips on a grin, a laugh bubbling free, and I want nothing more than to taste that very part of her.

Keep it.

Her body trembles like mine as I approach her, and we both admit with a shared glance that this moment is the one we've been avoiding.

"The person I thought you were," I start, aiming to apologize, to atone for ever thinking she was less than the powerful, intelligent woman she is, "I was wrong. Your father is wrong. You could do so much for the company, and—"

"You're doing a lot of talking for someone whose breath I supposedly took." She scrapes her teeth over her bottom lip, eyes shining with a dare. "If you want it back, come get it."

She dives into the water, the calm and quiet of before shattered to chaos in her wake.

I'm alone for an instant before she bobs to the surface, shaking her hair from her face. She grins like she's just won a million bucks, floating naked on a muddy shore. But considering she already had a million bucks, maybe this experience *is* the prize to her.

"Come in!" She splashes me from below, and I must admit, the cold water feels rejuvenating on my sticky skin. "Suit yourseeeelf," she sings on a backstroke. "But I'm getting clean, and you're still wearing Shaylyn's lunch, maybe even breakfast."

"Not a good image."

"Not a good smell, either," she quips.

"You're just replacing the puke with parasites," I tell her, examining the sign by the dock. "See? It's part of a reservoir." I point to the sign. "Look, it says it's a water moccasin habitat."

"Oh, come on." She switches to breaststroke. "I've been swimming in this very spot since I was a teenager, and I've never been made aware of any snakes or parasites."

"It literally says right here that you could encounter both snakes and—"

*Splash!*

I float to the surface after being yanked in by the temptress of the river, and all I can do is glare incredulously as I spit algae-ridden water from my mouth. "The sign says...*fuck it*." I slap the water in defeat.

She giggles, pleased with her victory. "I love it when you say fuck."

"I know." I roll my eyes at her this time, and she throws her head back on a cackle, her signature of pure joy. "I love your laugh." I draw her in and wrap her legs around my floating body.

"I've got you."

"You do?"

Our eyes lock beneath the stars.

"Yeah. I do."

The wind skips across the water, and she pulls me closer, her hardened nipples brushing my chest.

I free my hand and touch her there, and my cock pulses to life when she whimpers. I linger, and she moans, neither moving nor stilling, just breathing and squeezing as she rocks her body against me.

I wait for her to tell me what she wants.

"Please, Oliver."

It's all I need before I'm rolling her nipple between my fingers. Her head falls back, and I use my other hand to find the soft, wanting spot between her legs, the one clung to my wet body.

I play for a moment, squeezing and tugging, touching everywhere but the spot I know she wants.

"Fucking, please, Oliver! Nash! *Daddy!* Oh!"

"Don't call me daddy." I pinch her clit. "Naughty fucking nanny."

"Then what do I call you?" She gasps.

"Yours." I move to where I can stand and hold her close, drawing circles on her clit with my thumb. "Call me yours, Lem."

"Mine, Oliver. Fuck!"

I thrust my middle and ring finger inside of her, nearly losing my balance when she clenches around them.

"You're mine," she says again.

I capture her mouth, exploring the spaces with my tongue until a long, pleasured moan escapes her. "You like it when I do this?"

"Yes." She begs me. "Please, Oliver, keep doing it."

"Fuck, I love the way you say my name." I thrust my pointer finger in beside the other two, filling her up until she cries my name on loop. "Juicy little Lemon, all for me."

Her head drops to the side, and she presses her neck to my mouth, arching into my tongue and giving me full access. "So tight around my fingers," I say into her ear with a nibble. "Think I need something bigger to juice it properly."

She tightens her hold around my hand with each dirty phrase I speak, and even though it's not part of who I was, I'm finding it's certainly easy to make it a part of the man I'm becoming, my cock hardening impossibly more with the dominance I hadn't known I possessed.

For her.

"This pussy is mine, isn't it?" I stroke my fingers in and out, curling to hit the spot that makes her squeeze and sing my praises.

We wade to the dock, and I peel the wet clothes from my body.

Lemon, ever the performance artist, uses it as her private runway, taking the stage in the moonlight and draping her body across the planks dramatically.

And bare to me.

Neither of us says a word as I climb on top, dripping over her. Her hair fans around her body, tangled and wild, the way I've always known her to be.

This is the Lemon I love, so I tell her.

You never know when you won't get to say that to someone again.

"I love you, Lemon Perkins."

She sighs, but it's relief in her eyes, not disdain.

Not mistrust.

I see only reflected love, and I wrap my tongue around hers, teasing the moans and whimpers from within when I bite and suck on her bottom lip.

Her neck.

Then her chest.

I feed each nipple into my mouth, until I'm alternating between the two, her flesh pressed together, the hard peaks, a delicacy in my mouth. Moans and curses break free, and I slide my hand back down, palming my shaft that's growing harder and heavier each time her bare pussy presses into my thigh.

I frown at my cock, a first for me. But with how tight she was around my fingers, I suddenly worry she might not be wet enough for more.

Lemon's eyes sparkle as her body remains pinned beneath me. Her head is just inches from my hard on. "Do you want me to spit on it?" She bites her lip then adds breathlessly, "Oliver."

"*Jesus,*" is all I get out before she does just that.

She sucks and twists, feeding my cock into her mouth, encouraging my thrusts, praising me between mouthfuls, and lapping until I'm not sure if she's the one in control or me.

I wrap my fingers through her hair to hold her head steady, and her eyes gloss with lust when I take over, screwing her face. She moans around my erection, her throat tight and tense, and the pressure threatens to break me at any moment.

But... "No!" I growl, whipping my cock from her mouth, the animalistic beast from before clawing back out of me as I force her down and lick a trail to her ear and insert a finger in her sweet, dripping cunt. "I want to be inside of this when I come."

Her eyes light when I lean her back and kiss her center before I position myself at the entrance.

"Before we do this," I say, "I may have loved other women before you, but I haven't done this with anyone but...her."

Lemon's eyes gloss as she draws a breath, but they don't leave mine. Not to worry, or cast judgement, or compare herself to the ghost she'll never be.

She simply slides my cock deeper.

A single thrust is all we need to join completely.

"Like I said, we're a yin yang," she whispers. "I have done this with a lot of people before you, but you're the only one I've ever loved."

# Chapter Twenty-Six

## LEMON

Oliver Love Nashville pounds the shit out of my pussy.

And I am so here for it.

His cock slams inside me, stretching me open until his tip reaches my G-spot, each thrust pushing me closer to coming apart.

He hooks my knees around his shoulder, shoving deeper until he's all the way in.

Nine inches of pleasure pounding me with years of pent-up longing.

I moan around his tongue, loving how he moves around my mouth freely, taking what he wants, marking me as his. And his beautiful blue eyes shine when he sees what he likes.

Those slutty eyes that have granted me more orgasms than I could count.

I cry his name when he lowers his head to my breasts, still thrusting deep inside me, sucking each nipple in rotation as I'm moaning, meeting his thrusting with my own and begging for more friction between us.

He flares with dominance when he moves from my nipples to my center. He flicks my hardened buds, twisting them between his fingers and thumbs as he fucks me senseless.

"You don't have a tattoo over your ass, you lying little tease," he growls, wrapping my hair around his fist to yank me tighter, but if he thinks that's punishment, he may as well spank me more.

I love this shit.

A geyser releases between my legs, as my orgasm gushes over his cock, sliding down the back of my thighs. I scream profanities surrounding his name, and his thrusts get deeper, faster, until he's fucking me clear into the dock, and I'm creaming over his monster of a goddamned cock.

"Come for me, Love," I whisper.

That's all it takes. One last thrust, and his warmth explodes inside me.

It's perfect.

Until it's not.

"You two!"

Oliver's eyes flash to life. He withdraws his body, yanking me up with him.

I search for my gown, but it's no use. We have to move. "It's a ranger," I whisper.

"A what?" Oliver shoots his hands down to cover his crotch. Per usual, it triggers my eye roll.

"He can't see your junk from over there, you old idiot. Hurry!" I drag his arm when I realize he's no better than a deer in headlights. "Let's go!"

"We're going to prison."

"Relax," I tease. "They just take you to county jail for stuff like this."

"What?"

I take delight in my non-answer as he follows me from tree to tree.

A flashlight shines in the distance, and Oliver practically shits himself. It's evident I got us into this law breaking, and I will most definitely have to be the one to get us out.

"Don't make a sound and crouch behind this boulder until I say, got it?"

He nods, eyes wide and clearly terrified, but he trusts me, and I'm proud of that. He needs this kind of freedom I offer. Tonight, we'll go back...home...and he'll be Dad again, and I'll be...

Whatever it is we're deciding here, I suppose.

Either way, he doesn't need a visit to the Pine Forest precinct derailing our progress. I mean, Sheriff Percy's got some fun stories and all, but my partner in crime definitely can't handle that.

The ranger's light flits down the trail on the same route to the car. "We need a diversion," I whisper, crawling through the bushes to grab a rock.

"What are you doing? He'll hear you!"

"I'm gonna throw him off our trail. I saw this on TV."

"Yep. We're going to jail."

"Would you calm down, Nash? It's a diversion tactic."

"You only call me Nash when you're annoyed."

"That should be telling right now." I shush him. "Now lower your voice before Ranger Danger over there sees us."

My bracelets clank against my wrist when I chuck the rock through the air, bringing me luck, I hope, as it sails past the stoutly uniformed man. It lands in the woods with a loud rustle, and the flashlight glow immediately changes direction.

"As seen on TV." I curtsy.

"Well, now what? Got any sitcoms for when he turns back because he doesn't find two naked people within reasonable distance?"

"And what is the most reasonable distance for two naked people?" I snort, peeking back over the boulder.

He scowls, over my games tonight, I gather.

It's fair. He's worried.

It's not the same as me getting caught.

He's got kids.

My stomach unsettles with the sudden weight of this. That my little 'bending of the law' skinny dip in the river could easily be a dirty smudge on some parenting record in the eyes of a social worker.

A strike for this single father of four, who relies on rules and reason to guide him.

Is this how it will feel if we're together? Responsibilities weighing me down like a brick in my gut? People who depend on me not to fail but always doing just that?

*And what if I do?*

"I think he's gone," Oliver whispers.

I faintly hear him, but in the two seconds since he didn't laugh at my joke, I've gone to a place in my mind I'm not sure how to escape.

"You okay? Lem?""Yeah," I lie. "Let's make a run for it when I say go. I've got you, too." I repeat the words he professed when he held me in his arms and we floated beneath the stars. "Go!"

We run between trees, and the rustling beneath our feet is louder than the wind. Normally, I don't give a damn about being quiet, but nothing about this date has been normal.

If we're caught, it will be my fault.

Oliver will suffer because of me.

A reckless daughter and an even worse nanny.

And here I am, supposed to be helping this man raise his children, and I'm ruining his reputation instead, encouraging him to break laws and make messes.

"I'm sorry, Oliver." Sticks and leaves stab the bottom of my feet. This is when adrenaline should kick in, but all I feel is fear that at any moment, this thing we've started could come crashing down from the sky, falling to pieces, all because of me.

"Don't be," he yells back. We share a look of apprehension as the flashlight rounds the corner, and he smiles through his nerves. "You gave me an adventure, Lemon Perkins. You make me live."

I hop over the chain, scraping my knee. I hiss at the pain, but I don't care, as long as we make it out of this together.

"Hurry! He's coming." I open the door to the Mustang and start the engine. The car roars to life, matching the fear I feel in my soul. "Come on. Come on!" I shout to Oliver as he hurdles over the chain. He slings his body around the trail head, diving headfirst into my car at the very last second.

The park ranger races to the entrance. His light streaks the sky as he waves his hands in the air. "You two! Come back or—"

Oliver slams the door, and we catch our breath, watching the ranger do the same in the rear as we zoom away.

"We did it?"

"We did." I grin, hands still tight to the steering wheel. "I've never been surer I was going to get caught in my life," I admit.

"You said we'd be fine. You said trust you!"

"And you did. And we are."

"Barely."

His complaints fall flat when he smiles and the crow's feet I find so endearing crinkle proudly.

We laugh together for what feels like minutes, until my abs engage, and our stomachs threaten to burst.

"You should have seen yourself back there." He whistles. "The way your naked butt bounces when you run barefoot...it's something to watch." His eyes on my body heat it right back up. "You should add it to your workout routine at home. I might just watch."

There's the word again.

*Home.*

I'm still not certain how I feel about it.

"Whatever," I change the subject. "I looked hotter than Paul Blart back there."

"Can you imagine what he tells his co-workers tomorrow?"

"We made him a hero." I snort. "Haven't you heard? He saved a couple of unsuspecting nudists from the dreaded parasites of Pine Forest."

"Brat."

His smile tugs at my heart. I wish I could keep it at the front of my mind, but when I peer past it, my stomach drops, and I screech to a stop.

"Get dressed!"

"Easy, Lem. I was joking."

"Yeah, and for once, I'm *not* joking!" Without another word, I throw his Victorian pants in his face and shove the ugly shirt that came with them onto my own body.

It barely hits the top of my thighs, but it's all we have. I sigh when I see a Naked Oliver still sitting next to me, with a highly distracting cock slung across his thigh. "Get the damn pants on, Oliver!"

I slap his face toward the contact station ahead and point out the angry man, coming straight for us.

"Is that..."

I nod.

"Papa."

# Chapter Twenty-Seven

## LEMON

"*Quatsch!* This has no explanation, Zitrone!" My father, with power, wealth, and privilege, silences me, lip curling in outrage as he notes our clothes.

Or lack thereof.

I bite back the joke on the tip of my tongue, because I wasn't kidding when I warned Oliver.

Father is outraged.

"Sir, if I may—"

"You may not!"

It pains me to watch him crumble under my father's boots. It's not his fault he's in this, very under clothed, situation. It's mine.

I'll accept that.

But Papa doesn't know the whole story.

And he doesn't know about us.

"Please, Papa. Don't be angry with him for what I've gotten us into." I stand taller, pushing off the car and using nothing but my own legs to support myself when I face him.

He'll settle for nothing less.

"It's not Oliver's fault we're in this predicament." I toy with my bangles, noting his familiar scowl of annoyance flick there, so I drop my arm to my side and clear my throat. "If you'll give me a chance to explain—"

He cuts me off.

My shoulders drop with his eyes. I know from experience that was my one shot. He will hear nothing more, Emil Perkins, the all-powerful Alpha and Omega of opinions.

And my life.

"*Oliver*, is it?" His eyes shoot to the man in question. The one standing beside me, shaking in his goddamned half-a-suit. His pants aren't buttoned, and he hasn't got a shirt, since it's the only thing that covers me.

Papa's eyes gloss.

And that cuts Oliver Nashville deeper than any words ever could.

My father's disappointment wounds him.

"I trusted you, Oliver. You keep my daughter safe. Is this safe to you?" He gestures down my body at the *Risky Business* cosplay and shame heats me all over.

I cross my arms over my chest. I want to run.

Find a new adventure.

"I needed both of you tonight. My right-hand man and my daughter. Not because you are my right-hand man or my daughter, but because you are the future of this company. The two of you."

"What?" I flick my eyes to Oliver, who seems as stumped as me.

"I want to be free, Zitrone. Sylvie and me. He holds up his hand and a golden band wraps around his left finger. "We are to make it official soon. I..." His eyes drop.

He can't even look at me.

I disgust him.

"I wanted to share this moment with you tonight. With Sylvie."

The woman of the hour emerges from the car. I wish I could say I hate her and don't trust her, but I know Papa. She'll have signed a prenup.

Plus, I read that note about her 'inbox.'

Her eyes seem kinder than I remember as a teen, and people change, like Oliver and I.

"I'm happy for you, Papa...Sylvie."

But he cuts me off again. Sylvie holds a hand up, urging him to let me speak, but he'll have none of it.

"If you were happy for us, Zitrone, you would end the charades like this one. I track your stolen car here, thinking you are dead or worse. And you are off skinny dipping in the woods like your mother!"

His words sting, but I won't let them needle deeper than the surface. I reserve the right to be proud of this side of me. Flaws and all. So, I let his hurtful words roll into the dirt where they belong, back to earth from whence they motherfucking came.

My silence breaks him, and he fills it with more words aimed at cutting.

I can take them, though.

I will take them.

I will hold them in my pocket and collect them like a bunch of fucking charms, and when there are enough of them, I will dump them out and wear them on my arms, too.

Reminders of what I never want to become.

"There was a lot of talent at the banquet tonight, and you were there to scout none of it. You say you want me to take you seriously in this company? Well, this was your test, and you blew it, *Tochter*. And what's worse is you've corrupted my friend." He whips his heated eyes to Oliver and lets those words burn in the air. "You roped him into your childish schemes. He has a family, Zitrone! He cannot be careless like you."

I wait for Oliver to speak.

Blinking into the air.

Begging.

"Do you have no opinion, then?"

My heart drops to the pit of my stomach when it seems he doesn't. I'd suppose not, now that he's just learned he's the face of the fucking future.

I sniffle, tears on the brink of escape, but not in front of these two. "I'm sorry, Oliver. I'm sorry I've roped you into my wanton ways, lured you into my debaucherous lair with my sexual schemes and ideas of grandeur."

"Lem, stop. That's not..." He turns to my father, and I hold my breath. "Sir, I—"

"Save it. I know what's happened here. I'll make arrangements for her to stay elsewhere, starting next week. Better for the both of you."

"Sir, I don't think that's necessary."

"Yes, Oliver!" he snaps. *"Das ist es."*

"Lem," Oliver pleads before I walk away. "My job...and the girls. This isn't what I wanted."

"You don't know what you want, Nash." The pesky tear finally rolls down my cheek.

I don't wipe it.

I need him to see that I'm real.

"This is how you let yourself feel. Out loud, and in person, and for the whole fucking world to see, Nash. And *you*." I shake my head at my father. "You are so quick to judge that you don't even take the time to trust."

"I've trusted. Trust is what got me into this, Zitrone. Trust in you, and trust in him."

"Oliver is not the problem, Papa! Look at yourself. *Du bist das Problem!* People come to you with innovative ideas, and you chase them off, like the only way things can get done is if a bunch of old men in stuffy suits throw their dicks around about it! *Feigling!*" I seethe. "You are terrified of change."

"Watch your language, *Tochter!*"

"*Nein!* I will watch nothing. You will watch. You think you know everything, but you only know what you see with your own two eyes. You never feel with your heart, because you're scared it'll break all over again. This thing with her…" I point to Sylvie, who stands by his side. I can see from the outside she cares for him. Because she fucking feels something.

Not like these two. And I'm done being their handy dandy guide to trauma.

"This is your chance to feel something again, Papa. Because for the last few decades, you've boxed it up, only saw the good and fought for the best. But look at the other stuff, the raw parts of life, too." I gesture to my clothes. "Sometimes life doesn't let you stay in the goddamned box."

I storm to my car and whip out the napkin, chucking it forward, and letting it sail down to my father's feet in the dirt.

All eyes fall there immediately.

"My box was meant to be bigger than you planned today. *Das ist Schicksal!*" I spit. "Fate."

"Miss Tryst's signature?"

"I know my worth, *Vater*." I turn to Oliver. "I thought you knew it, too." I straighten my shirt and lift my chin. "I don't need to stick around while the two of you learn that those things you shove into boxes, power the same parts of you that could achieve your wildest dreams, as terrifying or painful as they may be. Feelings can change the world for you. What a privilege to be a man." I let out a confident exhale and look my father in the eye, once and for all. "You can leave your company to some other rich suit, if that's the future of Perkins Global, because I will never sit still, nor will I follow the rules. I'm done trying to reshape your molds."

# Chapter Twenty-Eight

## OLIVER

*F*uck.

For someone who rarely swears, my brain is doing a whole damn lot of it tonight.

I hit my head against the shower wall to accompany the fucks that have taken over it and let the water scald me in penance.

How could I not have defended her?

I froze.

I love Lemon, but my girls are my entire world, and her father has the power to disrupt everything they know with the snap of his fingers.

What's worse is I saw myself in that moment.

Is that how I am with Bry? Lashing out and demanding obedience without letting her get a word in? Without listening to her side of the story?

I rode back with Mr. Perkins and his fiancée. Lemon didn't exactly leave me a choice, speeding off in her Mustang with half my clothes and my phone.

It gave me time to set the record straight with her father. I explained Shaylyn's tire problems, how calm and collected Lem was in the moment, even saw his eyes light with pride when I told him about the roadside concussion screening and subsequent vomit.

"So, this is the reason for the missing clothes and the swimming in the river? You were...getting clean?"

My stomach dropped when he asked that question, and it's all I could do not to stumble over my lie of an answer.

"Of course."

I've saved my job, secured my daughters' futures, and gotten Emil off her back with two short words, yet somehow it feels like the beginning of the end.

I bow my head and try to pray, but all I see are her eyes and the tears I put there.

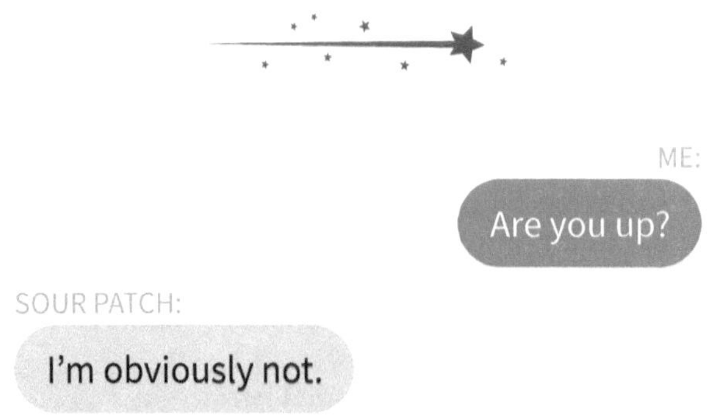



*B*rat.

I smile that she hasn't shut me out completely, and I prop myself against the headrest. I don't even know where to begin with this.

…Everything?

Several minutes go by while my texting dots blink empty promises.



That's what I thought.

S ix thousand sheep and twelve reps of pushups later, and I'm still staring at the inside of my eyelids, waiting for sleep to take me.

It does not.

At 2:33 in the morning. I flick my fingers through the blinds, drawn to the brightness that pours through the slats. The sky is dark, barely a sliver of moon, so it's the stars lighting the sky, sparkling even in the darkest night.

And now I'm thinking about Lemon.

Those are just things Lemon is.

*Ice cream.* I rise from the bed.

I'll sugar-crash at the very least. Or maybe I won't sleep at all after what we did tonight.

Broke laws. Got messy. Won bets.

*We lived.*

What would Lauren say to me now?

I wonder what she'd think about the man she fell in love with, the careful musical major with a promising future. The one who planned to open his own studio and play for the world. The one who wanted to be a loving father who provided his children with everything, even if he had to scrape the ground to obtain it.

The one who got on one knee to promise her the world and cried on those very same knees to a God who ripped her away when he was barely a whole man.

"You'd tell me to fix this, Lo. To stop being so *me*." I stab the metal spoon into the center of the carton and dig out the biggest hunk of cookie dough I can manage, then I shovel it into my mouth. "Lemon's probably thinking that, too," I mumble around the frozen mouthful. I swallow, letting the cold burn my esophagus so I can fucking *feel something,* as she says.

But I feel plenty.

I feel happy, proud, and hopeful one day, and terrified of those same feelings the next. Happiness means you can be sad. Pride allows for being humbled. And hope...

It died with my wife.

"You hear that, God? I stopped hoping, because she stopped living. How the hell am I supposed to hope and live and dream when those things are what cause the most pain?"

"You just grow a pair of ovaries and deal with it."

"Lem." I shove off my stool, but she stops me.

"Pain is life, Oliver. You should know that by now. But life is more than that. Look at me. Is there more to me than meets the eye?"

*Of course.* I struggle to say the same words I used as a lie to her father. I need to tell her what I said.

"Well, is there?" she hisses. "Answer me. Is there more than meets the eye?"

"Yes!"

"Pain only wins if you let it. You'll feel it whether you decide to or not. So be more than meets the eye, Oliver. Dare to live how you want regardless of the pain. Despite the consequences. Bend them to fit your life, like rules, choose what you want and fuck the rest."

"I choose you, Lem." My voice cracks. "I do. What we said in the river, what we did...it's real, and I want it, and I choose you."

"But you didn't." She swipes the ice cream from the counter. "You didn't choose me." Stepping into the light, she licks the spoon clean, eyeing me as she tongues the metal. "You didn't choose this." She runs the spoon down her chin, neck, and then I see it.

"Is that a Darkpath shirt?" I move closer, but as my jaw tightens, her eyes blaze.

"Oh, this old thing? She fingers the hem, drawing it up to the tops of her thighs. "Could be anyone's." She closes the distance between us, turning and pressing her ass against my erection.

And yes, I'm fucking hard for it, because she knows every one of my buttons to push. Including...

"Does it bother you that it's touching my bare skin? Skin that should be yours?"

My hands find her hips and fist the fabric. She grinds against my cock, punishing me with my own desire and taunting me with the reminder she could be with anyone she wanted right now, even an entire band, but she chose me.

And I didn't do the same.

"Makes me want to rip it off you," I hiss.

"Why?" she breathes. "Say it."

"Because you're mine." I finger the hem, brushing my fingers over the bare flesh beneath, but she shoves me away.

"No, not yours, Oliver."

My forehead pinches. "What about the river? What we both said. Your father understands about Shaylyn."

"How stupid can you be, Nash? Jesus Christ, you're a whole lifetime older than me and you can't even do simple fucking math. You say you want me, but when the time came to claim me, where was that same desire? Does my father know of our relationship, or does he still think I'm your nanny, and you're some persuadable older man who couldn't keep his dick dry around the boss's daughter?"

I drop my head.

"You didn't accept the title when my father was dangling the question in your face, and you didn't correct him when he assumed I was no better than some coochie casting succubus luring you to my womb."

"Womb?" I flick my eyes to her stomach, and my cock suddenly aches to fill it.

"Don't you dare think about it." She seethes. "No kinky stuff for you until you wake the fuck up."

"Lem, I'm sorry. I didn't realize—"

"You didn't realize anything, Oliver. That is the problem here. So, if you want me? If you really, truly want me like you say, you need to realize all the shit and then come back to this conversation once you have."

I swallow my words.

"Now, I'm still going on that camping trip tomorrow, because I promised your girls I would, and I do not break my promises, do you hear me? It has nothing at all to do with my uncontrollable feelings for you, or the ache I feel between my goddamned legs from the thrust of your gargantuan fucking cock."

She storms up the steps before I can respond, and she takes the ice cream with her.

# Chapter Twenty-Nine

## LEMON

"She's touching me again!" Bryar snaps.

"Ow!" Poppy shoves back. "I wouldn't touch you if you would just move your arm two centimeters to the right, but you're being selfish."

"You wouldn't need two extra centimeters if you would stop scribbling in that notebook and look up at the world."

"Maybe the world has too many bratty older sisters who think they're God's gift to humanity in it, and I'd rather sketch a better one."

"Dad!"

"Snacks anyone?" Oliver opens the glove compartment when all I can offer him in support is a look of pure shock. Over-stimulation is an understatement. All four of these girls in one car for hours on end?

This is going to be a long ride.

But then...silence.

"Thanks, Daddy." Cami sighs happily, chewing her granola bar. "Me and Kimmie's bellies were talking to each other they were so grumbly."

"You're welcome, Two-Bits." Oliver smiles, watching them from the rearview mirror. A sense of happiness warms my heart as I watch them, too.

"That was a neat trick," I offer. The first words I've spoken to him since last night.

"Thanks. One learns over time."

"I suppose one does."

We travel in silence for minutes on end while the girls' mouths are busy filling their bellies. We left just before sunrise, and finally, the light peeks its way above the mountain, pinks and reds, orange and purple, and every other color of life radiating from one common point.

It's beautiful.

"Are you crying?" Oliver whispers, nudging me with his hand.

I grab it.

"No."

"Liar." He flicks on the radio with our palms still joined and fingers twined. It's a step from last night. One to show him I'm still in this. I just need him to be, too.

My mouth wants to smile. My brain practically commands it, but my heart trembles so fast I can't ignore the warning.

Violin music plays from the speakers, a classical station, and I feel his fingers tap the back of my hand. "You make me want to play a song," he says softly.

We share a secret smile.

"Then play."

"Change the station, Dad," Bryar groans, slicing through the sentiment. *Kids.* We share a laugh about it as Oliver winks to the girls in the rearview and blasts the volume even higher.

"Daaaaddduuuh! You always make us listen to this boring orchestra stuff."

"It's good for your character," I say, whipping around in my seat. "And it is not boring, Bryar Elaine. It's classical." I wink at her and Poppy before turning back around in my seat, and they giggle at my dad impression as Oliver rolls his eyes.

"Fine," he concedes. "What'll it be?"

"Rock," Poppy calls.

"Boo! Country!" Cami yells. "We want country."

"Great." Bryar turns around. "We all want different stations, so Dad's just gonna put it back on his old man music like last time we couldn't pick. Nice going, Twinnie the Poo."

"Nuh uh!" Cami sticks out her tongue, crossing her arms over her chest. "Kimmie wants country, too, so that's two against you. We're the majority."

"You don't even know what that word means."

"Do to. We learned in social studies."

"Dad," Bryar whines, "tell her it doesn't count. She always just makes up Kimmie's vote, anyway. Kim, do you want country? Sign yes if you do."

Kimmie just purses her lips at Cami.

"Fine." Cami rolls her eyes at her twin. "Kimmie says she doesn't care."

"What about we sing a song?" I offer, totally out of my element with the parent thing. But Oliver is calm and collected, like he is on tour. This is his thing, being prepared and reliable.

It's why my spontaneity throws him off.

The kids laugh at my song idea, but Oliver's got it covered, like everything else today.

"How about the newest Shaylyn Tryst track?"

He holds up his phone, and the car blows into a million pieces.

Just kidding.

It doesn't blow up. But the screams are almost glass-shattering.

"How?" Poppy gasps.

"It's not supposed to be out until next month!" Cami squeals.

"Let's just say your nanny here is a very persuasive businesswoman. She signed Shaylyn Tryst to Perkins Records last night, and her sound designer sent us these sample tracks this morning. It's not the final version, though. You guys probably won't like it..." He grins.

"*Dad*!" they collectively scream while I giggle profusely.

We laugh as one, even Kimmie.

It feels...

"Happy," a small voice says from the back.

We all pause, sharing a single thread of energy, feeling the same miracle fall as light as a feather.

"Yeah." Cami sniffles from her side, a wide grin and soft tears falling from her tiny eyes. "Me, too, Kim." She signs something to her sister, and they link pinkies. "Happy."

"Happy!" Bryar shouts through her tears.

"Happy!" we all shout.

A tear rolls down Oliver's cheek, too, and when he squeezes my hand, despite my trembling heart, I squeeze it back.

*Happy.*

# Chapter Thirty

## OLIVER

Today was nothing I could have imagined.

Kimmie *spoke.*

My youngest daughter, who rarely chooses to sign, let alone speak, has been laughing, smiling, and emoting more than ever before. For the first time in her life, her twin isn't the only one who can tell what she's thinking.

I watch her by the fire now. A glowing pink haze highlights the freckles across her nose, the ones that match Cami's identically, and my breath catches.

I can barely tell them apart like this.

"Are you crying, Oliver?" Lemon whispers. Leaves crunch behind me as she rounds the side of our tent. "Is that why you're hiding?"

"I'm not hiding."

"But you're crying?"

"I'm gonna get you a little necklace that says, Brat."

"Kinky." She winks.

I tickle her to my lap, and we watch the kids together by the fire. The sparks flicker to the sky, and I watch those sail to the stars, too.

I wonder if Lauren can see this, all of this.

Can she hear that Kimmie talked?

But I realize now, as I look at the stars and the moon and the great expanse of everything around us, that she's part of it all. She's in the girls, every which way, and I'm believing more each day that she's the angel who guided me to the answers I've been praying for.

To Lemon, bringing me back to life one adventure at a time.

"I used to be able to tell the twins apart easily," I say. "But can you tell the difference when they smile like that? When it's not just one set of eyes shining back?"

"No." She grins. "I can't."

"Yeah." My heart swells. "They're growing up quickly. Before I know it, they'll be pissed at me every day of the week like Bryar or stuck so far in their headphones like Poppy that I'll never get a moment in unless I flag them down."

"You'll definitely have to flag them down because I'm teaching those little ladies to rollerskate. It's about time they had a way to ditch you properly when you start getting how you do."

"Hey!"

"Maybe Bryar wouldn't be so mad if you gave her freedom. Trust her once in a while."

"I do trust her."

"Yeah, and you sound like Papa again. You give her as much trust as you do the twins. She's going to start high school in a few short months, and you better believe she'll be faced with choices and situations outside of your control. She's a beautiful girl in a small town. She has every option ahead of her, whether you want it or not. She has your spirit."

"But sleepaway cheer camp? After the sneaking out and terrorizing her last five nannies?"

"Give her respect, and she will learn how to give it back. You don't understand girls at all."

"Nope." I cock my head at the four huddled around the fire. "But I sure do have a lot of them."

She laughs at my joke.

Loves me, even when she says she's mad.

And I want to apologize for not coming clean to her father. I had a chance to tell him how I feel, ask for his blessing... Hell, I should have begged him. Anything but what I did, which was nothing at all.

Like she's unimportant.

Temporary...

"I'm sorry, Lem. I should have told your father we—"

Her phone buzzes, shattering the silence of the forest, and we break away.

Bryar twists her body and skips to the log when she sees us. "Come dance with us, Dad!"

"Yeah, Daddy. Come on!"

I glance at Lemon, scanning a text on her phone with a worried look on her face, but before I can address it, her eyes soften to mine.

"Go ahead, *Daddy*." She winks, setting her phone on the log. "I have to pee. I'll be right back."

It's when she disappears behind the trees that I see the screen she still leaves unlocked.

TINA:

I mean he's one spicy silver fox, sure but you need to be single for this show. The end game is a couple falling in LOVE on the mountain.

TINA:

Are you sure you're still up for this?

TINA:

Tell me by Tuesday night. They lock us into the contract if you don't.

It's been left on read. She's seen this news.

And she did not reply.

The first message was sent on Saturday, and it's Monday night.

"Dad! Come on."

I leave the phone where I found it and dance with my girls.

*Single,* Tina said.

Love.

Is she still up for that?

And if she is, what are we?

"What'd I miss?" Lemon emerges from the bushes. "That's where this is." She plucks her phone from the log and shoves it into her pocket without another glance.

She doesn't text Tina.

"Why should you care?" I find myself snapping beneath my breath. "You'll be getting plenty of camping experiences soon, won't you? This will just be one in a bracelet of many."

*I will be one of your flings,* I say with my eyes.

Does she hear it?

Since seeing those texts, all I hear is I'm not a permanent person.

"What are you talking about, Oliver? We were just fine."

But I'm angry because I want her, not because I don't. How do I say that after all I failed to profess to her father? This is Lemon, crawling beneath my skin at every turn, digging and frolicking and blowing violently like a string-cut kite on the wind. "Get a lock screen for your phone," is all I manage.

I stomp to the bathhouse, my heart pounding so heavily in my chest, it might crack my ribs open and part with my body altogether. Right here in this goddamned forest where I only camp for the girls.

So they'll have a piece of Lauren in these woods.

I can't lose her, too.

"Oliver Love Nashville!" she snaps from behind me. "How dare you invade my privacy again and assume things? You stormed out of there like a child. Even the twins were baffled by your behavior."

"Well, these are my feelings, Lem. You wanted me to learn to show them? Here they are." I grind through my teeth.

"Fine. Do this, then." She exhales. "Let it out. Say it all right here, so we can get on with it and figure this shit out."

"This shit?" I balk. "This shit is my life. My family. My fucking *daughters*...don't you see that? You aren't just toying with my heart when you throw the cards in the air. You're playing with theirs, too."

She pulls back, brow pinched, as if I've just now opened her eyes to that fact.

Maybe it's new to her, but it's one of the hardest parts of letting myself love again.

Having children is constant fear.

"They love you, Sour Patch." My breath comes out ragged. "*I* love you."

"And I love *you*, but—"

"But nothing. You love us or you leave us, Lemon. There is no in between. Twist your adventures around my heart, but don't you dare play with theirs."

"So, what you're saying is you don't trust me?" Her nostrils flare, eyes narrowing to wear mine down.

She doesn't know they're already half defeated by the thought of her being gone.

"I'm not saying I don't trust you."

"But you are. Just like Bry and cheer camp. You don't trust that she will behave herself there any more than you trust I'd make the right decision for our relationship if given the chance. You assume. And you're always right when you've made up your mind. Just like him."

"Don't make this about your father, Lemon, please. This is about us."

"And so is he," she groans. "You want me to tell Tina I'm not going on that show so bad? Tell Papa you love me. Tell him you fucked me right there in that river with the parasites and all. Made me yours in mind, body, and soul, and then tell him you'd do it again, even if he said not to. Even if his money never crossed your fingers."

I freeze, our eyes locked for what feels like eons, until they break with the silence.

"Right, then." She pulls a hammock from her backpack and ties it between two trees by the tent. "I'll be sleeping here tonight." She climbs in and turns away. "Enjoy your tent."

T ent is right.

Not just in the physical sense.

I tossed and turned in my sleeping bag for what felt like hours. My phone's been dead for two, and I won't get a chance to charge it in the car until tomorrow, so I can't pass the time on that.

I fell asleep twice, but the first time I woke to a dream I was being chased, and all I could think was getting back to Lemon and the girls in one piece.

Sounds insane considering three weeks ago she was the promiscuous star of the tour bus and an ever-present splinter beneath my skin.

But she's always been an adventure.

Funny she searches for them like she needs them to breathe, yet her entire existence is a wild storm to me.

The second time I woke, I dreamed of her again. But this one had me stroking my own damn cock in my sleep, and that brings me to the tent in my sweatpants.

I unzip the real tent and peek at her, asleep in the hammock with one leg dangling over the side.

Am I afraid to tell her father about us for fear of my job? For the sake of the girls?

Or is she right...am I afraid to trust?

The moon's as wide awake as I am, lighting the gravel trail that connects the campsites. A walk might suit me, so I head down the path where sticks and pine needles crunch beneath my feet.

I'm lost in thoughts of the fight with Lemon, stuck in that spot in front of her father, screaming at myself to tell him I love her. If I could go back in time, and…

"Dad!"

"Bryar?"

"You'll never guess who I ran into at the bathhouse."

"What are you doing up this late?" I look around suspiciously. Or is that mistrust? The wind blows against my arms and forces my hair to stand on ends.

Lemon's right.

"I was peeing. What are you doing on the trail that leads to the place where everyone pees, Dad? Can't you give me a break for once?"

"Sorry, Bry. I didn't mean to accuse you. I'm working on that."

"Okay." She scrunches her nose, joining me on my walk. "I know you and Lemon had a fight. Are you guys, like…a thing?"

My eyes drop to the ground, and she pats my arm. "Were you?"

"Ouch, Bry. Too soon."

We walk to a bench and sit against the river breeze. This one was built by Troop 284. "Neat." I point to the plaque. "Remember when you did Girl Scouts?"

"Brownies." She squeezes my hand with a cheesy grin. "I hated every second of it, but…" She beams. "Mom was so proud, wasn't she?"

God, the way I laughed at Lauren in the front row, snapping pictures of a tiny Bryar earning patches pinned to a vest that swallowed her whole. You couldn't see her legs beneath the length of the pleated skirt.

"You were such a little kid." My eyes water. "You're a young woman, now."

"Ew, stop." She swats my arm and rests her head on my shoulder.

My baby girl, not too grown after all.

"Thanks for not freaking out when I mentioned Mom." Bryar sighs. "It's been a long time since I could talk about her freely. It feels less lonely this way."

"I never meant to make you feel alone. You or your sisters." I look my daughter in the eyes. They shine, just like her mother's.

Lauren's legacy—*her past*—lives on in our children.

But it's time to look to the future, and when I do, the eyes I see are other-worldly violet.

"Lemon probably didn't mean to make you feel alone, either," Bryar says. "With the hammock. She's great, Dad," she gushes. "She helps me with stuff you just don't get sometimes, and the twins...*Kimmie*, Dad. I don't know why you're fighting, but I know she looks at you the way I hope I look at someone one day."

I could cry, but it's not her blessing that's got me choked up, it's the wisdom. My baby girl is so much more than I give her credit for.

"I appreciate your vote of confidence, sweetheart, but it's...complicated."

"No, it's not. I think she could be your one."

"I had my one." I throw a stone at the woods.

She grabs a stone of her own and chucks it the same direction, turning her not-so-tiny face to mine. "Who says you don't get another?"

"That doesn't even make sense, kiddo. It's one."

She laughs, nudging me so hard she almost shoves me off the bench. "Logic doesn't matter when there's magic, Dad."

"Magic, huh?"

I'm glad she still believes in it.

"Remember what Mom used to say?" She wags her finger, looking so much like her mother, I almost see her there. "There's no such thing as—"

"Coincidence," I finish, meeting her eyes. "But it's not that easy, Bry. She has to want to stay. What if she decides there's something more out there?" I gesture to the open forest.

"Then I guess we'll all be sad. I've been sad before, real sad. Haven't you?"

*Wow.*

"In cheer, we call that a bail, stopping mid-trick to avoid injury." She grins like the moon. "But wouldn't it be sick if you stick the landing?"

I don't know how long we sit in the dark, but when I crawl in my tent and my head hits the ground, I finally fall asleep.

# Chapter Thirty-One

## LEMON

Piece of crap, three-dollar, monstrosity!

I twist myself silly in the unbearably snug hammock, rearranging my limbs until I'm tumbling from the sheath and ripping it off the trees altogether.

"Stupid fucking flash sale."

And it's not just the hammock. I'm angry and hungry, because I was not about to eat that fish we caught, what with all the parasites in the water...

I also hate fish.

Blah.

I hate it even more than him.

*Oliver.*

I practically sigh his name into the wind, pining at the moon like the damsel in every movie I pretend not to love, hopeless.

And then there's Tina. She keeps buzzing my phone. It's only got about fifteen percent battery, thank fuck, because then she can't ask me for the trillionth time if I'm doing the show.

I'm not. I made up my mind in the river.

But every time I try to type that sentence, a brick weighs down my entire arm and I'm back to shoving the phone away for another day.

What if this is my last chance for adventure?

What if I say no, and I miss out on destiny?

*But what if destiny is here?*

Does having the choice even make it destiny?

*Ugh!* I can't breathe.

I slide open my speed dial tab and hit the first contact, fanning myself with my shirt collar.

"Hi, Papa," I crack.

"Zitrone? *Bist du in Sicherheit?* What is this?"

"Papa, I'm fine!" I sigh. "Everything's fine. I'm just...I can't sleep."

I hear Sylvia mutter something soft in the background, and he whispers back to her, "No, it is okay. It is Lemon. Go back to bed, my sweet."

"Gagging internally," I tease him. "My sweet."

"Oh, hush. You call me at four in the morning and expect me to be alone in bed? I am not such the old man you thought." He chuckles, and yeah, it's my papa, and it's gross and all, but I'm genuinely happy he's got someone to fall asleep beside. That he's moved on from the pain of my mother, or he's starting to.

Maybe you never really move on from pain, like with Mom or Randall. You always feel the connection, but it isn't so painful.

Not anymore.

"Do you really think I'll make a good CEO?" I ask.

He grumbles, and I can hear him readjusting to the squeaky leather sofa of his office. "Did you call me to ask this at four in the morning?"

"No," I admit. "It's...it's Oliver, Papa."

"Olly? What is wrong? At the campground? I'll send a car."

"No, he's fine, Papa. That's the problem. He's fine. He's perfect and kind and responsible and smug, and he labels his leftovers and makes adorable faces when I switch up the sticky notes to fuck with him."

"Leftovers?"

"Papa, I love him."

A long stretch of silence follows.

Footsteps sound on the line.

Liquor pours in the background.

And when I finally hear the squeak of his sofa again, he speaks. "Zitrone, you are a beautiful young woman."

"Papa, ew, that's not what this is."

"But he is an older man, is what I mean. Not my age, no, but he has a family." He pauses, choosing his words carefully. "Is it possible you just think he wants more?"

"No!" I snap, silencing the very thought. "It's not possible, Papa. He loves me, too. He's just too afraid to tell you. Scared for his job, or because he thinks I'll just leave him like the others...I don't know."

"Won't you?" Papa asks. "Leave him like you have left the others? I know about the mountain show. The one where you are to appear naked and survive on what? Nuts and berries?"

"That's the other part of why I can't sleep."

"Are you going to do it?"

"I don't know," I say honestly. "I wanted to at the start of this summer, but then—"

"You fell in love."

"Yeah."

"It hurts, *oder?* Love." He hums into the phone, and I know what he's doing. He's rolling both rings in his palm, one from Sylvie on his finger, and the other around his neck, my mother's.

I noticed it there when he caught us at the park.

"Does it hurt you?"

"Every time, every day, my Lemondrop. But ask yourself a question. When have you ever turned your back on an adventure before?"

*No.*

That isn't where he's supposed to steer me.

"You're supposed to convince me that love is worth everything or some shit like that, but you're saying I should go on the adventure? Choose the mountain?"

"I'm saying you need to choose the adventure you wish to take. They don't always look how we think, Zitrone. When I met your mother, I never could have imagined one kiss would lead me to this country, to Perkins Global, or to fathering you, my biggest adventure. And my proudest."

"Stop," I tease. "We all know your company is your pride and joy, not your mess of a daughter."

"Like I say, adventures can sometimes be hidden right in our own home. Ask yourself one more question tonight, *Mäuschen.*"

"Shoot."

"Where is home for you? Maybe that's the answer you seek."

"Wait." I stop him before he ends the call. "Just to be clear, you're still going to let me be the CEO even if I get naked on a mountain on national TV?"

"No. *Definitiv nicht.* You choose your adventure, like I say, but *Zitrone*?"

"Yes, Papa?"

"You are my pride no matter what. *Ich dich liebe, Kind.*"

I pad barefoot back to the campsite, where my tangled and tossed hammock mocks me from downriver, the light of the moon over the water creating a spotlight for said mockery.

Not my best judgement call.

A branch crunches in the woods, and I startle, but I check the girls' tents, and our whole group is sound asleep, so I hurry into Oliver's as quietly as I can and pray I'm not eaten by a bear.

I hear a few more crunches before there's nothing but crickets and frogs humming a tune. I slow my breathing and lie beside him.

I'm more confused than before after my call with Papa.

If I go on the show, I lose Oliver and the company.
But If I stay, I lose my freedom, don't I?
For tonight, I curl around the man I love and close my
eyes, drifting to sleep to the beat of his heart.

# Chapter Thirty-Two

## LEMON

"Y ou snore." I slap my hand over Oliver's face, just as my eyes fly open. "Oliver!" I'd forgotten I'd moved to the tent. My thighs are still wrapped around his, and my head on his chest.

"Lem?"

"The one and only." I hide my face in his arm "The hammock was tangly."

"Oh? Is that all?" He tickles my sides.

"Stop it! Okay, okay." I sit on my knees and push him back down. "I also got scared a bear might eat me."

"And you needed me to keep you safe?"

"Well, I figured at the very least if it slashed through the tent, it would have a choice between you and me, and there's a lot more of you. You'd be tastier."

"Brat." He flips me over and lowers his face to the apex of my thighs. "You're tastier, I assure you that."

He blows against my center, and I want him, fuck do I want him, but wait...

I lift his chin. "We never cleared the air last night. I'm sorry for not cluing you in on my decisions about the show. What I decide for our relationship also affects your girls, and that wasn't fair of me. It's been just me for so long. I'll have to get used to that."

"So, you're staying?" He grins, moving back up my body.

"I'm staying." I kiss him. It's everything I want and need when I'm with this man.

"I was wrong, too, Lem." He shakes his head. "I was wrong not to trust you. I promise I'll—"

"*Help*! *Daddy, help*!" Cami screams through the campground, her voice somewhere downriver.

Downriver!

"Oliver, my hammock! It got snagged on the bank last night. What if she tried to get it?"

I scramble to my feet, not bothering with pants. The sleep shirt from last night will have to do.

Nothing matters more than Cami.

"I see her! Wrapped around that tree."

The hammock twists around her sandal strap, tossed and turned by the rapids threatening to tug her under.

Oliver sprints ahead, falling over his feet in haste to the river's edge, to the same tree branch that snatched up the stupid thing I should have stored in the backpack last night instead of thrown.

This is my fault.

And it could cost Cami everything.

"Daddy!" She hiccups. Water sloshes into her mouth and she coughs it up, pulling herself farther up the branch that bows beneath her weight. "Heee-eeelllp!"

"Grab my hand, Two Bits! There you go, there you…Two Bits!"

"Ahhh! Daddy!" Cami's foot slips farther down the branch. "Daddy, I'm falling!"

"Hang on!" My heart races as Oliver scrambles the bank, scanning and assessing the risks. Everything in his position at Perkins Global should have prepared him for fight or flight, yet he looks hopeless.

"I'm not small enough to get between those two branches. We could pull her in from the base and hoist her up the rocks to the bank, but—" He attempts the squeeze, but the branch cracks beneath his weight.

Bark crumbles in heavy chunks to the water below, and a horrifying thought passes between us of what could become of the little girl that holds our hearts.

His eyes turn red, tears of frustration streaming with his labored grunts. His attempts to shift his weight in any way that could save his baby. "I-I can't get to her, Lem!"

"I can." I nod. "I can jump from this ledge and land on the wider part of the base. It's rooted to the bank."

"No! Lem, it could break. You could—"

"Oliver, I could save her!"

"Ahhh! *Daddy*!"

He tenses with each scream.

"You'll be swept through the gorge if you miss."

But all I see is Cami. The loud one, the proud one, the first one to hug me, and she feels like home.

"I love a good adventure."

And then I jump.

# Chapter Thirty-Three

## LEMON

Time crashes over destiny, air assaults my skin, and tiny metal charms slap my wrists.

The gorge roars beneath me, a thirty-foot drop to raging rapids and boulders cut like glass, but nothing spikes fear more than the thought of losing one of these girls.

This is my family.

*My home.*

I choose this goddamn adventure whether it's the end of me or not, and even as I fall, my heart flies, knowing I did everything in my power to preserve it.

My body slams violently against the sideways cypress, my knees taking the force disgracefully, but nothing could slow me while Cami fights not to fall to the thunderous whitecaps beneath.

"Lemon! Lemon, help me, I can't hold it anymore!" She coughs on the water rising above her chin.

"I'm coming, Cam!"

I'm up in an instant, fuck the pain that stings my shins, or the splinters in my palms, and screw the fate that thinks it can take one more person I love without a fight.

"I got you, Cam! I'm coming."

I shimmy up the trunk. Slabs of deadwood sluff to the water below, and the farther I travel, the narrower my support beam becomes.

Distantly, I hear the man I love focusing my fears, calming my chaos. His words of encouragement easing through the brush as the branch bows beneath me.

"You can do this, Lem. Help is coming!"

We were right. I fit right through the section that traps her. "I'm through!" I yell up. "Cami, can you reach my hand?"

Her fingers brush mine, but...

*Crack!*

The branch breaks completely, and her fingers slip through mine. Everything in my body wars against my brain. What I see can't be what it is. What it is can't possibly be what I see.

Stringy brown hair wisps around a small porcelain face, peppered with freckles beneath two icy blue eyes that look like his, and all I can do is pray.

"*Why?*" I scream to the God, who takes and takes and takes from me despite everything I try to give. "Why her? *Fucking take me!*"

Oliver's sobs echo in the distance, and I can't bear the thought of him losing her after he's lost so much.

"Take me!" I launch my body from the branch and leap to the river, grabbing hold of her and wrapping her tiny body in my arms.

I will not let her go.

We fall.

Fast and hard.

Tears in our vision and blood over our skin, and we cry together. We scream and we hug, and we pray.

And just when everything feels like it could end, I'm yanked back.

Suspended in air at the end of a whiplash.

Not flying. Not falling.

Not ending this adventure before it's over.

I twist my neck and search the skies to find an orange rope wrapped around her sandal.

"The hammock…"

We dangle by the grace of God and a sparkly pink shoe. But relief is only momentary.

"My shoe! It's slipping!"

"Cam, I need you to trust me," I decide. "I'm gonna let go with one hand to grab the rope, but—"

"No! I'm scared! Lemon, don't!"

"I need to, sweetie. It's the only way, okay? Can you trust me? I'm very strong. I lift bigger weights than your dad." I offer her the best smile I can while we hang horizontally over our potential end, and I wish I could change this for her.

But that's the thing with adventures. With life… isn't it? You just never know.

"You know how Kimmie says things with her eyes?"

"Y-yes," she sobs.

"Look at my eyes, Cami."

*I've got you.*

"Okay," she whispers.

In one swift motion, I tighten my grip on Cami, wrapping my legs around her tiny body, and swing my arm up to the rope around her foot, gripping it in my palm just as her sandal strap brakes.

I twist my wrist, coil the rope around it, and squeeze Cami between my legs and other arm as tightly as I can. The rope cuts and rubs between my bracelets, bending metal and flaking charms into the water like confetti, but all I can think is *we're okay.*

"Your bracelets." Cami sniffles. "I'm sorry, Lemon. I shouldn't have tried to get the hammock by myself. I thought I could reach it. I—"

"It's okay, shh," I soothe. "You took a risk. You chose to follow your heart, and you ended up on an adventure.

Sometimes they turn out a little more than we planned. I know how that goes." I squeeze her tighter as my muscles burn. "Can I tell you something?"

"I don't have a choice while we're like this."

I laugh at that. "You're so much funnier than your dad."

My wrist burns from the circulation being cut, and two more charms split from their metal loops as the rope digs deeper into my skin, but that's what I'm trying to tell her.

"None of those charms matter, Cam. I'd toss every one of them right now to keep you safe. My whole hand, even."

"You would?"

"I would," I say. "Someone once told me you should never settle for a life you don't love with every breath. Well, you girls and your grumpy old dad are the reason for my breathing, and there's not a charm on those bracelets more important than the five of you."

**B**efore long, a fireman from the neighboring camp is sent down with a harness. He cuts my wrist from the coiled rope, and my hand immediately throbs as feeling comes back to my fingertips. "I'm Dom," he says. "I'd shake your hand, but I need to rescue you first. And your hand looks bad. We'll get it fixed up. Hold on tight." He wraps his arms around us, and we're hoisted back to the bank.

"Thank God!" Jeremy screams, scrambling past Oliver to wrap me in a bear hug. It doesn't bother me, though, not when I peer over and see the look of a miracle in Oliver's eyes as he rocks his baby girl in his arms.

"Wait, why are *you* here, Jer?"

"Excuse you!" He scoffs. "Forgive me for coming to my best friend's aid when she's dangling to her fucking death by a rope. What have I told you about leaving kink toys around? It's dangerous."

"It was a hammock rope." I swat him. "Thanks for coming to my aid, but seriously, why are you here?"

"Cheer camp," he says. "Bryar came and got me when your sugar daddy sent for help."

I snort. "Wow. How is that for fate? She wanted nothing more than to go to that camp, too."

"I heard." He smiles. "Look, we have plenty of food, and there's a special ceremony tonight. Why don't you all come and fill your bellies by the fire once the EMT dude checks you out?"

I eye the man in question. Dom, the firefighter. "He's kind of hot as fuck, right?"

"That's what I said!" He leans in. "And I have intel that he's got a serious thing for your cousin."

"The fire daddy!" I gasp.

"Mhm." He smirks. "They have been canoodling at the neighboring soccer camp we do recreation stuff with. I guess they're coaching or whatever."

"Katie, coaching a sport? In nature?"

"Right? Isn't it going to make the best story? Anyway, get your knees and hand cleaned up. You look highly unattractive, this way. I'll see you at camp."

"Bye, Jer." I shake my head as he shimmies away, and I step back into Oliver's arms.

"Sour Patch," he rumbles in my ear. It's painful and passionate, the most feelings I've ever heard him share in one sound. "Thank you."

# Chapter Thirty-Four

## LEMON

"**Y**ou'd be an okay CEO, I guess."

"You guess?" I shove him off the path. "Jerk!"

"Those were prickly plants, Lem. That hurt. My body is still raw from our morning."

I laugh out loud, brushing the prickly things off his back. "Now *that* is what she said."

"Oh, I get it." He rolls his eyes. "Even if you're not the best CEO, you'll still be hilarious to have around the office, you know? Distracting, that's for sure." He curves his lips.

"Shut up. You'll be working for me, you know. Don't forget that."

He narrows his gaze, squeezing my ass as we walk.

The girls hold hands while we follow Jeremy, Katie, and Dom to the cheer camp Bryar finally gets to attend, on a team ceremony day and all. How's that for destiny?

Kimmie hasn't left her twin's side since this morning, the once protected one turned protector. Their bond is amazing. With so few words, they say everything. They feel it in their hearts and shout it with their eyes.

Like someone else I know.

"You know," he goads, "I bet you're gonna be the first CEO in the history of all time to have a *Bone Me* tattoo on your ass."

"Very funny." I shake my head. "You've seen the proof I was joking."

"Have I?" His eyes drop to my waist. "I don't think I remember. Maybe I hit my head back there on the branches and you should jog my memory."

"My first order of business when I take over, in fact, will be to have you sign a big, fat NDA. A whole stack of them, come to think of it." I rise on my tiptoes and brush my nose against his. "You know too much. And I'm only agreeing to any sort of partnership if thirty percent of all proceeds go to the Pine Forest homeless shelter."

"I wouldn't expect anything else. And I don't mind. As you know, I'm a lousy millionaire." He boops my nose. "So, you're gonna take your father up on the offer, then? Work with me? Be the next CEO?"

I turn my head and look at the valley below, the one we scaled above in a single hike. What could we accomplish together with a lifetime?

"Or have you decided to climb the mountain?"

"What if I do both?" I ask.

He mulls that over, chewing on the question between his plump, kissable lips. "Depends on what you want your next charm to be, doesn't it?"

I twist my naked wrist. "I'm not doing those anymore."

"No?"

"I never realized how much they felt like chains, my symbols of freedom. Isn't that funny how they could be one in the same?"

"Good thing the parasites have them, then." His lips curve.

"Oliver Love! That was a good one! Look at you."

"You like it?"

I kiss him.

"I like it more than your 'she said' jokes." I smile. "But I'm just glad to see you joking. I always knew there was a fun part of you, deep, deep, like way deep down inside."

He swats my ponytail. "You made your point."

"I'm sorry I assumed you were just a hot, sexy grump. If I'd known you were learning to grieve...or avoiding grieving, rather..."

He rolls his eyes.

"Sorry. You know what I mean. Death is not easy. And it never will be. But neither is life, right? We just have to trust the process and enjoy the adventure."

"You're wise beyond your years, Lemon Perkins." His hand captures mine. "How did you know all that, about grief? About learning to live with it?"

"My mom," I admit. "I'm still healing from that grief, I think. Piece by piece, every day." I frown. "But when Randall, Shana's father, passed, I was gutted. Losing him was like losing my mother all over again. But then there was you and your girls, and somehow, Oliver, healing your family was what I needed to heal my heart."

"That was beautiful, Lem."

"Thanks for listening," I say as we cross a narrow creek. "I know I can be a lot."

"That's where you're wrong, Sour Patch, I like you that way. Please don't ever be less."

"You mean it?"

"I do." His eyes find mine. "You can climb that mountain and search the skies for starlight, Lemon Perkins, but you'll never find it there. It lives in your soul."

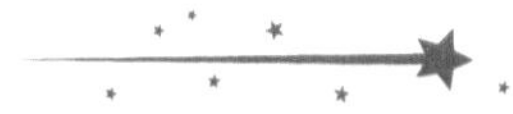

The evening fades into orange and yellow wisps as we gather around the cheerleading camp, singing songs and watching skits performed by the fire. The peace and calm of the evening is almost enough for the strife of before to fade away.

The twins learn a dance from the older girls while Poppy props against a tree sketching the sunset, and I could live right here in this moment for a lifetime, surrounded by joy and love.

I grab Oliver's hand, and we sit back in a pair of Adirondack chairs to people-watch.

"Some of these kids have really weird clothes," he whispers.

"Don't you dare judge them. You're just too old to know fashion. I happen to like that one girl's...is that a skirt or a top?"

He gives me the side-eye. "See, the fact you can't tell is the problem. And what about the hair styles? Some of them look bald!"

"You're right...most of them...look bald."

Oliver stands. "Are those razors?"

Around the campfire, several students have already begun shaving their heads.

"For Coach Jasmine," a girl says. She shaves a strip of her long dark hair in one confident stroke, and she smiles as the others cheer.

Jeremy comes beside us and smiles. "We're proud of your daughter, Daddy Nashville."

"Please." He shoots me a glare when I snicker. "Call me Oliver. But why do they have razors?"

"That's why we're proud of her. She organized this whole ceremony for Coach Jasmine."

"Bryar planned this? This whole event? The food and the songs and the..."

"Shaving heads." He nods. "Mhm. In honor of her mom."

"Bryar?" Tears spring his eyes. "That's why she wanted to come here. Not to sneak around or..."

"It's okay," I tell him. "Remember? We're here for each other's messes. Go fix this one, Love."

"Bry!"

His daughter's eyes snap to his, tears and determination spilling over lashes.

"Do it, then." He nods.

And I sing with pride when she does.

Rebellious, brave, passionate Bryar follows her own damn heart.

"For Coach." She buzzes a strip of hair to the ground. Without looking away, she does another, meeting her father's stare this time. "For Mom."

Oliver says nothing, just watches his daughter and breathes. When he holds out his own hand, Bryar's brow pinches.

"For Lauren," he croaks.

A tearful Bryar throws her arms around his neck and cries into his chest as silver hair sifts to the dirt.

"For Mom!" Poppy shouts.

Jeremy winks at Oliver. "Told you old men with sweatpants were in." He hands me the razor. "For Randall Holiday?"

"For Randall Holiday," I agree, and we shave our heads straight down the middle, too. "For the record," I gather our girls around, "I'm staying, even after the summer's over, if you'll have me."

They squeal, jumping and laughing and singing a thank you to the sky as love connects our souls.

"Something like starlight?" Oliver asks.

But I shake my head as the tears fall happily from my eyes, and I hold the world in a single hug.

"Something like us."

# Epilogue

## LEMON

"So, tell me, *Lemony Slickett*, is it?" I giggle as Oliver moves the phone around my face dramatically. "What makes you want to be one of Daddy's little girls?" He turns his phone upside down, feigning another camera angle, and I can't help it, I spurt with laughter at this total square of a man I've fallen for.

"I can't take you seriously when you chew your lip and circle around me like that. Oliver!" I snatch the phone. "Just as I suspected. You didn't even hit record."

"It's roleplay," he argues, adjusting his rock hard cock in the super distracting sweatpants I made him promise he'd always wear for me. "What if someone sees the video one day?"

"You would be the only one to show them. Are you gonna show someone a video of you fucking me senseless?"

I smirk when the grumbling sound comes from his throat, and the scowl of disapproval rests its gaze on my body.

"Maybe I'll just bend you over my lap and spank you for being such a filthy little tease. Usually has you as wet as a river."

I meet his sparkling eyes at the word *river*, the adventure neither of us will ever forget shining through.

"Besides…" He bites my neck, licking where he's just marked me as his. Goosebumps prickle my body, and his arms wrap around me. "The only man's couch you'll ever be cast on again will be mine, Sour Patch."

Oliver Nashville slides the belt from his loops in one single motion, and then he drags it against my lips, leaning over me on the couch with a smirk.

"Lie back while I play my favorite instrument."

I do as I'm told, and very rarely is that a thing, but this man? I trust him implicitly.

And isn't that what relationships are about?

Trust? Love.

"Ahhh!" I cry when his lips come down over my pussy and he sucks the entire thing in his mouth. He hollows his cheeks as he holds me in, and the blood rushes to the front until my clit pulses recklessly.

I wrap my thighs around his head, crying his name as he lashes at my aching pussy with his tongue, flattening it all the way down my ass.

"More!" I cry. "Need you inside me. Please!"

"Brat. Think you can have everything you want when your pussy's wrapped around my tongue?"

"Yes!" I scream.

"God, you're right." He moves atop me and slides into my wet slit with the full force of his passion.

"Yes! Harder!"

My head falls back across the armrest as he thrusts all the way to the hilt, and I scream when it hits the back, the pressure building until it threatens to break free between our love.

He moves in and out, slowly at first, and his eyes pierce mine with a sly smile.

"What is that look for?" I gasp when he slams back inside and has me clenching every muscle below my waist. "Oh!"

He smirks, lips brushing my ear. "I was just thinking about when I finally take this tight little ass. How much you'll clench around me then. How I'll have you lie there while the cum spills back out."

*"Fuck!"* I scream again, his thrusts penetrating deeper than before just like the filth of his words.

I lock my lips with his as his cock slides in so far he might split me open if he goes any deeper, but when I moan and whimper, he just swallows my songs with a kiss.

"Told you I'd make you sing."

"Cocky old millionaire." I wrap my legs around his hips as he pumps into me, and we come as one.

"I want to keep you, Lemon Perkins."

"Then fuckin' keep me."

"Forever?"

He gets to one knee, naked, freshly fucked, and there's a giant purple dildo on the floor, but I couldn't care less about any of that right now, because for the rest of my life, Oliver Love Nashville is all mine.

"Forever."

"**O**kay, you guys, one last time, let's go over it. I don't need anyone falling again before we make it to the park. Bend your knees and march to get yourself started."

I demonstrate to the family on my own skates, clapping my hands happily when Poppy executes my lesson perfectly.

"You got it, Pop! I knew you'd be a natural. You've got the legs for it."

"What about me, Lemon? Do I have the legs for it? Does Kimmie?"

"You have identical legs," I remind them, "and they are identically excellent for skating."

"Yay! Did ya hear that, Bryar?" Cami sticks out her tongue as she jets by her eldest sister, who has fallen on her butt more times than I can count. "Lemon says my legs are excellent. Wonder what happened to your genes."

"Little twit," Bryar mutters under her breath, but I catch her frustrated eyes and glide over the asphalt to her side.

"You can do it, too. It just takes some time."

"And you'll be here to teach me?" She presses her lips together.

"Promise, Bryar Patch."

"How far are we skating?" Jeremy whines. "My piggies are tired. Most of them already left for the market."

"Or to go wee wee all the way home." Cami giggles.

"Touché, small child." Jeremy crosses his arms. "I'll allow it."

I love this, everyone spending time together and creating an adventure just being in our own backyard. I steal a glance at the entrance to Pine Forest Estates, at the bars I once thought I'd grow to hate but now seem to love.

*Home.*

"You've come a long way from scaling the bars of your own mansion, have you not, Zitrone?"

My father chuckles in my ear.

"Yes, Papa." I smile back at him. "I have, huh? And so have you." I nod at Sylvie, who's being pulled along by Kimmie and Cami, one on each arm as they laugh.

"Sylvie has certainly turned my life inside out."

"Oliver, too," I say, nudging the man in question with my elbow. I'm pleased he doesn't fall over, my skating lessons being helpful after all. "You give me an adventure every day, Nashhole." I tug his tie until his body rolls to mine.

"I'll put an adventure in you." He chews his lip as his eyes drop to my belly.

"Don't you think about it, you dirty old man." I swat his arm away. I may not be ready for my own baby yet, or ever, but I get heart eyes all the same.

*Maybe*. I touch my stomach. It would certainly be an adventure.

We swerve past the school and through the park, where we plan to end our day with a picnic I've packed in our backpacks, each of us carrying a different dish.

That was Oliver's idea, the planning and all, but see? We go together perfectly like that, unnatural pieces fitting where you wouldn't think they might.

And speaking of unnatural pieces…

"Is that Katie in a park?" I swing my eyes to Jeremy's, and he raises a suspicious brow back. Two times this year I've found Katie in nature. And that is two times more than our whole lives.

"Hey, girl!" I flag her down, sliding to a stop at the table of positively steaming firemen who surround her.

And the shiny, fat rock on a very specific finger.

She arches a brow when she sees my hand linked with Oliver's. "Something long term?"

I arch mine back.

"Fire daddy?"

We share a knowing smile.

Honestly, I wondered if anyone but family would ever love her. She's not always warm.

But here? Surrounded by these men who accept and seem to approve of her, by people who could be, dare I say, friends?

She ignites.

"Don't take this the wrong way, Katie Kat, but you seem like…"

"Less of a cold-hearted bitch?"

She laughs when my eyes widen, but I can't negate her statement.

"Z, I'd like you to officially meet the new Pine Forest Fire Captain, Dominic Reston. We're engaged!" She holds up her hand.

"How?" I squeal as Jeremy and Sylvie swoop in at my side to peep the ring.

Katie and Dom share a heated look. "It's a long story," she starts, "but if you want to hear it…"

"We do!"

"Well, it all started with a spark."

If you enjoyed this story, please check out the other stories in the *Pine Forest Something Series*:
**Something Like Sunflowers**
&
**Something Like Sugar**
For updates, sneak peeks, or to follow my publishing journey, subscribe to my newsletter at www.elsiebeabooks.com or connect with me on social media. For professional inquiries, please email elsiebea@elsiebeabooks.com.
Thanks for reading something that brightens my soul.
*Something Like Starlight*
XOXO,
Elsie
**As a thank you, please enjoy a teaser chapter to follow from**
**Something Like Sparks**
(Coming 2026)

# Chapter One

## KATIE

I wonder if pain took my father's mind off death.

Or does death take your mind off pain?

"Are you okay, Katie Kat?" Jeremy slides my usual vodka across the bar.

My gaze lifts from the candle I keep deliberate distance with, and I sigh. "It's this time of year. Rookies." I nod to the gaggle of red helmets that strolled into Cowboy's Paradise like they owned the place. "It's the same every year. They'll take on two or three new guys, one of them will last, and all of town will have to deal with their idiotic hazing rituals for the next month."

I chug the entire vodka in one motion and slam it back down.

"Damn, icy much?" Jeremy cocks his head to the fire squad in question, playing some variation of flip cup with three of Dustin's handcrafted tables smashed together like cheap plastic folding things.

"Yes. I am very icy. My father was fire captain of an entire district. It's a position of honor, about saving lives and putting others first." I sneer at the men across the room, cheering like it's Friday Night Football when a quarter lands in a cup.

It's wrong to wonder why he had to die while absolute morons walk the streets every day contributing nothing but fluff to society, yet here I am.

I roll my eyes when the youngest looking of the bunch slides his arm around a hair-twirling Macy Honeycutt. "Picking up women with uniforms so new they still show a factory crease isn't honorable. They haven't earned anything." I cross my arms over my chest. "Just look at the way they take zero regard for this town's woodwork."

"I didn't think you cared about wood. Well, certainly not *firewood*." He snorts.

"I'm pretending you didn't say any of that, so I don't barf across your bar." I roll my eyes when he gives me an innocent wink. "Don't fall for their hotness, Jeremy. It's all fake outerwear. Real firefighters are out on the streets manhandling apparatuses and busting through windows, not pounding back pinkies at the town dive bar."

He gasps. "I take offense to that. I happen to make exquisite pinkies, thank you very much." He fills a beer from the tap without breaking his glowering eye contact. "And anyway, Miss Single-and-way-too-sexy-not-to-mingle, some of those guys are straight hotties. Unfortunately, emphasis on the straight part." He sighs.

"Oh, shut up. You are so horny." I shove my glass his way for a refill. "How is Corbin, anyway?"

Jeremy stills at the mention of his partner.

"He's staying at his mother's...indefinitely."

"Oh, Jer. I'm so sorry. I had no idea."

"It's fine." He pours himself a drink this time. "A story for another day. Besides, I have my sights set on bigger and better things."

"Oh, yeah?" My heart tugs for Jeremy and whatever he feels he must go through alone, but his genuine grin eases my mind when he whips out a sparkling pair of blue poms.

"You are looking at Pine Forest High School's interim varsity cheer coach!" He shakes the sequin monstrosities in my face. "Only until Coach Jasmine finishes treatment, but it's the perfect distraction."

"I'm happy you have this, Jer."

"Me too." He sighs. "But what about you? I am so proud of what you and Lem are doing for this community. The families you two house in the apartments upstairs are wonderful people who deserve every chance you're affording them. I've met every one of them."

"I believe that."

Jeremy Callahan is one of the good ones.

Not that people in Pine Forest are bad. They don't understand circumstances, though. If it's not something that affects them directly, they develop blinders to the problem altogether.

I always wondered how people could so easily paint pink over blue and not see purple.

"We're trying everything we can, I'll be honest," I admit. "But it's exhausting being the only social worker in this town. Between guardian ad-litem meetings, placement appointments, family check-ins, food bank organization, and the group home, I hardly have time to brush my own hair." I hold up a matted mess of red curls and sigh. "See, I didn't even today."

"I wasn't going to point it out." We both laugh, but it's dark how comedic it is.

My job is humanity. That weight can be intense most days, even before Ryder runs to my side at the group home and tells me about his day.

The mother I wish I could be for him.

For all the kids who don't have someone assigned to them by circumstance. The truth is, he's not mine. None of the kids are, even if their fears and hopes and all their firsts are embedded into my heart.

"Did you know some places have departments full of people like me?"

"God, that's terrifying." He gasps, sending us both into a fit of self-deprecating laughter again. "But can I ask you something?"

"I don't like it, but yeah."

"Do you think you're spending too much time working? I know the town needs it, but you can't pour from an empty cup." He nods to the glass I already chugged yet am still trying to swig down again, and my face heats.

"I should turn in for the night."

Dissecting this part of me might seem fun to Jeremy from beneath the glow of the bar lights and the buzz of liquor, but my past isn't smooth as ice, like he thinks.

It's a wildfire.

"Don't leave just because I got real with you. You're being a total Lemon. Sulk when you don't get your way." He folds his arms across his chest and waits for me to tell him he's right.

He is, as it were, which just annoys the hell out of me.

I hate being wrong.

"I can't settle down and have a life, Jeremy. I have sixteen children under the age of twelve in my adjacent-guardianship on a daily basis, foster parents to counsel and license, thousands of dollars in relief checks to disburse to families all over town, and just when things couldn't get any busier, Ryder has soccer camp coming up, and if the youth programs don't show a successful turnout this season, the county is threatening to cut the funds for children under ward of the state to play in youth sports. What the hell do I do with that? Snag a fire daddy over there and dance around his pole until he puts out all these goddamned fires?"

Jeremy's lips twist, eyes locked in cartoon hearts behind me.

"It's a fire daddy, isn't it?"

"We prefer the term 'first responder,'" an amused voice says.

A deep, grumbly, not-attractive-in the-least sort of voice.

I do not give the rookie the dignity of turning to face him. *First responder, my ass.* They're all so young they respond to the Flinger app more than emergencies.

Firefighters are a hard fucking no.

He doesn't know this, though, and Jeremy is not a lick of help smirking behind the tap as this absolute skyscraper of a man twists my body to face him, and I see full-on red.

Instincts fit like armor, and I throw the hulking stranger over my shoulder and pin him to the ground before either of us can exhale. "Do not touch me."

"Okay!" He holds up his free hand in surrender and meets my icy stare, the clear blue weapons that cut if I use them right.

*But that's not how I'm using them now, is it?*

Disobedient is what they are, curiously tracing his neck tattoos, even as my brain commands they cease and desist this charade, but the unmistakable 5's across his throat gives me pause. Four of them in a row.

It signifies a fallen firefighter.

I know it all too well, and even if this asshole did just touch my hips like death-wish is his middle name, my heart breaks for the fact he knows it too.

For a breath of time, we share the same heartbeat, and eyes darker than night pierce my own in a flash of pain that slips from my mind just as quickly as it comes.

Dark hair stubbles a chiseled jaw that flexes so precisely I feel it in places I shouldn't dare, and full sleeve of tattoos I can't make out beneath the haze of bar lights rolls over biceps that could lift ten of me.

"What huge arms you have." I don't mean to say. It's the vodka, I'm sure.

I measure his palms against my own before I realize what I'm doing, and a heated spark passes through our bodies when the tips of his fingers curl over mine.

"The better to put out goddamned fires with." He grins.

So why does it feel like one just started?

# Acknowledgments

When I set out to publish my first romance novel, I never imagined there would be a second, let alone a third. My passion has only grown thanks to the opportunities made available to me, and I consider myself incredibly lucky to be able to say I did not do this alone, so thank you.

To my children, for your patience and belief in my words. T, for making bracelets and PR boxes, and for leaving endless smileys on my notebooks. G, for saying the funniest, most intuitive things, and inspiring the spirit of Cami. And K.P., most of all, for giving me every reason to write romance. You're my sunflower, my sugar, and my starlight, and I couldn't do it without you.

To my family and friends, for showing up to my local events and tricking people into thinking I'm a celebrity. It really does sell more books. Who knew?

To Molly, for jumping headfirst into the romcom world with me and bringing us another gorgeous Pine Forest cover.

To my editors, Kimberly, Lori, and Ramona, for being there from start to finish as my wild ideas get polished enough to shine. My stories and craft improve thanks to your guidance. And to Evelyn, for your detailed eyes on the final format.

To my beta readers, Johanna, Natalie, and Milena, thank you for your feedback on characters, plot, and the German/Denglisch translations. Your help to make Lemon and her father's relationship more dynamic through dialogue has been invaluable.

To the Bea Hive, for hyping up my series and consuming my words. Your support feels warm and reassuring in the growing world of indie authorship.

To Erika, for literally everything. Organizing my chaos, curating my content, reminding me that yes—release dates do need to be chosen at some point, and then making me stick to them. For listening to me whine, reading my messiest early drafts, and encouraging my 2 a.m. smut-writing and spin-off ideas with slutty little graphics, I can't thank you enough. Publishing and marketing romance is one of the craziest things I've ever done, and "best assistant ever" doesn't even begin to describe the role you play in my world.

Lastly, to my readers. From the bottom of my heart, thank you for coming back to my stories and choosing my words.

# About the Author

Elsie Bea is a contemporary romance author from Richmond, Virginia. She lives 'out in the sticks' with her incorrigible husband, crazy kids, and a gaggle of dogs, chickens, and ducks. When she's not reading or writing, you can find her singing and dancing through her kitchen and spending time with family.